We hope you enjoy this bo
renew it by the due date.

You can r
by usi

SILE
WITNESS

BOOKS BY CAROLYN ARNOLD

DETECTIVE
AMANDA STEELE SERIES

The Little Grave
Stolen Daughters
The Silent Witness

BRANDON FISHER FBI SERIES

Eleven
Silent Graves
The Defenseless
Blue Baby
Violated
Remnants
On the Count of Three
Past Deeds
One More Kill

DETECTIVE
MADISON KNIGHT SERIES

Ties That Bind
Justified
Sacrifice
Found Innocent
Just Cause
Deadly Impulse
In the Line of Duty
Power Struggle
Shades of Justice
What We Bury
Life Sentence (prequel
romantic suspense)

McKINLEY MYSTERIES

The Day Job is Murder
Vacation is Murder
Money is Murder
Politics is Murder
Family is Murder
Shopping is Murder
Christmas is Murder
Valentine's Day is Murder
Coffee is Murder
Skiing is Murder
Halloween is Murder
Exercise is Murder

MATTHEW CONNOR
ADVENTURE SERIES

City of Gold
The Secret of the Lost Pharaoh
*The Legend of Gasparilla and
His Treasure*

STANDALONE

Assassination of a Dignitary
Pearls of Deception
Midlife Psychic

THE SILENT WITNESS

CAROLYN ARNOLD

bookouture

Published by Bookouture in 2021

An imprint of Storyfire Ltd.
Carmelite House
50 Victoria Embankment
London EC4Y 0DZ

www.bookouture.com

ISBN: 978-1-80019-022-1
eBook ISBN: 978-1-80019-021-4

To Max and Sophie

CHAPTER ONE

Someone was in the house.

Angela's eyes sprung open, and she looked around the dark room. Her heart was hammering, but the bedroom door was still closed, and all she could make out were the familiar shapes and shadows of the furniture.

Then another small thump.

The thunderstorm might still be raging outside and playing tricks on her mind. She strained to listen but didn't hear the storm. The noise had to be her imagination.

She looked over at her daughter, who was wedged between her and her husband, Brett. Zoe's fear of thunder always sent her running into their room, and even though she was six, they didn't have the willpower to turn her away. Zoe was in a deep sleep, her favorite stuffed doll, Lucky, hugged to her chest. Her breathing was heavy, and her eyelashes were fluttering against her cheeks. Nothing like a child's carefree slumber.

Angela glanced at the clock on the nightstand beside her. *4:03 AM.*

She should be asleep herself, floating in a fictional world where there was no stress or worries, no doubts or concerns about the future. Even Brett was lightly snoring, off in some dreamland, escaping reality. This was ridiculous. She had to get some rest because she had to be at work in less than four and a half hours.

She closed her eyes.

The door banged against the jamb.

She bolted upright. The bedroom door only vibrated like that when an exterior door was opened and the air pressure changed. That wasn't in her head. Someone *was* in the house.

She strained to hear anything else but was met with the haunting assault of silence.

Still, she had this horrible feeling something wasn't right.

"*Psst*, Brett." She reached out, over Zoe, and poked his shoulder.

He mumbled something incoherent. Zoe squirmed, tugged from her dreams but not fully waking up.

"Brett," she repeated more urgently.

"Yeah… Huh… What?" Groggy, he flipped onto his side to face her.

"I think that someone is—" Fear froze her vocal cords, her words lodging in her throat.

Someone was on the staircase. The unmistakable groan of the third step from the bottom hit her ears.

Brett jumped from bed—he must have heard it too—and proceeded to nudge Zoe awake. "Come on, honey, time to wake up."

Zoe moaned. "What?"

Angela could feel her husband's gaze drilling through her in the dark, urging her to act.

"Zoe, let's play hide-and-seek," she said.

"Yes, Mommy's right. Let's…" Brett was now talking at a whisper, as was she. "Come on, it's important," he added.

"Right now?"

"Yes, and you can bring Lucky with you," Angela told her daughter.

Another groan on the staircase, this one about halfway up. They had to move.

"Hide," Brett pushed out urgently.

Angela grabbed her cell phone from the nightstand and pulled Zoe from bed. She looked around the room, thinking about places where Zoe could be protected. Even if whoever it was got to her and Brett, Zoe needed to be safe. They only had a matter of seconds. Her gaze landed on the perfect spot, and she got her daughter secured just as the landing creaked. Whoever was in the house was just on the other side of the bedroom door.

Her breath remained trapped in her lungs.

"Go!" Brett hissed and shoved her into action.

She ran past him to the walk-in closet and ducked into the corner behind a rack of clothing. She was having a hard time getting her fingers to work. It was just three digits that could save them, but her hands were shaking so badly.

9... 1... 1...

She held her phone to an ear. No ringtone. *What the hell?*

She tried again as the bedroom door was opened. She heard Brett and the intruder talking, but her heartbeat was pounding so loudly in her ears she couldn't make out what they were saying.

There was a bang, followed by Brett screaming. Two more cracks, and a thump on the floor.

Her brain was slow to process what had happened, but layer by layer the stark reality sank in. Brett had been shot! Probably killed!

Oh my God!

She gasped and slapped a hand over her mouth, shoving herself as far back into the closet as she could. She tried to hold her breath, but her body wasn't listening, and she was heaving in air.

Why is this happening?

Footsteps approached the closet door, and as she heard the handle turn, she knew she was next. The clothes were swept back, and she came face to face with her killer. Tears streaked down her face, but she no longer feared her fate. She closed her eyes and heard the click of the gun—three taps in quick succession. Time slowed right down. At first it was like nothing had happened. Then, for the briefest of moments, a searing pain overwhelmed her entire system. Following this was a warmth accompanied by an incoming darkness. But just before she left this world, she sent up a silent prayer.

God, please, please let my little girl live. Please.

CHAPTER TWO

Triangle, Virginia
Tuesday, September 7, 4:05 PM

Solving murder was nothing like riding a bike. Every case was different and came with unique challenges. This one was a double homicide involving a missing girl. But Detective Amanda Steele appreciated her job more than ever after recently having been suspended, and she was especially invested when the victims were children. She'd been pulled from her mother's court trial for this one and hadn't been able to arrive on scene fast enough.

The girl was Zoe Parker, only six years old. The same age Amanda's Lindsey had been when she'd died. That thought made her nauseous, but she wanted to think positively about the girl's fate. In the photo, Zoe was smiling and waving at the camera. Her blond, curly tendrils reached a couple of inches past her shoulders, and her skin was milky white with a sprinkling of freckles across her nose. She had the bright, blue eyes of a spitfire, with a zest for life. She looked fearless and ready to take on the world.

Amanda pulled back and straightened up. She'd been looking at the photo on Becky Tulson's phone. Becky was her lifelong friend and a police officer with the Dumfries Police Department. She had been a first responder to the Parkers' home in Triangle, a small town in Prince William County. Amanda and her partner, Trent Stenson, were homicide detectives with the PWCPD. Dumfries

PD called their unit when a death was suspicious. "You said the woman who found the Parkers provided you with this picture?"

Becky nodded. "Yeah, Libby Dewinter is her name. Says she's a close family friend and Zoe's godmother. Apparently, Mrs. Parker texted the photo to her last week before the Parkers left for vacation."

It was the Tuesday after Labor Day weekend, and it wasn't uncommon for people to get in a vacation just before the start of school.

"What was she doing here today?" Trent asked.

"She normally watches Zoe on Tuesdays and Thursdays from the close of school until Angela Parker gets home from work at six. Dewinter's out back when you're ready to talk to her."

"Thanks," Amanda said. "We'll be there shortly. First we need to…" She pointed up the staircase to the second story. There was a slew of officers already searching for Zoe, and Amanda and Trent's main responsibility was piecing together what had happened in the house, starting with the two murder victims.

"It's not pretty," Becky said. "I'll give you that warning."

"Murder never is." With that, Amanda led the way upstairs to the primary bedroom, Trent following her. Becky headed in the opposite direction, toward the front door.

The home was certainly spacious, with three levels of living, or so she'd heard. She and Trent hadn't yet taken the tour, but officers were searching every nook and cranny for little Zoe Parker. Amanda was holding out for a happy ending but had learned a long time ago not to get attached to the idea. Life had a way of blowing up in your face when you least expected it. Possibly cynical but born from having the ground fall out from beneath her feet.

She entered the bedroom and looked at the body of Brett Parker, age forty-five. Already silver-haired with a closely groomed mustache and beard, he had kept himself trim and fit. He'd been a handsome man in life, but death had a way of painting even the most attractive with a macabre brush of horror. She'd witnessed many expressions on the dead during her years as a homicide detective. Everything from frowns to smiles to grimaces, but Mr. Parker's face relayed shock. His brown eyes were open wide, like the bullets had come as a surprise, but it would seem he might have been aware of the intruder and may have even confronted him or her.

He was on an area rug at the end of the king poster bed and was supine, as if the bullets that struck him had knocked him straight backward. To mock the tragedy of what had transpired, luxury was all around. A crystal chandelier was overhead, and flames in a gas fireplace to the right of the body flickered like sparkling diamonds in the large puddle of congealed blood. Amanda wasn't a medical examiner, but her experience with the dead told her Brett had been deceased for several hours, and the attack probably happened sometime in the night. That was also supported by the clothing he'd conceivably worn to bed—a pair of blue-plaid shorts and a white T-shirt.

"A double tap to the chest, one to the head," she said. "Looks small. Maybe a twenty-two caliber. This looks a lot like an execution."

"The work of a professional?" Trent pointed to the floor with the tip of his pen. "I'm not seeing any bullet casings."

She agreed. "Definitely looks like the shooter policed their brass. May also mean they have a record and don't want to leave anything behind that could lead us to him or her."

"A professional then." He smirked at her.

She shook her head but smiled. "Fine. Let's say a 'professional' for now. But we'll see just how professional if we get bullets from the bodies—and a lead as a result." She knew it wasn't beyond the realm of possibility that a killer would remove bullets from their victims and/or use rounds that became forensically useless.

She took in the entire bedroom. It was more like a suite than just a place to sleep. There was the enormous bed, a bench at the footboard, and nightstands on each side. A sitting area was off to the left with a full-size couch and more tables. A large flatscreen television was mounted above the fireplace and would have been viewable from anywhere within the room. There was an attached bathroom with a walk-in shower and a soaking tub—enough marble for a mausoleum—and another crystal chandelier. *For a bathroom?* Amanda might be the only woman who didn't get the fascination.

There was a walk-in closet where Mrs. Parker's body was, according to the recap from Becky when they'd first arrived. They'd get to her, but Amanda couldn't kick thoughts of the missing girl and the discrepancies. Parts of the house had been tossed. Even the nightstands had been ransacked, their drawers hanging out and bric-a-brac strewn on the floor in front of them. "What are we really looking at here?"

"I'd say burglary…" There was a question to Trent's voice, like he wasn't completely sold on the idea.

"But?" she prompted.

"It wouldn't explain the missing girl."

"What I'm thinking too. But if we're looking at a kidnapping gone wrong, why would someone want to take Zoe? Presumably the people that could have paid a ransom—if this was what it's about—are both dead." For now the question was rhetorical, but it was hard to get her mind off the girl. Libby Dewinter, the family friend, might be able to shed some light, but Amanda also thought it important to look at the crime scene in case it provided some insights. That was the only reason she and Trent were here and not talking to Libby right now or joining in the search for Zoe.

She started toward the walk-in closet, careful to not disturb the scene around Brett Parker. It was a long and rather narrow space with track lighting. The wife's clothing was on the left, the husband's on the right. Beyond that was an in-wall safe, its door swung open. But Amanda was more interested in the second body.

She stopped in front of Angela Parker. Just forty-one years old, the woman had long, blond hair the same shade as Zoe's that fanned down around her face. She and her husband had been an attractive couple. Angela was in the corner slumped slightly to her left side. Her head hung forward, her chin resting just above two bullet entry points that had scorched the fabric of her pajama top. It was part of a matching set she wore—pink cotton with white ribbons and daisies imprinted on the fabric.

Amanda crouched down and saw there was a hole in Angela's forehead to match her husband's. Clutched in one of her hands was a cell phone. She'd probably tried to call for help.

"She didn't stand a chance…" Amanda got back up and took a few breaths. She could only imagine how terrified the woman had been. A home invasion, her husband shot, then herself… but where had her daughter been, and where was she now? If someone had broken into her home, Amanda wouldn't have left her girl's side—that is unless she felt the child was safer elsewhere or had no say in the matter.

Amanda walked to the open safe and looked inside. Empty. "Completely cleared out," she informed Trent.

"None of this is looking good to me, Amanda," Trent said. "What I mean is, you have a professional shooter, a scene that looks like a robbery, but also a missing girl. The Parkers, it would seem, were targeted. But by whom—and why? What could they have done?"

"Everyone has enemies." A sad, but sober truth. She hated to think that even a young, innocent girl could have enemies, but Amanda's experience told her it was entirely possible.

CHAPTER THREE

Amanda was leaving the walk-in closet when Sergeant Malone called her name. She emerged to see him near the bedroom doorway.

"How's it looking?" he said.

For a moment, she wasn't sure what he was really asking. Scott Malone was her and Trent's boss, but also a friend of her family. He was best buddies with her father, Nathan Steele, former police chief for the PWCPD. Malone had known that he'd pulled her from the opening day in her mother's trial. What he didn't know was that just before he'd called, her mother's defense attorney, Hannah Byrd, was requesting the removal of a prosecution's professional witness: crime scene investigator Emma Blair. Something that Amanda tried to put out of mind—easy to do with an ugly case like this one. But upon seeing Malone, it was all back. Not that she was a true fan of Blair's, as the woman always treated her with disdain for no reason that Amanda could think of. But Blair was good at her job and had the evidence in order, so Hannah's request really made no sense, and Amanda had to leave before getting the answer.

"Seems like it was a professional hit," Trent answered Malone.

"Any sign of the girl yet?" The question hurt Amanda to raise, but she needed to know, even if the answer was a horrible one.

Malone shook his head. "So professional... Burglary gone wrong, a kidnapping, something else?"

Everyone wanted answers, but there weren't enough to go around. "Too soon to say," she told him. "We're just going to talk to Libby Dewinter, who found them. See if she knows of anyone who might have reason to kidnap the girl."

"Hopefully, she can help."

"Yeah." She gave Malone a pressed-lip smile as she walked around him and into the hall. He caught her in the crook of the elbow.

"You all right?"

Trent glanced at her on his way past and headed down the stairs.

"I'm good," she told Malone.

"If you need anything, Ida and I are here for you—for all your family. You know that?"

Ida was Malone's wife and a sweet woman. "I know. We all do."

He patted her shoulder, and she carried on down to the main level. Her thoughts wandered to her mother's trial. Her mother, Julie "Jules" Steele, had killed a man—cold and premeditated. Amanda had heard the confession, though it had never gone on the record. Everything was left in the prosecution's hands to prove beyond a doubt that Jules had committed the murder. Given the victim, Amanda carried some associated guilt herself. If she'd been there for her mother and the rest of the family and shared her grief with them about Lindsey—and Kevin, Amanda's husband, who had also died in the accident with their daughter—maybe things would look a lot different right now. Instead, she would have that regret with her for the rest of her life.

"Ms. Dewinter's on the back patio with Officer Tucker," Trent told her as she reached the first floor, interrupting her thoughts.

Three crime scene investigators entered the house, but they were probably only the beginning for a house of this size. One was a new face to Amanda. The other two she knew, including Emma Blair. They exchanged brief greetings, except for Blair, who just grunted in Amanda's direction. The CSI obviously held something against Amanda, and all she'd been able to figure out was it was personal rather than professional. What that was specifically, Amanda had no idea. But today she seemed more miserable than usual. It was probably because her testimony had been dismissed, and she, sent packing.

Amanda and Trent walked to the back of the house, and she glanced through every doorway they passed. Some rooms were tossed while others appeared untouched. The dining room seemed unaffected, and she found that kind of strange. In a home like this there would likely be expensive silverware and china. Then again, if this had been a burglary, the thieves were probably looking for what would convert quickly to cash, such as electronics and jewelry. And it could be surmised given the size of the house and neighborhood that the Parkers would have had their fair share of such items.

Trent got the rear door for Amanda, and they stepped out onto a spacious deck with an iron-slatted railing that went the width of the house. It was south facing, and back here, the September evening sun still packed a lot of heat. She pushed up the sleeves of her shirt.

There were a couple of outdoor furniture sets and a built-in grilling station in the corner, but there was no sign of the woman or the officer. She heard voices, though, and followed them down a set of stairs to the yard. She found herself on a flagstone patio on the edge of a beautifully landscaped yard with more stone, a fire pit, a shed, and fencing that lined the entire perimeter. There was also one section devoted to Zoe with a large playground area that had swings and a slide.

There was another outdoor seating space nestled under the upper deck, and that was where she found the two people she and Trent were looking for. Like above, there were two groupings of furniture. One required cushions and remained bare, while

Officer Tucker and, presumably, Libby Dewinter sat in two of four cast-iron chairs that were positioned around a matching table.

The woman's head was bowed, and she held a pair of black-framed glasses in her left hand. She had been pinching the bridge of her nose when Amanda and Trent walked up, but now she let her hand slowly fall and looked up at them. Her eyes were blood-shot, and her cheeks blotchy. Tears had caused tracks through her makeup, and fat drops clung to her eyelashes and threatened to fall.

Officer Tucker rushed to his feet and, in the process, caused the legs of his chair to scrape across the stone. "Libby Dewinter"—he gestured with an open palm to each of them in turn—"this is Detective Steele and Detective Stenson."

"Please, call us Amanda and Trent," Amanda amended, wanting to offer up their first names to put the woman at ease. But Amanda wasn't about to let her guard down. It was possible that Libby was involved in all that had happened somehow and her "discovery" of the Parkers nothing more than a strategy to make her appear innocent.

Libby put on her glasses and sat just a bit straighter, but the display of strength quickly diminished. Her chin trembled, and she pulled a tissue from her jacket and dabbed her cheeks, pressing it carefully under the lenses of her glasses. Amanda would guess Libby was in her early forties, and she suited her pageboy cut and long bangs. "Did you find Zoe?"

Amanda shook her head. "Not yet. Do you know of anyone who might have wanted to take her?"

"I don't understand why any of this is happening... happened."

"What about any family members or estranged family that might have been around and wanted Zoe for themselves?" As sad as it sounded, it was far more common than one might think, and hiring a professional to take care of things was easier than anyone wanted to acknowledge.

"No." A huge sniffle. "They had no one. Angela's parents were never in the picture. She was put into the foster system when she was a young girl. I think she was only a couple of years old, if I remember right."

"And Brett's?" Trent asked, leaning forward, his right elbow on the table, a pen in one hand, his notebook in the other.

"His parents died a few years ago, within a year of each other."

"That would have been rough," Trent lamented in a way that left Amanda wondering if he knew that pain firsthand. She didn't know about the losses he'd faced in life. They were relatively new partners—their pairing became official nine months ago, in January—but she tried to carve a line between the personal and the professional. It was getting harder to enforce given they worked together quite well, and he was one of the most loyal people she'd ever known.

"I just... I'm terrified for Zoe." Libby wiped her brow.

"Did either Brett or Angela have any brothers or sisters?" Amanda couldn't get sucked into the emotional aspect of the case. She had no problem being the strong one.

"I don't think so."

"We were under the impression you were close to the family." Phrases such as *I don't think so* didn't fully support that claim. "How long have you known them?"

"I met Angela ten years ago when I had her firm do my personal tax return. We just hit it off."

Amanda and Trent had been given a brief recap on the victims when they'd arrived, so they were aware of the Parkers' places of employment. Angela was an accountant at Mind Your Own Business, and Brett worked at Falcon Strategic Technologies, a defense contractor out of Washington.

"Do you think Zoe has been taken for ransom?" Libby's voice was small.

"I'm not seeing that at this point," Amanda admitted, without coming out and saying the Parkers couldn't exactly pay one.

A small nod. "I just can't imagine anyone doing this to them. I assume that Angela looked much like Brett? I turned around and left when I found him." A shiver visibly tore through Libby, and she rubbed her arms.

"I'm sorry to say this, but yes, Angela was also shot. She was found in the master walk-in closet."

Fresh tears fell down Libby's face.

"You're sure that Zoe Parker would have been here last night?" Trent asked delicately, earning Libby's gaze.

"Definitely. The unmade bed gave it away. The Parkers are—were—so meticulous. The beds would be made every morning. Who would have—" Libby gulped. "I just had a bad feeling something happened when Zoe didn't come to school today. They'd never let her miss the first day back. And Angie and Brett would have been due to return to work today."

"So just to rule this out, is there any possibility Zoe could have spent the night at a friend's?" Amanda asked, but doubted the likelihood. As a mother herself once, she never would have allowed a sleepover on the eve of the school year.

"I wouldn't say so." Libby traced a finger around a pattern in the tabletop.

"When was the last time you spoke to the Parkers?"

"I spoke to Angela on Saturday."

"This past one, three days ago?" Amanda asked.

"Yeah."

"How did she seem to you?" Amanda was trying to get a sense of what had happened here, what could have triggered a double murder.

A light danced in Libby's eyes, like something came to her mind but she didn't want to say it out loud.

"What is it?" Amanda was curious if the hesitation on Libby's behalf was due to loyalty to the Parkers in some regard.

"She was a little upset."

"Did she say why?" Amanda was starting to question the stability of the Parkers' marriage, but she'd give it a few minutes before probing that area. Libby might get defensive of her friends if she pushed the matter too soon.

"Brett dragged them back early from vacation. They were supposed to return home this past Sunday, but they came home on Thursday."

"Why was that?" Trent asked, angling his head.

"Apparently, Brett told her he wanted to beat the traffic."

That could make for a valid point, but the timing of the cut-short vacation was noteworthy, though not necessarily related to the murders and Zoe's disappearance. "But you and Angela sensed there was more to it?"

"Yeah."

"Any idea what?" Amanda countered.

Libby shook her head.

"Where did they go for vacation?"

"Lake Chesdin. It's less than a couple hours away. They rented a cabin on the water in Sutherland."

"Oh, yeah, I know where that is." Amanda's parents used to bring her and her siblings there as kids. "Sounds like it would have been a peaceful getaway."

"Should have been. They never vacationed."

An out-of-character vacation *and* it was cut short. "Were Brett and Angela having marriage problems?" Amanda's mind was spinning now with more theories. The Parkers had a beautiful house and family, but maybe it wasn't so perfect behind closed doors.

Libby chewed on her bottom lip, then offered, "I don't think so."

"I realize it might be uncomfortable for you to talk about your friends' marriage. You might even feel like you're betraying them in some way, but if you know something… You could help us find out who did this to them and where Zoe might be."

"As far as I know, they were doing their best, working at it. Angie was the maddest I'd seen her at Brett about him cutting the vacation short. And for that, I don't really blame her."

Amanda was tossing that around along with the seeming secrecy surrounding the reason for returning home. He'd said it was to beat traffic, but was that really all it was? "You said 'working at it.' Did they have marriage problems before?"

Libby sighed. "I probably shouldn't be talking about them now that they're…" She hiccupped a sob, and Amanda gave her a moment to collect herself.

"Anything you know could help us." The rare vacation, the marriage that was being worked on, doing their best… The most common motive for a domestic murder was infidelity. "Had Brett cheated on Angela or vice versa?"

Libby met Amanda's eyes and blinked deliberately. "Angie, but it was several years ago now and long over."

"How long ago?" Amanda asked.

"Six, seven years ago."

Zoe Parker was six… "Was Brett Parker Zoe's biological father, or was this other man?"

"Angie was adamant she was Brett's, but I don't know if she ever got a paternity test."

"We're going to need the name of this guy."

Libby shrunk back. "I… I don't know it. It was someone she worked with then, at the accounting firm. That's all I know. She greatly regretted the affair."

Could this mystery man have come after Zoe all these years later, thinking she was his? If so, why wait? It didn't seem likely. Or had Angela been cheating on Brett with someone more recently? She could have ended things, and the man could have been of the mindset that if he couldn't have Angela, no one could. But how did that explain Zoe's disappearance? "Was she seeing anyone recently?" Amanda asked.

Libby shook her head. "I don't think so." This time as she said the words, her voice lowered.

"It's okay. We can find that out." A look at Angela's phone records and talking to other people in her life, starting with those at work, might reveal someone.

"I can't believe I might never see Zoe again. She sent me this…" Libby pecked on her phone before flipping the screen for Amanda and Trent to see. It was the photo of Zoe that Becky had shown them. "Angie said she just had to say good—" She sobbed and put her phone away again.

"We're very sorry for the loss of your friends, Ms. Dewinter," Amanda started. "But let's not give up hope about Zoe."

Libby sniffled and blinked more tears from her eyes.

"You were really close with her. Her godmother," Amanda said softly.

"I was—I *am*. You're right, I have to think positively that we'll find her, and she'll be all right."

"Exactly how we need to think of it." Amanda touched the back of Libby's hand, which was resting on the table.

Libby bobbed her head, blinking back more tears. She patted her wet cheeks. "I was more than a family friend to Zoe, more than a godmother… I was Aunt Libby. The Parkers were my family. I'm not in communication with any of my blood relatives. My parents are alive, as far as I know, and so are my brother and sister, but they all shunned me when I came out."

"I'm sorry to hear that."

Libby waved a hand of dismissal, but it was rather easy to see the pain burrowed in her eyes. "I'm not the only one dealing with that. It's just their minds are too small to accept what is different from their norm. But I don't need them in my life, and through all the hurt and pain, I discovered my strength and what real love is. I've read before that people don't leave us, but the universe gets them out of our way. I kind of like that… Comforting. And I have since found my soul family. The Parkers were very much a part of that."

"I'm so sorry for your loss." The words purged from Amanda's throat raw with meaning and settled as an ache in her chest.

"I appreciate your saying that. I just wish it would bring them back."

There was no response for that. Amanda had made the same wish a zillion times after losing her daughter, Lindsey, and her husband in the same accident. She'd even wished that she would have had a chance to meet the unborn baby she'd lost that day. Most of the time she couldn't bear to think that, because of her injuries, she was left unable to have any more children. It was just all too painful. "So, we need to ask you some questions. They're ones you've already answered, but I'd like to run through them again."

"Okay," Libby dragged out.

"What brought you here today?"

"I sit with Zoe on Tuesdays and Thursdays after school. Those are the days Angela works until six. Brett's rarely home before seven, given his commute into Washington and all. It's really no inconvenience for me. I teach third grade at Dumfries Elementary, so I'm already there to drive her straight home and then sit with her."

Amanda went to Dumfries Elementary growing up, and her niece Ava just graduated from there. She'd ask her about Libby Dewinter when she got the chance.

Libby continued. "When I found out that Zoe didn't show for class, I had a bad feeling, but I tried to dismiss it. Then Angie and Brett weren't answering their phones. They're tied to those things, so I figured something was wrong."

"Always trust your gut." Amanda's dad had drilled that into her.

"You're right, and I did. Wish it had been wrong this time, though. I got here and saw their cars in the driveway. I tried her again, then Brett. No answer from either one of them, but then I peeked in the window and saw the mess in his office."

Amanda recalled seeing the office right off the front entrance when they'd arrived. It was one of the rooms that had been tossed.

Libby went on. "I know I should have called the cops right away, and I really wish I had, but as you know, I went in the house, and I…" Libby's eyes glazed over and took on a faraway look. The dropped words were obviously something to the effect of *found them.*

Amanda could reprimand her for going inside, but there was no point in making this woman feel worse than she already did. "You have a key to the house?"

"Uh-huh. Thinking back, I didn't disarm the security system. It must have already been." Her brow pinched in confusion.

"And that would be unusual, for the Parkers not to arm it before bed?" Trent asked.

"Oh yeah. They were meticulous. Very much about ritual."

Amanda met Libby's gaze. "Did you touch anything in the house?"

"Nope. Not a thing. I watch those cop shows and know better."

Those same shows should have taught her to stay outside and call 911 rather than enter the home, but Amanda wasn't going to beat Libby over the head. She did need to ask something else, though. "As a matter of procedure, where were you between last night and this morning?" It was a wide span of time, but she wanted to know if Libby's schedule was accounted for.

"You need my alibi?" Libby sank into her chair, deflated.

"Just procedure," Amanda reiterated.

"I was at home with my girlfriend all weekend—including last night. Never saw Angie, just spoke to her on the phone. This morning, I left my girlfriend at seven to go to work. Her name's Penny Anderson. Would you like her number?"

"That would be great." Trent had his pen poised over his notepad, ready to write it down.

Libby recited it from memory, and Trent scribbled in his book.

"Thank you for being so helpful, Ms. Dewinter." Amanda stood and drew a business card from a pocket and extended it to Libby. "If you think of anything, all my information's on there. Call any time, day or night."

"I will. I won't be sleeping until Zoe's found."

"We'll update you as soon as we know anything. In the meantime, we're going to have an officer escort you home. We'll need you to stay in town and be available in case we have any more questions for you. We also might require that you formally ID the bodies."

"I understand." Libby tapped Amanda's card against the table a couple times and then stuck it into her phone case.

Amanda could only imagine what the woman was going through. She'd shown up probably trying to convince herself she was being paranoid, only to find that her intuition had been right all along. The Parkers had been in trouble—only Brett and Angela no longer felt any pain. But what about Zoe?

Where are you, little girl?

Whoever had taken Zoe might not know it yet, but they had a whole lot of hell coming their way.

CHAPTER FOUR

Amanda and Trent stood as Libby Dewinter and Officer Tucker walked away. The door next to them was opened by a CSI, and Malone came out. He didn't need to say a single word. His face and slumped body language said it all.

"No sign of the girl," Amanda concluded.

"None. I've ordered an Amber Alert."

"We just spoke with Ms. Dewinter, and she said that Mrs. Parker had an affair several years ago," Amanda offered. "She doesn't think there's anyone now, but we can't rule out the possibility. We'll look into Angela's phone records and pry into her life. Brett's too, of course."

"No name on that boyfriend?"

Amanda shook her head. "He worked where Angela Parker did—at least at the time of the affair. Dewinter didn't know his name. But we'll go over to the accounting firm tomorrow morning." Unfortunately, given that it was after five in the evening, it would be closed now. "Not seeing a reason for him to take Zoe, at any rate," she added.

"Dewinter also mentioned a security system in the home," Trent said. "It wasn't armed when she arrived."

"Just more proof whoever did this knew what they were doing." Malone perched his hands on his hips.

"We'll check with the security company to see if they have a time when it was disarmed." If it was the perp, it would narrow the timeframe for the investigation. "Do we know where the shooter gained entry to the home yet?"

"Yep." Malone pointed back through the door he'd just come through. That explained the presence of an investigator there. His phone pinged, and he looked at it. "Oy vey. I better get out front before Hill makes a mess of things."

"Hill? What's she doing here?" The animosity between Amanda and the now police chief Sherry Hill wasn't a secret from anyone. She'd been behind Amanda getting suspended in the spring, though the rivalry between Sherry and her family dated back to Nathan Steele—neither could tolerate the other. Amanda just did her best to avoid the woman whenever she could.

"You know what she's like for the media limelight, and it's shining here."

"Let me guess. She's spinning things to make the department look good, but it's really all about her image," Amanda said.

"Wouldn't put it past her." With that Malone hustled off, through the yard, around the side of the house to the front.

Amanda followed in his wake, across a flagstone path that led to a gate. Malone flicked a latch and went through, held the gate for her, but she shook her head. He let go of the gate, and it sprung shut. She stepped closer to inspect. "No lock on the gate, and it swings open toward the driveway." She turned and looked at the yard again, then at Trent, who'd been right behind her. "Fully fenced and the next-door houses don't look over the space."

"Completely private and isolated," he added.

"Making it perfect for someone wanting to get in and out without being seen." She returned to where they'd been seated under the second-story deck, to the door that had been deemed the shooter's point of entry. This section offered even more seclusion as it was sheltered from three sides. The fourth was open to the yard.

She nudged her head toward the back door. "Let's walk through the house the way our shooter would have."

The CSI who had held the door earlier for Malone was still there. She was a new face, and introductions were made. Cassie Pope had doe-like eyes, light-brown hair which was pulled into a ponytail, and delicate facial features. Cassie was probably early to mid-thirties, like Amanda and Trent, and she couldn't stop looking at Trent. Amanda swore the woman's cheeks flushed a little when they exchanged names. "Pretty horrid scene upstairs, so I hear," she said.

"You never… uh… went up and saw for yourself?" Trent shook his head. "Never mind. You just said…"

Amanda raised an eyebrow. She'd never seen him like this before, and his cheeks were getting some color too.

Cassie smiled at Trent and chuckled.

Before this attraction between the two of them gets out of control… "It is pretty horrid. Whoever did this is cold and calculating. And the couple's daughter is missing." Her words brought the mood down instantly, and she nudged her head toward the security system panel near the door. "Is there any sign of tampering?"

Trent cleared his throat and met Amanda's gaze briefly—her point made. Flirt after hours, not at the site of a messy double homicide with a missing kid.

"Ah, no, nothing that's obvious anyway. I'll process it for prints, see if I get anything."

Amanda didn't want to be completely skeptical, but given the indications thus far of a professional, she doubted there'd be prints to find. "How did you conclude this door was the point of entry for the shooter?"

"It was unlocked. I've swabbed the door, and no prints there. Hardly even a scratch to the lock. The shooter must have had a lock pick set and was skilled at using it."

Given the couple who Libby had described, they'd have made sure all access points were secured and the security system armed before bed. "Do we know who the Parkers used for their security?"

Cassie stepped back and pointed to a label on the side of the box. "Says 'Protect It.' Looks like a Washington phone number."

"Yeah, I know who they are." The case she and Trent worked back in April had brought them to the Fosters' door, the founders of that security firm. It was also the same investigation that had culminated in her suspension, as well as Trent's temporary relegation to desk duty. She pulled out her phone and brought up the note app. She often switched between jotting things down old-school with a pen and notepad and doing so digitally. *Check with Protect It on Parkers' service. Disarm time?*

She finished and looked at Cassie. "It's likely if the shooter came in here, they left this way too. Regardless, it would be a good idea to check the side gate and yard for any possible trace evidence."

"I'll make sure that's taken care of."

Amanda smiled at her. "Okay, we'll leave you to your work." She started to move but realized Trent wasn't joining her. She looked back and saw that he and Cassie were locked in eye contact. "Ah, Detective Stenson. You wanna join me?"

"Oh, yeah. Sure." He grinned at Cassie, and she at him.

When they were steps away from the CSI, Amanda leaned in and said to Trent, "Cool it, Romeo."

"Yeah, sorry. She's pretty, though, eh?" He looked over a shoulder.

"Seriously?"

He held up a hand.

"On your own time. Right now, we have serious things to focus on." *Like a missing little girl and her murdered parents.* She started walking.

They'd already passed an oak pool table and a wet bar, which was to the side of the entrance. A length of hall ahead likely led to the stairwell to the main level. There were several framed photographs on the wall. Many were of the Parkers, but others were of landscapes. As they walked, they came to a sitting room with a fireplace and a TV set up in the corner. Nothing looked tossed down here. Even the electronics appeared untouched.

"If this was a robbery, they'd have started here."

"Do you think the shooter's main goal was to kidnap Zoe and kill the Parkers? Then he tossed some areas of the house just to cover that motive?" Trent gave her a skeptical sideways look.

"I'm not sure about motive yet, but as you've pointed out a few times already, we're likely looking at a professional. This person policed their brass and probably got in and out with no one noticing. And when they left, did they take Zoe?" Officers would canvass door to door, but she wasn't holding her breath for a lead. "They had to know the Parkers had a daughter—the room, the pictures on the walls in the home. I wouldn't think a professional would want to leave a loose end. And I'm not sure how all this gels with robbery."

"Huh, good point."

They resumed walking through the basement, and nothing down there appeared to have been touched or removed. If the perp had gone through the cupboards in the kitchenette, it wasn't obvious.

They went upstairs to the main level. They found themselves in an eat-in kitchen that was next to another sitting room. More pictures on the walls, but the space itself had been tossed. There was a lidded ottoman, its top gaping open. Pillows were on the floor and drawers in the tables were opened. It appeared that the contents were spewed over the couch cushions. Just ordinary things: some candles, a lighter, assorted remotes, and other bits of bric-a-brac. The Parkers might keep an orderly home, but what they kept stored out of sight was a different story. It was just an assorted mishmash. But like downstairs, the electronics remained.

"You know, it's almost like the shooter was looking for something, not that they were robbing the place," she said.

"So kidnapping, murder, and looking for something... But what?"

"Not a clue."

They walked toward the front of the house and found CSI Isabelle Donnelly processing the office. She currently had her eyes to a camera, working on capturing every square inch of the space. Earlier, Amanda had peeked her head in quickly, but this time, she took a closer look at the room. It appeared as if high winds had blown through and had their way with paperwork and books.

"They did a number in here," Amanda said quietly so as not to startle Donnelly.

She lowered the camera. "You could say that again."

"You find a laptop?" There was no desktop computer, although there was always a chance it had been taken.

"Not yet, but I still need to work my way through the desk drawers."

"Okay. Keep me posted?" Amanda requested.

"You got it."

Just outside the office, in the main entry, Amanda faced Trent. "The only rooms that were tossed were high traffic—the office, main level living room, and the primary bedroom. If the shooter was looking for something, they must have felt it was likely to be in one of those areas."

"And if it was information, it would likely be on the family computer."

"Right..." She chewed on that. "But they didn't just walk off with the computer—assuming they even did. So what were they looking for?"

"Something digital?" Trent tossed out with a shoulder shrug.

"Maybe they were looking for a backup drive?"

"Well, Mrs. Parker worked at an accounting firm. She could have uncovered something illegal in a client's records. Maybe she was going to expose them. This person or company could have deep pockets and thought if they killed her and took the files, their problem would be solved."

"Sure," she said slowly. "But then you'd think they'd target her workplace."

"Not if she also brought her work home."

"I guess, but that's going to a lot of trouble when the leak might not be fixed. Considering possible backups."

"Then there's Brett. He worked for a defense contractor. Maybe he had something someone wanted to get their hands on," Trent suggested. "It would be easier to target him at home, I'd think, than at his workplace."

"And that's assuming Mr. Parker brought his work home with him," Amanda said. "We also can't rule out a possible affair—on either side. And if one of the Parkers was cheating, their lover could be married and have something to lose. They could have been trying to find incriminating evidence and seeking to protect themselves."

"Hiring someone who's professional, though? Sounds like that would be expensive, and I'm not so sure it would happen in the context of an affair."

"You don't know what they might have at stake. Could have a signed prenup—then it's not just a matter of a divorce but kissing their way of living goodbye. We need to consider it."

"Then they didn't consider we'd be checking the Parkers' phone records and text messages and could be led to them that way."

"Could be, sure. But I really don't think the Parkers' marriage was that rosy. They go on a sporadic vacation and come home early. The wife is supposedly offered no real explanation—or did she just not want to tell her friend Libby why they returned ahead of schedule? I don't think it had anything to do with traffic."

"Me neither." Trent got this sort of dazed look to him. "But can you imagine if the murders are connected to Brett's work? It would have the makings of the plot for a thriller novel."

"You a writer now?" She'd play along for a minute or two.

"No." He smiled at her.

"Then let's focus on the evidence and not get carried away."

"You got it."

She didn't know about Trent, but her nerves were frayed thinking about Zoe. She hated the nightmares circling in her mind—the ones that included a sex-trafficking ring she knew was operating in Prince William County and knowing what they'd do with a little girl like Zoe. She tried to push the thoughts away, but they lingered there in the back of her mind.

CHAPTER FIVE

Amanda stepped into the primary bedroom to find CSI Emma Blair and another investigator at work. He was another new face, bringing the total number of CSIs in the house to four. He must have arrived when she and Trent were talking to Libby. Hans Rideout, Amanda's favorite medical examiner, was also there. He worked out of the Office of the Chief Medical Examiner in Manassas. It was a town about thirty minutes away and was also where her mother's trial was being held.

The investigators didn't acknowledge their arrival, but Hans looked up from where he was leaning over the body of Brett Parker.

"Hi, Hans," she said.

"Hey. Why is everyone dying to see me?" Rideout snickered at his not-so-funny joke, but that was morgue humor for you—and Hans. He loved his work and didn't let death dampen his spirit.

"What can you tell us?" Amanda nudged her head toward the body.

"Death happened quick. Given the lack of blood loss around the gunshot to his head, I'd say his heart had already stopped pumping by then. Of course, I'll know better once I have him back at the morgue, but I'd say one of the rounds to his chest had done the trick."

"Can you estimate time of death?" she asked.

"All I can say is probably over twelve hours ago as he's in full rigor. His internal temperature can give me a better idea now, but

I'll know more once I conduct additional tests at the morgue." Rideout rooted in his bag and withdrew a thermometer, which he pierced into Brett's abdomen, likely his liver. A moment later, he pulled it out and said, "Looks like it's well done."

She had a hard time finding amusement in his humor today. "Which means?"

"Give me a minute." He scribbled in his notebook, then struggled to his feet and set off into the hall. Amanda realized it was likely to get the ambient temperature of the house. He returned and mumbled, "This place is bloomin' huge. Not sure why a family of three would need such a large home."

"Different people, different strokes... something like that?" She was quite sure that she got the cliche wrong, but hopefully close enough that Rideout knew what she meant.

"Different strokes for different folks. Uh-huh." Rideout wrote down something else next to his first entry, and his lips started moving while his eyes stared into space. "The body has cooled to about seventy-five degrees Fahrenheit. Calculating in what I know about the stages of rigor, etcetera, and the surrounding temperature, that would mean Mr. Parker here has been dead for a minimum of twelve hours. I'd say TOD's likely somewhere between that and sixteen hours."

She pulled out her phone and woke up the screen to see the time. "Five thirty now, so that would put TOD between one thirty and five thirty this morning."

"I'd say that's good math." He smiled at her.

"And for Mrs. Parker?" She nudged her head toward the walk-in closet.

"I still have to get to her, but I'd say the two murders likely took place in rather fast succession."

Amanda nodded as that made sense to her. She could only imagine how horrifying those last moments had been—especially for Angela, who would have heard her husband shot and had to know she was next. She probably didn't even have time to call 911. This thought reminded her of the phone in Angela's rigored hand. "CSI Blair?" Amanda called out.

The CSI stopped what she was doing, which appeared to be taking inventory of what had been tossed from the drawer of a table in the sitting area. "Yes?" Just one word, but the way her voice arched, it was full of derision.

"Mrs. Parker had a phone clutched in her hand," Amanda began. "Did you collect that yet?"

"I did."

"Any evidence that she tried to call nine-one-one?" She wasn't sure why this mattered to her so much, but she was curious.

"It's locked," Blair said. "I was going to submit it to Tech."

"Is it looking for a pattern, a fingerprint, or just a—"

"A code."

"Have you tried any that are commonly used? Relevant dates such as birthdays or anniversaries?"

Blair didn't say anything and went into her collection case and extended the phone in an evidence bag. "Be my guest."

Wow. She is *chillier than normal.* "Ah, thank you." Amanda took the package and gloved up. While she was getting the phone out, she considered what Angela might have used as a passcode. If the Parkers were having marital problems, it likely wasn't their anniversary. "Ah, when was Zoe's birthday?" She looked at Trent.

"Let me find out…" He made some quick calls, then gave her May second and the year.

Amanda punched that in. "No luck…"

"Not getting anywhere?" This from Blair and obviously a rhetorical jab.

Amanda ignored her and tried something else. Success. She held up the unlocked phone, the screen toward Blair, triumphant.

"What was it?" Trent asked.

"One, two, three, four."

"Really? You would think people would learn."

"Wouldn't you." Her gaze took in what was on the phone—the keypad with 911 keyed. "She got as far as typing the numbers, but why not press call?" She went to recent activity, and it showed two failed attempts. She shared that with Trent.

"Interesting. I just made a call, so there's a signal here."

"Ah, maybe there wasn't at the time of the break-in. We've kicked around the idea of a professional shooter, one that's also skilled with a lock pick, disarming a security system… Why not bring a signal jammer too?"

"Not much of a leap."

"And no landline here?" Amanda directed the question at Blair.

"Nope."

Not a surprise as many households were converting over to cell service only. It was interesting, though, that the shooter left Angela's phone. But had he been interested in Brett Parker's? "Is the wife's the only phone you've found thus far?"

"Yep," Blair answered but kept working as she did so.

Amanda went through more of Angela's call log. There were a couple of missed calls from her work and one from a man by the name of Warren Kennedy. She noted the voicemail envelope in the top left-hand corner. She went back to the log and scrolled down. Warren called and spoke with Angela on quite a regular basis, even when she was on vacation last week, and the conversations lasted several minutes. She asked Trent to make a note of the name and number. Then she put the phone back in the evidence bag and handed it to Blair, who tossed it into her case. Amanda told her the passcode in case she hadn't heard and added, "We'll need a compilation of her contacts, the call log, any of her texts and emails."

"It will get done." Blair gave her a blank stare that sent a chilly spike right through Amanda's core. "Standard procedure."

The way she'd tagged on the last bit, Amanda would think she'd called Blair's abilities into question, but she certainly hadn't meant to. "Thank you." Amanda tried to be polite, but it wasn't easy. And as a thirty-six-year-old woman, Amanda shouldn't care if the investigator didn't like her, but for some reason she did. One day—not now—she was going to come out and ask Blair what her problem was.

Trent turned to Amanda. "If Angela was having an affair, and part of this was to cover that fact, why not take her phone? Sure, we can get what we need from the cell phone provider, but it's left for us to work through."

"I don't have the answers to every— Oh, maybe they want us to think the murders have something to do with Brett. They take his phone, and now we're scratching our heads again."

"You do have an answer for everything."

She smirked. "It's a gift. But we'll subpoena the records from the provider. Could you make that call to the security company now?"

"Sure. What about that guy Warren Kennedy? You want me to call him too?" Trent asked.

"One minute…" She took out her phone and googled his name. "Interesting. He's the owner of Mind Your Own Business, the accounting firm where Angela worked. What was that number again?" Trent told her, and she put it in a Google search. "He called her from his personal number, not the business line."

"So is Warren the man she'd had an affair with before? Or did she ever end things? Or pick them up again?"

"*Or*," she mocked him, "it could be a lot of things, but it might just be that he was calling about business."

"On her vacation and from his private phone?"

"Why not? Besides, some bosses don't relinquish control well. But in answer to your question, no, don't call him. I'd rather see him in person and get a feel for him. Let's go." She headed to Zoe's room.

Trent was talking behind her. A quick look over her shoulder confirmed he was on the phone, and from what he was saying, it would be with the security company.

She took in the space that clearly belonged to a young girl. Pink was the color of choice from the walls to the bedding. Stuffed dolls were lined up against the wall, all seated there as if ready to be called into action. Posters were tacked up. One in particular stood out to Amanda; it was covered with various butterflies of assorted colors interspersed with fun motivational sayings to encourage individuality and personal power.

The comforter was flipped back, and the sheets were pulled out from under the mattress, like the little girl had been tossing and turning in her sleep. Given what Libby had said about the Parkers, Zoe would have slept here last night.

What if Zoe had been afraid of thunderstorms? Lindsey had been, and every time there was one she'd come running into the bedroom to sleep with Amanda and Kevin. They could never refuse her. Amanda remembered savoring the time, realizing how fast she was growing up. She'd hold her daughter and nuzzle into her.

What if?

She rushed back to the primary bedroom and ducked, looking under the bed. Nothing. Of course. Officers would have looked there. Amanda stood, hands on hips, heart pounding. She had gotten carried away with the notion that the girl was here. Even if she'd been in her parents' bed at the time of the intrusion, that didn't mean the shooter hadn't taken her.

"Amanda?" Trent called her name. He was no longer on his phone.

"Yeah?"

"The security company was very cooperative. Said the Parkers regularly armed and disarmed their system."

"As Libby thought. When was it last disarmed?"

"They said the code was entered at four-oh-three AM."

"Guess we have a better idea on time of death, then," Rideout interjected as he must have overheard.

"Seems so," she said mindlessly. She was still thinking about Zoe—now obsessively. She had to be okay. Though she knew that Zoe didn't *have* to be, she refused to give that thought power.

"As we discussed before, Amanda, the killer was prepared," Trent said.

"Definitely a professional, it would seem." The theory left so many questions unanswered. Where was Zoe, and if it was a hired gun who took out the Parkers—what was the motive? What did the Parkers have or know that got them killed and had their girl vanishing without a trace?

CHAPTER SIX

Amanda took another look around the primary bedroom. Rideout had left Brett Parker and was in the closet working on Angela. The CSIs were still processing the room and would be for a while yet. She paced. "Hitmen are usually paid to kill, not kidnap."

"You really think the girl is here somewhere?" Trent countered. "Everyone's been looking for her."

"I know, but I think they still missed something." She considered the possibility that Zoe had hid then managed to get out of the house and flee. She could be in a neighbor's yard, and Amanda knew people were out there looking for her. It would have taken a lot of guts on Zoe's behalf to run. And she may have been aware that her parents had been killed. If so, she was more likely to stay put in a safe, secure hiding spot. Wherever that was. She talked it out. "The perp shoots the Parkers, searches the house, we can only assume afterward. Then what? Collects the girl when he or she finishes trying to find what they're looking for? Makes no sense. That's taking too much of a gamble, and to search the house before coming upstairs and killing the Parkers doesn't make sense. The Parkers could have ambushed him, but there's nothing to indicate that. If the Parkers tried to do either, they probably wouldn't have been shot in the bedroom. They could have been found on the stairs or another level. And I really think that Zoe was in her parents' room when the break-in occurred."

"Due to the storm?"

She nodded.

"So… what? You think she's in here somewhere?"

"I'm starting to think that. Yes."

"All right… But here's one thing standing out to me. If Zoe was in here, why wouldn't Angela have taken Zoe with her into the closet? She could have at least tried to protect her."

"How? She wasn't armed. I'm thinking she may have placed Zoe somewhere safe to give her a chance of surviving." Amanda racked her brain to figure out where that might be. She crept around the room, avoiding trampling on blood and other possible evidence. "Zoe?"

"Aman—"

She held up her index finger to silence Trent. "Zoe, if you're here, it's safe to come out." She rapidly searched the room with her eyes again, and her gaze landed on the bench at the end of the bed. There had been a storage ottoman downstairs. *Could it be…?* She walked over to the bench for a closer look. Rattan wicker with a removable cushion on top. She passed it to Trent, keeping her eyes on the bench. It was hinged! "Zoe?"

There was the faintest sound of a sniffle. So faint, Amanda wasn't sure if she was imagining it, but she lifted the lid.

She gasped at the sight of the little blond girl who was inside—alive—burrowed into a blanket. She looked so small and fragile. Amanda's heart melted, and she just wanted to scoop her up and hug her, console her. Amanda got down on her haunches and drew back a bit at the very faint, yet pungent, smell of urine that hit her nose now the lid was open. But she'd probably been in there since the moment before her parents were murdered. It was surprising they weren't looking at more of a mess here, but Amanda's foremost concern was the girl. "Oh, sweetie, you're safe now. I'm a police detective. My name's Amanda, and this is Trent."

The girl's eyes skipped to him.

Trent smiled kindly at her, then said to Amanda, "I'll go stop the Amber Alert."

The CSIs were watching from the corners where they were working. Rideout ducked his head out from the closet and put a hand over his heart and pinched his eyes shut when she met his gaze. Then he returned into the closet.

Amanda helped the girl out of the ottoman. She was clutching a stuffed dog with large, floppy ears. Her little face was pale, and her eyes bloodshot.

"You're Zoe, right?" Amanda offered a gentle smile, knowing who she was, but she wanted to see if she could get the girl to talk.

She stroked the ears of her doll and said nothing. She looked at Amanda briefly, but her gaze landed on her dead father.

Amanda had to get Zoe out of there.

"Come on. You're safe now." As Amanda held out her hand to the girl, she noticed the rather loose weave of the wicker and the pinholes of light. Zoe had probably seen everything, including her father's murder. She might be safe for now, but if the shooter found out that there was an eyewitness, Zoe could be in grave danger.

CHAPTER SEVEN

Amanda didn't want to let the girl go but had no choice. She'd gotten an immediate change of clothes for Zoe, and Malone swept her off to the hospital to have her checked over. Child Protective Services had been called and would meet him and Zoe at the station afterward. A department psychologist specializing in dealing with traumatized children would also be speaking with Zoe. And Amanda was on the sidelines… Even farther away than that. She needed to push the girl out of her mind for now and get on with the murder investigation. But how could she separate the two? After all, who would rob a little girl of her parents? The thought enraged her and only fired her forward. "We need to go talk to this Kennedy guy," she told Trent.

She stepped outside and was blinded by the lights of a full-blown media circus—Chief Hill right in the middle of it. The star clown putting on her best performance. Amanda hoped Hill would be smart enough to hold back about Zoe. Surely the woman had enough brains to prevent her from outrightly endangering the girl.

Hill really had no business even being here. It was the Public Communications Office that normally handled such things. In Amanda's eyes, Hill was just trying to make herself look good at every opportunity—no matter how distasteful—since she'd recently taken over the position of police chief.

"Unbelievable," Amanda muttered to Trent as they made their way to the department car.

She'd let Trent look up Warren Kennedy's home address while she made a call to Libby Dewinter.

"Oh my God, she's… she's…" Libby started crying at the news—happy tears, to be sure.

"She's being looked at by a doctor, and everything is under control." The latter bit sounded a little off. How could something like this be *under control*?

"So happy. Can I see her?"

"Let me get back to you on that, but I'm thinking there shouldn't be a problem. Stay by your phone."

"I definitely will."

Amanda ended the call, and Trent had Kennedy's address. He started driving, and her phone rang.

"Detective Steele," she answered without consulting caller ID. She figured it was probably her mother or one of her siblings. She had four sisters and a brother—all vested in the outcome of their mother's case, obviously. Her father rarely picked up the phone.

"Amanda?" It was Logan Hunter, a man she'd been seeing since January. The relationship was still at a very much casual stage, probably more due to her desire than his, but he had been a little different in the last few months. The dynamics of their relationship had changed a bit. Her job had ended up putting him in danger, and as a result, he seemed far more sensitive to what was going on with her. She wouldn't be telling him about the case she was working today. "How are ya?" he asked.

"You really don't want to know the answer to that question." She would have loved to just strip off the badge, her clothes, and sink into bed, enveloped in his arms. He did have a way of making her feel safe—even if she knew it was temporary, a few hours here and there. Just like everything in life really. Fleeting. Unpredictable.

"Oh, the trial was that bad? I'm so sorry I couldn't be there."

Logan worked in construction and couldn't get time off easily.

"I understand." And she did.

"But how did it go?"

She gave herself a few seconds to consider how to answer that question. Before she'd left, the trial was hung on Emma Blair, and not a whole lot else had happened all day. "It's just getting started." There was no need to get into the details. Besides, she didn't have any.

"I see…"

"Not really much to say. You doing good?"

"I am. I was hoping to come over to your place. I could pick up something for dinner and meet you in an hour. That work?"

She glanced over at Trent as he took them this way and that, and from the looks of it headed to Woodbridge, another town in Prince William County. It was also where the Central Police Station was that they worked out of. "Actually, I'm working a case right now."

"Right. Of course you are."

"Don't say it like that." She wished that evil didn't exist just as much as he did, but she wasn't living in a fantasy world.

"Just miss you lately."

"Me too." And that was the truth. She could conjure his cologne—a heady concoction that smelled like a campfire—if she inhaled deeply enough. "What about Friday? We could go out…"

"Or stay in?" His smirk traveled the line.

"Could work."

"What about Thursday instead?"

She didn't know where she'd be in the investigation Friday, let alone Thursday. "Sure, let's plan on that."

"Okay. I'll be at your place about six thirty on Thursday."

"Sounds good." She ended the call and looked over at Trent. "Oh, the boyfriend wants a piece of me." *Did I just say that out loud?*

Trent laughed, and so did she. Sometimes on this job you just had to find the time to laugh.

*

Amanda had knocked three times before the door was opened. A trim man in his fifties with salt-and-pepper hair and an aura of charisma stood there. She held up her badge, and Trent did the same with his. "Detectives Steele and Stenson. Are you Warren Kennedy?"

"I am." He drew his gaze from her to Trent.

"We need to speak with you about Angela Parker," she began. "Can we come inside?"

"Ah… yes… come in." He seemed flustered and awkward at the mention of Angela's name, but he had to know if cops were on his doorstep about her, something bad had likely happened.

Warren took them to a living room with a fireplace, not that it would be needed until the evening temperatures started to dip. He sat on a wingback chair, and Amanda and Trent sat in two others.

"What is this about Angela Parker?"

"We understand she's an employee of yours," Trent started.

"That's right. Is she… is she okay?"

"Unfortunately, Angela and her husband, Brett, were murdered in their home this morning," Trent said.

Warren didn't utter a word or a gasp, but his eyes widened, then narrowed. He became stiff like he'd stopped breathing.

"Mr. Kennedy," Amanda prompted.

"Wow. I'm speechless. I don't know what to say. Their little girl?"

"She's alive." She wasn't going so far as to say *fine*. That ship was a long way off. "You were close with Mrs. Parker?"

"She worked for me for fifteen years. One of my best employees." He massaged his brow. "Everyone at the firm's going to be devastated."

"Were you and Angela ever anything more than employer and employee?" Amanda asked delicately.

"Me and—" His mouth twitched, and Amanda wasn't sure if he was offended or going to snicker at the idea.

She waited for him to get himself together.

"That's a no. She was just my employee. By a stretch, my friend. But it's not like we socialized—unless you count company events."

From his reaction, she believed him, but she wanted to clear up something. "You called from your personal phone and spoke to her last week when she was on vacation. What was that about?"

"Oh. Well, my calling from my personal cell phone wasn't unusual. It's always on me, just what I reach for. You'll probably notice that I called her regularly from that number."

"We did," she admitted. "And the purpose for calling her last week?"

He sighed dramatically. "She handles this one client who is, let's say, a little difficult. I just needed to ask some questions about his account."

"You spoke a few times," she pointed out.

"Yep, all about this client."

"And who would that be?"

"I'd prefer not to say, for confidentiality reasons."

"While I can appreciate that, we're investigating her murder," Amanda said. With the weight of the word *murder* slung into the fray again, the tension in the room intensified.

"Surely you don't think a client killed her?"

"No one is ruled out yet."

"Including me?" He blanched at his question.

"Where were you this morning between four and six?" she asked matter-of-factly.

"I was here sleeping until five but was at the office by six."

"Can anyone substantiate that?" Trent asked.

"I don't see how. It was only me there."

"What about a security system?" Amanda said. "Could you provide us with a report showing when you clocked in?"

"You really think I'd kill her—and Brett? You must be crazy."

She bristled somewhat at that comment but also noted the familiarity he had with Angela's family. Surely that was expected since she had been a long-time employee. Brett had probably been to some of the company functions Warren had brought up.

"It's procedure," Trent ended up saying when she hadn't responded.

"I'll see what I can do."

Amanda pulled out a business card and handed it to Warren. "My email's on there. You can send the report from your security system there."

"Sure." Warren crossed his legs. "Anything else?"

"Back on the subject of Angela's clients, were you aware of any who were upset with her? Anyone whose records she flagged for some reason? Maybe she was going to expose someone for fraud?" She wanted to check off what questions she could while she was here.

"Not that she ever mentioned to me."

Amanda nodded. The next bit might be a little harder to bring up, but that was the thing with death, it had a way of exposing everything—even our darkest secrets. "It's come to our knowledge that Angela had an affair with someone she used to work with at your firm."

Warren flushed. "That's why when you saw my calls you assumed that Angela and I had more than a business relationship."

"That's right," she admitted. "This affair I'm referring to, though, goes back about six or seven years. Do you know who that might have been?"

Warren seemed to give it some real consideration. "I suspected something was going on between her and Colin Brewster, but I didn't want to believe it. I'd caught them here and there—just the way they'd look at each other. Quite sure I saw him smack her butt in the copy room once, truth be told."

"Mr. Brewster still work for you?"

"Oh, no, he moved on a couple of years back. California, if memory serves. I got a call from some firm out there."

If that were the case, they could probably take Colin off the suspect list. Angela would have been in his rearview mirror. Not likely they'd rekindled things long distance. If they had been in communication, though, it would show up when her records were reviewed.

"Was Angela seeing anyone else that you know about?" Trent asked, leaning forward, elbows on knees.

"If she was, I didn't see evidence of that. Not around the firm anyway. Can't say if she was meeting up with a man outside of work."

"Thinking about it, looking back, any impressions she may have been cheating on her husband recently?" Amanda asked.

"I'd say no. She was just as obsessive about her family as her work. She'd go out for lunch with Brett when she could and was always bringing in Zoe's drawings and taping them to her filing cabinets."

"So she had recently become more, shall we say, *attentive* to her family? Why do you think that is?" Amanda was thinking that guilt over her infidelity could have moved her to overcompensate.

Warren shrugged. "I have no idea."

Amanda nodded and stood. "All right. Thank you for your time and cooperation, and we're sorry for your loss."

"I appreciate your saying that. I'll send over what I get on the security system report." He held up her card, and she nodded.

Out in the car, she turned to Trent. "Warren Kennedy didn't kill them."

"I don't see it either."

And just like that, one visit potentially marked two suspects off their list—Warren, Angela's boss, and Colin, her old flame. But it didn't eliminate a new lover. Amanda and Trent needed to do some more digging into Angela's personal life.

CHAPTER EIGHT

As Amanda and Trent were leaving Warren's house, Malone called to inform them Zoe was being taken back to Central where they would be meeting with the woman from Child Protective Services and the police psychologist. He assured her that Zoe, by all accounts, was physically healthy if a little dehydrated and in need of food—two matters the doctors at the hospital had seen to. It was likely she hadn't left the ottoman from the time of hiding there around four in the morning until around five forty in the evening when Amanda had found her.

Amanda called Libby Dewinter and told her to head to Central if she wanted to see Zoe. Not that there was really a question about that.

Central was one of Prince William County PD's three stations. The PWCPD was rather large with about seven hundred officers. Central housed the Homicide Unit, along with some other special-ized departments and administration. The building had opened a few years ago and was mostly a single-story redbrick structure and situated on a country lot surrounded by trees. It would have been a serene setting if not for the nature of the investigations that went on inside the station's walls.

Trent went to the warren of cubicles where Homicide was set up. They were down a few detectives and had been for a while. One male officer had started while Amanda was suspended and Trent was on desk duty, but he'd come and gone in no time. The only detective in the unit who seemed to stick around for the long haul was Natalie Ryan, a.k.a. Cougar, because she'd dated a guy who was young enough to be her kid *once*. That was all it took for the nickname to stick. Amanda resented the judgment on Natalie's behalf more with every passing day.

While Amanda went to visit Zoe in one of the interview rooms, Trent would be pulling some quick reports on the Parkers, Libby Dewinter, and Colin Brewster. And he would get a trace started on Brett's phone and request subpoenas for the Parkers' call histories.

Amanda peered through the glass at Zoe. This particular interview room was made up like a living room with plush furniture, potted plants, and framed landscapes on the wall. It was meant to be soothing, comfortable, familiar. And there was a small table for children with matching chairs, buckets of toys and building blocks, coloring books, crayons—anything to assist in calming a child.

Zoe was sitting at the children's table, clutching her stuffed dog like it was her best friend in the world. Amanda just wanted to run into the room and scoop up the child, reassure her that everything would be okay, but just the thought had her feeling like a hypocrite. There was nothing okay about losing one's family—especially because of murder and maybe having witnessed it, no less. Amanda tried to remind herself that they didn't know for sure if Zoe had seen anything, but at the very least she likely would have heard everything.

Seated next to Zoe was a woman whom Amanda recognized as Colleen Frost, the police psychologist.

Malone came up behind her, holding a coffee cup.

"Decaf, I hope?" she jested with him, though her heart was shattering for Zoe.

"Nope. The real deal. Not going to sleep tonight anyway."

"But she was found alive." She had to cling to that. It meant something—or at least it would once Zoe had a chance to heal. "She say anything?"

"Not a word." He gestured with his mug toward Colleen. "I mentioned that to Frost, but she wasn't concerned. Said it was completely understandable given the circumstances."

"Detectives." A female voice came from behind them.

Amanda spun, and Libby Dewinter was standing there, having been escorted back by the front-desk receptionist. She barely appeared to be holding herself together, let alone upright. "Ms. Dewinter," Amanda said, "this is my sergeant, Scott Malone."

They shook hands, then Libby pressed her forehead to the window that overlooked the room. Tears were streaming down her cheeks. "I can't thank you enough for finding her." Libby sniffled and swiped at her cheeks with her palms.

"Don't mention it."

Libby turned and wrapped Amanda in a hug before she had a chance to react. Libby started sobbing heavily, and Malone met Amanda's gaze and left.

Libby pulled back. "Can I see her now?"

"It would be best if I talked to you first... just filled you in." Amanda guided Libby to the room next to the one Zoe was in, which was pretty much a mirror image, and searched for a tissue box. "Sit wherever you'd like," Amanda told her. "I'm just going to get some tissue."

"No, it's okay. I came prepared." Libby dropped into an armchair and pulled a wad of tissues from her purse, which she then set on the floor next to her feet.

"I see you have." Amanda shut the door and headed for the couch. Usually it was the people she was speaking to who chose the couch. It was a piece of furniture that offered comfort and was associated with relaxation. But Libby wasn't relaxed, wasn't even looking to be soothed based on her body language, which was rigid as if she were braced for more bad news.

Libby dabbed at her face and neck and blew her nose. "Who is that woman with Zoe?"

"Her name's Colleen Frost. She's a psychologist with the police department. I can assure you that Zoe's in good hands."

"She looked nice. And Zoe even looked like she was okay. She is okay?"

"She's been through a lot, and there will be a long road ahead."

"Kids are resilient," Libby interjected, looking at Amanda as if seeking confirmation.

"Children can handle a lot more than we think, but they're also far more vulnerable than we can necessarily imagine." Amanda spoke slowly and in an even tone, trying to maintain a sense of calm.

"She's... she's *not* okay then? I mean, I know she lost her parents, but... Ah, where did you find her?" Libby kneaded the tissue in her hands.

So much for calm. Amanda leaned forward just slightly. "We ended up finding Zoe in her parents' bedroom."

"She was there all that time?"

"It would seem so."

"Why didn't anyone find her sooner? I don't understand."

"She was in the ottoman at the end of the bed. It was lidded with a compartment inside. She was very good at staying still and quiet."

"Thank goodness the killer didn't..." Libby touched her throat, unable to finish the sentence that would have undoubtedly ended something along the lines of *find her.*

"Definitely a blessing she remained unharmed, but she was in there for a number of hours." There was more to tell Libby and to ask her, but Amanda would take things slowly so as to not overwhelm her. "The ottoman was made of rattan wicker, and the weave would have made it rather see-through." She let that sit with Libby, then added, "We believe that Zoe may have witnessed her father's murder."

Libby gasped loudly, and her eyes widened. Fresh tears snaked down her cheeks, and she didn't bother wiping them away. Maybe she didn't even notice them at this point. "She... she... Oh my God."

"I know. It's a horrible thing to imagine, and obviously she's been put through something no one should have to face." She waited a few moments for Libby to calm down. "It's why we arranged for her to speak with a police psychologist right away. Also—"

"There's more?" Libby's face was a mask of heartbreak.

"Since she may have seen what happened, it's possible that Zoe isn't safe. That is *if* the shooter finds out about her."

"Well, who's going to tell them?"

"Her face was all over that house—in the framed photos. Her room's right down the hall. It would make sense that the shooter knew they'd missed someone." As Amanda laid out the ugly truth, a pain knotted in her chest.

"Oh… I'm gonna be sick." Libby rubbed her stomach as she rocked back and forth.

"I tell you this so you're aware of the situation, to be upfront, but she's in good hands. We won't let anything happen to her." The statement came out as a promise before Amanda could prevent its birth.

"I… trust you." Libby sniffled. "Did Zoe say she saw her dad get killed?"

"Not in so many words," Amanda said, doing a little dance around the truth, then figured it was probably best to be forthright. "She hasn't actually said anything since I found her."

"Not one word?" Libby blinked, her lashes loaded with unshed tears.

"No. But that's completely normal for what she's gone through." People sometimes shut down after traumatic events. Amanda had herself, when she'd lost her family.

Libby nodded. "Her mind's trying to make sense of it." She met Amanda's gaze. "As am I. Why did someone do this to them? The Parkers were nice people. They didn't deserve this." Anger fired in her eyes.

"No, they didn't. Really, no one does." Just for an instant, Amanda felt a touch hypocritical. There were days she could justify her mother's actions, given who her victim had been. "I know that my partner and I asked you this already, but can you think of anyone who might have had something against them?"

"No. Absolutely not." Libby rubbed her arms. "And I'm guessing, since you keep asking, this was no ordinary break-in?"

"We have reason to believe it may have been something else."

"Like what? I said they were nice people. Minded their own business."

Now wasn't the time to point out that people who kept to their own affairs weren't typically targeted for murder. And the evidence was pointing to the Parkers possessing something that the shooter wanted. "There was a safe in the walk-in closet, in the primary bedroom. Would you happen to know what they might have kept in there?"

"Angela had some pricey pieces of jewelry. Maybe that?"

The thing had been empty, so maybe the shooter helped themselves to some bling, even if it wasn't the main purpose. "Okay. Anything else you could think of?"

"Isn't that enough?"

"The safe was completely empty." Amanda's mind was stuck on the possibility that the shooter had been after information. "Do you know if Angela or Brett took their work home with them? Maybe had something on their computers that someone might find valuable?"

Libby met her gaze. "I think they only had one laptop, but if you had it, you wouldn't be asking me that question. It was taken?"

"It seems so." Amanda hadn't received the official word on that yet. "Do you have any idea why someone would want it?"

"Not the foggiest. Though Brett did bring work home on his laptop. I know because Angela would complain about it sometimes."

If Brett brought sensitive files home, that could explain why someone wanted the laptop, but why all the other rummaging? Was that simply to throw off the investigation? "Do you know what Brett did for Falcon?"

"Honestly, my eyes would blank over whenever he talked about it. Some top-secret things, though."

"And he talked to you about it?"

"Just in generalities," Libby said. "No details. You'll have to ask Falcon directly. All I can tell you is he was a type of programmer."

"We'll be talking to them," Amanda assured her. She wondered if Brett had discussed his job with other people, and if that had factored into the murders, but she refused to get sucked into conspiracy theories. "Is there anything else that Brett may have used the laptop for other than his job?"

Libby chewed on her bottom lip. "He loved taking photos. It was almost an obsession with him. Maybe he kept some pictures on his computer."

Brett's interest in photography would explain the numerous framed photographs, but how could a picture get him and his wife killed? Unless he took pictures of something highly confidential and the wrong person found out. Or he was going to sell images of that *something*, and the deal went south. She shook aside the thoughts, feeling she may be getting carried away.

"You probably found his cameras," Libby prompted.

"I'm not sure if we did or not at this point." She'd make a note to follow up on that. "But *cameras* plural?"

"Yeah, he had two. One for digital and one for film. Come to think of it, he was a bit of a nut when it came to backing up his pictures. Probably his computer too. He had rolls of negatives around the house and more than his fair share of hard drives. Maybe he kept some in their closet safe?" She shrugged. "I'm not sure. I think he also stored things on the cloud." She pointed toward the ceiling as if digital storage were up in the sky somewhere.

Amanda would make sure she followed up with the investigators on a laptop, backup drives, cameras, and film negatives. Maybe the shooter wasn't looking for a file, but a photograph. Maybe they'd decided to take everything just in case… or to avoid tipping their hand as to what they were after. Did that also explain the rummaging in different rooms of the house? And at what point had the Parkers come into the possession of something the shooter wanted? One would assume more recently, and there was the random family vacation that had also been cut short. "You said that the Parkers rarely took vacation?" she asked.

"They haven't as long as I've known them. A day here or there, and relaxing some on weekends, but never week-long getaways."

"Who planned the trip—Brett or Angela?"

"Oh, it was his idea."

Amanda's mind was taking her in such fantastical directions—again. Had Brett, through his work, obtained knowledge of something that he was trying to sell, but the plan backfired? Had he divulged what he did for work to the wrong person, and that had somehow led to the murders? Then it hit her that Brett's phone seemed to be missing and not Angela's. Maybe that *did* mean something? Had he attracted evil to his home?

"Do you know why the desire for a getaway?" Amanda asked. "They just wanted a quick break or was it for some other reason?"

"I don't really know."

"Where was it they went again?"

"Lake Chesdin."

"Right. Lots to do there."

"Golf, fishing… Not that Angie or Brett were into any of that."

"Why go there, then?" Her voice was barely its regular volume. She was getting carried away with plots that existed in blockbuster movies. Defense contractor defects and sells information to the highest bidder. It *could* explain a professional killer.

Get a grip, she coached herself.

"Just for fresh air? To go hiking," Libby said with a shrug. "You could probably tell from their gorgeous property, they loved nature and the outdoors."

There was a knock on the door, and then it opened slowly. It was Trent.

"Dr. Frost has finished with Zoe," he told them.

"Can I see her now?" Libby gathered her purse and looked at Amanda. "Take her home?"

"That would take a while to get sorted out. It's something you'd have to arrange with child services."

"Oh, I guess that makes sense. I just assumed that I…"

"Unfortunately, we can't release her into your care tonight. Something may be able to get worked out, but these things take time. And remember, we have to think about her safety foremost."

Libby bit her bottom lip and nodded.

Amanda continued. "Trust me. She will be cared for and protected. I just wanted to let you know this ahead of time so that later, when they come to get her, you're not surprised and don't make any fuss in front of Zoe."

Libby jutted out her chin. "I understand."

"Good." Amanda offered a small smile and stood.

As she and Trent proceeded to take Libby next door to Zoe, Amanda couldn't help but wonder whether she'd be so understanding in Libby's position. But then, Amanda had a beautiful girl who'd slipped through her fingers once; if she ever had a chance to go back and change that, she would. She'd spent over six years wishing that she could. And while her daughter was beyond saving, she still had the opportunity to be there for Zoe.

CHAPTER NINE

Amanda watched through the window as Libby ran across the room to Zoe, dropped to her knees in front of the girl, and enveloped her in a huge embrace. In response to Libby's affection, the girl appeared rigid. But, eventually, she raised her arms and hugged back. Libby cupped the back of Zoe's head, and by this point, tears were streaming down Libby's face. Zoe was devoid of emotion and was the first to withdraw, but she tapped the chair next to her. Libby sat her adult frame down gingerly on the child's chair.

Amanda turned to Trent to let the two of them have their privacy. "You checked Dewinter's background?"

"She's clean—squeaky, as some might say. Teaches at Dumfries Elementary, as she told us. Not so much as a parking ticket. Shares a place with Penny Anderson, her girlfriend."

Amanda nodded, recalling the name. "As she told us."

"I highly doubt she's involved in what happened."

"I don't think she is either. What about any next of kin for the Parkers?"

"Again, as Dewinter told us, there's no one. Also Colin Brewster's current residence is in California."

Amanda glanced back at Zoe. She was mostly alone in this world—well, except for Libby. At least Zoe had that. She faced Trent again. "Had an interesting conversation with Libby…" She filled him in about the photography and Brett's work as a programmer, adding, "He was big on backing up his photos and files to various hard drives. Even had some actual negatives kicking around, according to Libby. We'll need to see if the CSIs recovered any. It might give us a direction as to what the shooter was after—file or photo. In the meantime, we should also get ahold of the Parkers' internet provider…"

"It's the same company who handled their cell phones," Trent inserted. "I found that out when I was getting started on the subpoenas for their call history."

She nodded. "We'll also need access to their cloud drive. Apparently, Brett would use the cloud for backup purposes as well. Again, it might be our best chance, maybe only chance, to figure out what the shooter was after."

"I'll handle that."

She looked around, now curious where Colleen had gone. "Did Dr. Frost leave without speaking to me?"

"Right here. Was just getting a coffee, Detective."

Amanda turned to see Colleen smiling and holding a steaming mug. She raised it, blew on it, and took a tentative sip. "Shall we?" She led the way to the room that Amanda had just left.

Following behind the psychologist in a glorious haze of aromatic coffee, Amanda had a strong craving for one. But the desire to hear what Colleen had to say about Zoe was more powerful.

Colleen sat in the chair that Libby had vacated, and Amanda and Trent sat on opposite ends of the couch.

"I'm afraid she's not doing well," Colleen started. "But it's very early yet, and it may take her a while to open up. Her mind has a lot to process. A child's mind works slightly differently than an adult's." Colleen paused, crossed her legs, perched her mug on a knee. "As a grown-up, we have life experience to pull from. We can apply one area of understanding to a new endeavor and draw similarities until we grasp the new that's before us. In other words, we have a platform and plethora of wisdom to build upon. Think how one uses a metaphor to aid in the understanding of a new thing. Well, a child doesn't have this store of knowledge. Even in the case of an adult witnessing or hearing something as traumatic as Zoe Parker has, their mind would be struggling to make sense of it. Assign logic, rationalize it. A child doesn't do this exactly, and it's a benefit for them really."

Amanda glanced at Trent, back to Colleen. "How is that?"

Colleen took another sip of her coffee. "She's simply processing what she witnessed—nothing more. Unlike with an adult who longs to assign reason, purpose, the answer to *why*. This is probably why people think of children as resilient. And they are. But as they get older, memories will resurface. When that happens to Zoe, she will then try to come to grips with it, make sense of it from a more adult perspective."

"It's the long-term that wreaks havoc," Amanda concluded.

"Exactly. That's why how we handle the situation now will have a great bearing on how Zoe processes this into part of her life experience."

"Sounds like you believe she did see her father's murder," Amanda said, clutching her gut.

"I do, yes. Not that she's saying."

There went Amanda's next question about whether the child had begun talking. But to hear Colleen discuss Zoe's forming mind, Amanda was happy the weight of that responsibility wasn't on her shoulders.

"I should clarify. Not one *verbal* word. However, body and facial language, as you know, also talks." Colleen smiled kindly at Amanda and Trent. "Whenever I asked questions about what she might have seen and presented hypotheticals, she would tense at times. When she did, I knew that I was getting somewhere. This is why I feel confident in concluding she did see the killer."

Amanda's heart sped up with rage. "Not just her father's murder, as in him going down, but the shooter's face?"

"Keep in mind that for a child, 'seeing' can mean sensing as well. It doesn't mean she literally saw the shooter. I do get the impression it was a man, but not someone Zoe knew."

Amanda was impressed that the doctor got this much from Zoe, even though the child hadn't spoken. "Was there any exchange of words between the shooter and her parents?" The minute Amanda asked the question, she knew it was a long, long shot.

"I suspect that there was some conversation, but I have no way of knowing what was said until Zoe starts talking. I will meet with her again tomorrow and keep spending time with her for as long as it takes." Colleen uncrossed her legs and stood. "Obviously she will return to school at some point too, but let's take this one day at a time."

Amanda hated how the world wanted to inflict normalcy after tragedy—as if busyness or going through the motions would ease the pain of a broken heart. "Thanks for working with her." She smiled at Colleen, and the doctor dipped her head.

"My job, Detective." Colleen left the room, letting the door stay open behind her.

Amanda faced Trent. "Zoe saw and heard her parents' killer, and if that person finds out, she could be in real danger. We need to keep her safe, Trent."

"We will."

She met his gaze and slowly nodded. But her eye ended up catching the time on the clock on the wall. It was going on ten at night. Zoe needed to get some rest. "Hopefully, someone from child services gets here soon." She got up and went next door.

"I'm gonna see what progress I can make on that cloud drive," Trent said.

"Good idea."

He headed off to his desk, and she knocked and entered the room where Libby was still with Zoe.

Libby looked at Amanda, pressed her lips into a flat line, and very subtly shook her head, which Amanda took to mean the girl hadn't spoken.

Zoe lifted her gaze to meet Amanda's. A spark of light flashed in her eyes, and Amanda half-expected her to say something—but she didn't.

"Zoe, you've been incredible," Amanda said, smiling at the girl. Then she went over and kneeled in front of her.

Zoe was still clutching her stuffed dog against her chest. She seemed to be keeping a close watch on Amanda, but she remained mute.

"I'm sure you're getting tired." Amanda lowered her eyelids slowly, opened them just as slowly.

A nod, barely perceptible.

A rap on the doorframe, followed by, "Hello, are you Zoe Parker?" A middle-aged woman entered and was coming toward Zoe. She had a friendly face and kind presence. Zoe didn't react at all to the woman's question, but she looked at Amanda.

Amanda stood between Zoe and the woman. "Can I help you?"

"Erica Murphy. Child Protective Services." She produced a card in quick fashion like a gunslinger in the Wild West.

Amanda took the card. "I'm Detective Amanda Steele."

"Yes, I was told I'd find you in here." The woman smiled pleasantly but took another step toward Zoe.

The girl squirmed and tugged on Amanda's hand. Amanda tried to put herself in the girl's place—Erica was just another stranger thrust upon her.

"It's okay. You're safe, Zoe." Amanda put a hand on the girl's shoulder but removed it just as quickly. The physical contact was inappropriate under the circumstances, even if it was motivated by fellow feeling. Zoe grabbed Amanda's hand and pulled it to her.

As her small hand melded into Amanda's, the memories crashed over her. Amanda's breath froze in her chest. She had to calm herself. This wasn't Lindsey… She wasn't back from the dead. And, that, *that* was okay. *That* was *okay.* Maybe if she repeated it enough?

Somewhere in the room, she heard voices—Erica and Libby exchanging names—and eventually Amanda felt her mind and heart come back to her.

"Ah, Erica's here to take you on a sleepover," Amanda inserted. "You know what a sleepover is?"

Zoe's gaze flicked to Libby then back to Amanda, and she nodded.

"They're fun. Right?" Amanda smiled at her. "You go to Libby's sometimes and stay over?"

Another nod.

"Tonight, Erica wants you to go with her for a sleepover."

"Don't talk to strangers." The voice was small and quiet, so much so that Amanda wondered if she'd imagined it. But it was the sweetest sound, and it had Amanda's heart bumping off rhythm.

"That's right, but Erica isn't a stranger."

Zoe pierced Amanda with her gaze, calling Amanda out.

"She's not a stranger," Amanda repeated. "She's a… new friend." That would hopefully make the proposal more appealing.

Erica advanced on Zoe again, her movements a little rash even to Amanda, and Zoe jumped to her feet.

"No!"

"Zoe, I'd love to be your friend." Erica smiled.

It was starting to feel like this woman was more in a hurry to check Zoe off her to-do list than take the girl's feelings into consideration. But maybe Amanda was allowing herself to get too personally vested in this case, specifically regarding the six-year-old girl she was looking at right now. Zoe's blue eyes met Amanda's and made her chest ache, but she was done for when the girl took her hand and hugged it to herself again, next to the floppy-eared dog. Amanda tried to free her hand from the girl's, but she had the grip of a wrestler.

"I go with you… Sleepover. Can I?"

Amanda peered down at the girl, but as much as she felt for the child, she just couldn't allow herself to get that involved. If she took her home, it would certainly become personal and—

"Of course she can." Chief Hill strode into the room. She refused eye contact with Amanda and kept her gaze on Zoe.

Amanda looked back at Zoe, and the girl was peering back at her. She tapped the back of the girl's hand. "I just need to have a word with our new friend Erica. And this is Sherry Hill."

Now the chief met her gaze, derision sizzling there. Probably because Amanda hadn't used her title, but kids didn't care about them, and Amanda certainly didn't think the woman deserved the one she had.

The three of them stepped into the hall, leaving Libby with Zoe.

"I can't take her home." Amanda glared at Hill, not really caring if Erica picked up on the hatred she felt for the woman. "I never said that I was willing to take her home. Besides, I don't have any place for her to sleep."

Hill contorted her face into an ugly mask. "You live in a two-bedroom house all by yourself." She crossed her arms and turned to Erica.

Wow. Amanda felt like she'd been physically struck. Hill knew about the accident and how Amanda had lost her husband and daughter in one blow. Hill was a monster. Amanda opened her mouth, about to tell the woman off, when Erica spoke.

"It just doesn't work like this. There's protocol that needs to be followed."

"Amanda Steele is a detective with the PWCPD," Hill began. "You may not be aware, but Zoe Parker's life is potentially in danger. Her parents were killed, and she was left alive. The killer might return for her."

At the mention of Zoe's predicament, Amanda softened just slightly.

THE SILENT WITNESS 69

Hill turned to Amanda. "I am right, yes? Zoe is in danger?"

Amanda's throat was constricted and dry. All she'd love to do at this moment in time was haul off and punch the woman.

"Detective," Hill prompted.

"Yes," Amanda hissed.

"Then it's settled. Zoe Parker will go home with you." Hill rubbed her hands together and looked at Erica. "She'll cooperate with you to get taken care of whatever needs taking care of." With that, Hill slithered away like the snake she was.

Bitch!

"Detective," Erica started, sounding tentative, "are you good to take her home? You do have a place for her to sleep?"

Amanda thought of her daughter's room. It had basically become a shrine over the years. Reluctantly, Amanda nodded.

"All right. Well, it's clear the girl has taken a shine to you." Erica smiled, but Amanda couldn't get herself to form the expression. She'd become locked in the past in some ways, but in the present, she felt like she would be betraying her daughter by taking Zoe home.

"It's for one night," she clarified to Erica. "We'll have to work something else out tomorrow."

Erica held eye contact with Amanda for a while longer, then eventually nodded. "Let me make some calls." She walked off, her cell phone to an ear, leaving Amanda standing there in shock.

"I got all the subpoenas rolling."

She heard Trent's voice, but she was locked in a daze. She wanted to hurt Hill. She flexed her hands into fists.

"Amanda? What's…"

She took a deep inhale. "Guess Zoe's in my care tonight."

"Oh… *Oh.* Really?"

"I'd never joke about that." She went into the restroom and splashed water on her face, then met her eyes in the mirror. Zoe did like her; more importantly, she trusted her. Amanda shut her eyes and spoke to Lindsey's ghost… or her memory. "Mommy needs to help another little girl. I hope you'll forgive me, baby. But please know she's not taking your place and never could." She gripped the edge of the sink and opened her eyes again. "One night," she swore to herself in the mirror and left the room.

CHAPTER TEN

Amanda signed some paperwork for Erica Murphy, but otherwise the process had been rather straightforward—though not entirely painless. The pain entered in with the little package Amanda had in the front seat of her car. Zoe Parker.

She was driving them to her house, a modest bungalow that she'd once shared with her husband and daughter. She hadn't been able to bring herself to empty out Lindsey's room, and while it would be the most suitable for a young girl, she didn't know if she could allow Zoe to sleep there. Maybe they could bunk in the living room—Zoe on the couch, Amanda on a blow-up mattress. Like a fun slumber party, only without the party.

She glanced over at Zoe, but the girl was staring at the stuffed dog in her lap. "What's his name?" Amanda asked.

Zoe stopped stroking the dog's ears, but she didn't say anything.

Lindsey had a favorite doll she called Twinkle. While she had proudly declared the name, she and Kevin had a hard time not laughing. But when they'd asked Lindsey why she'd chosen it, she gave them a serious reason. It was because the doll's eyelids opened and closed, and to Lindsey, they twinkled. She took Twinkle with her everywhere. It had been in the car that night and "died" with her daughter, stained with her blood and discarded. At this moment, Amanda wished she'd had it cleaned and buried with Lindsey.

She pulled into her driveway and turned off the car. "Well, this is it." She took off her seat belt and reached over to unclip

Zoe's, but the girl beat her to it. Amanda held up her hands in apology. "Sorry, I should have known you're big enough to get that yourself." She realized then just how long it had been since she'd had a child to care for.

"It's okay."

Every time Zoe spoke, it warmed Amanda's heart.

Amanda got out of the car and reached into the back seat to retrieve Zoe's bag of things that Erica Murphy had gathered from the family home. Zoe remained in the passenger seat, looking not so sure, and Amanda walked around to her and opened the door.

"I've got you. You have nothing to worry about." Amanda flung the bag's strap over her shoulder and held out a hand for Zoe to take—and she did.

They walked, holding hands, to the front door. Amanda only let go of the girl because she had to pull out her house key and stick it in the deadbolt. She stepped inside and turned on the light. "Just make yourself at home."

Zoe kicked out of her shoes while taking in the house from the entry.

It was a rather open concept home, something she and Kevin had taken care of long ago with numerous renovations. There was a living room to the left, the kitchen beyond that with the dining room to the right. Straight ahead led toward the back of the house. Around midway back, a hallway branched off on the right. Not that Zoe could see this or know, but that led to two bedrooms and a bathroom. The basement was partially finished, but not used except for when Amanda had laundry to take care of. The home certainly wasn't what Zoe was accustomed to.

"It's smaller than your house, but—"

"It's nice." Zoe didn't look at her when she spoke but shifted her stuffed dog from one arm to the other as she slipped out of her coat.

"Here, let me help." Amanda bent down and—

"No!" Zoe burst out and stopped all movement, except to hug her fluffy dog tighter to herself, the one sleeve of her jacket abandoned and draping to the floor.

"Sorry, honey, I wasn't going to touch your friend." She pressed her lips in a kind, understanding smile, while making the mental note that the girl was particularly fond of the stuffed animal. Amanda could understand why. After all, it was all she really had left of her life. "I was just going to help you out of your coat."

Zoe clenched her jaw, and after a few moments, she resumed the balancing act with the dog and took her other arm out of the coat. Amanda retrieved it from her, slowly, and Zoe relinquished it.

"I usually just hang my coats here." Amanda proceeded to hook it on a coat tree that stood next to a table near the front door. She'd have to dig out the small one that she and Kevin had bought for Lindsey—one Zoe would be able to reach.

Amanda stopped herself. This was for one night. She cleared her throat. "How about a quick tour? Then we should both get some sleep."

Zoe bobbed her head but didn't say anything.

Amanda proceeded to show Zoe the house, ending with Lindsey's room. She opened the door.

Zoe's eyes widened at the sight of pink, similar to the decor of her own room, less the motivational posters. Lindsey had a shelving unit full of books with stuffed dolls on its top. She also had a craft table with an open coloring book, crayons haphazardly sitting on the pages and nested in the spine as if Lindsey had just stepped away.

"Whose room is this?" Zoe looked up at her, and Amanda sucked in a ragged breath.

"It was my daughter, Lindsey's."

"You have a daughter? Where is she?" Zoe had made her way to the far end of the room that faced the street. It was where the craft table sat under the window.

Amanda glanced away as tears sprung to her eyes, but she refused to allow them to fall. *Life moves forward.* Her new motto. "She died. It was a while ago now."

Zoe met Amanda's gaze and stroked her dog's ears a little more fervently.

"Hey, you never told me his name." Amanda flicked a finger toward the stuffed animal. Anything to change the topic.

"He's shy right now."

He… Okay. Amanda added that to the list of mental notes she was compiling. "Okay, well, it's still good to meet you." Amanda spoke to the dog as if it were a person and lifted an ear as if it were a hand and shook it.

Zoe didn't giggle as Amanda had hoped, but the corners of her lips twitched slightly. "He likes you," Zoe said.

"That's good. I like him too. Well, should we get the living room all set up? I thought we could sleep out there together."

"Can I sleep in here?" Zoe's eyes went up to the ceiling, and Amanda was reminded of the light on Lindsey's nightstand that projected stars. Lindsey had insisted on having it on every night.

"Can you—" Amanda rubbed her throat.

"I like it in here."

Amanda's heart was melting, and she was torn. She looked at the bed, remembering the last night that Lindsey had slept there.

"Please?" Zoe had the puppy-dog eyes going on.

Amanda sniffled. "Ah, sure… why not? Let me get your bag, and you can get changed into your pajamas."

"Okay." She jumped up onto the bed.

"While you're doing that, I'll change the sheets."

"To other pink ones?"

"You betcha." In fact, that was the only color she had for Lindsey's bed.

"Thank you."

"You're welcome." Amanda retrieved Zoe's bag, rooted through it, and produced a pajama set that was pink and patterned with puppies. She handed them to Zoe and directed her down the hall to the bathroom to change.

With Zoe out of the room, Amanda dropped onto the edge of the bed, her shoulders sagging. How was she supposed to get through this night? This new little girl sleeping in Lindsey's bed. She pinched the tip of her nose and let a few tears fall. She could have sat there for hours, just thinking and processing her emotions, but Zoe needed to get to sleep, and it wouldn't do her any good seeing Amanda a wreck. Then there was Amanda's new motto about living forward, born from necessity to keep herself from unravelling. She mustered herself and got the bed made.

Zoe returned just as she'd finished. Her dog was still in her hands, and there was no sign of her previous clothing. It caused Amanda to smile. She was remembering in glimpses what it was like caring for a child, the constant picking up behind them. And Lindsey had just been starting to understand the concept of putting things away. Not that it was obvious with a quick glance around the room, namely the coloring book, abandoned crayons, and the eternal Barbie doll picnic.

"Here you go." Amanda flipped back the sheets and comforter and gestured for Zoe to get in.

She climbed into bed and snuggled her head against the pillow. Her exhaustion gave itself away in a brief closing of her eyes and the red rims, but her stubbornness had them shooting open again.

"It's okay to sleep. I know I'm going to." That might be a lie. Amanda's mind was a mess, and she often went to bed with the aid of a sleeping pill, but with Zoe in the house, she wouldn't be taking one. She might even sleep with a gun under her pillow—just in case the killer came for Zoe.

She pulled the blankets over the girl. "I'll just get you a glass of water, then leave you be. But if you need anything, I'll be down the hall. You remember where my room is?"

A very tiny "yes."

Amanda got the promised glass of water and set it on the nightstand. Zoe was already drifting, her eyes closed. *Ah, the deep, peaceful slumber of a child.* But there was a good chance the dreams she'd have tonight—and maybe for a long time yet—would be more nightmarish in nature. She resisted the motherly urge to kiss the girl on the forehead. *Not appropriate*, Amanda reprimanded herself, *and she's not Lindsey!*

She flicked on the star-projection light.

"Where's Lindsey's daddy?" Zoe's question arrested Amanda just as she had her hand on the light switch. She turned it off, and stars were cast across the ceiling, to which Zoe gave no reaction.

"He died too." Amanda turned back to look at Zoe's small form in the bed. For a trace of a heartbeat, she imagined Lindsey had returned or that she'd never left. The bit of moonlight that spread through the curtains and seeped around the edge cast a haunting spell on her mind.

"I miss my daddy and mommy."

"I'm sure you do, sweetheart." With that, Amanda pulled on the door but left it partially open. That was the way Lindsey had preferred it.

Amanda went into the hall and leaned against the wall, gathering her emotions. She had to get a grip. *One night. That's all this is.* A place for a young girl to get some rest and be safe. Nothing more, nothing less. And while the girl would survive, Amanda wasn't so sure that her own sanity would, let alone her heart.

CHAPTER ELEVEN

It was still dark when Amanda slipped out of bed, and she had done so very quietly because she wasn't alone. At some point around one in the morning, Zoe had come into her room and made herself comfortable on the other side of the bed. Zoe was still resting peacefully—a miracle, given what she'd gone through in the last twenty-four hours or so. Amanda had spent a lot of the night staring at the ceiling. It was so strange having a little girl in the house, let alone *her* bed, and it not being Lindsey. And just when Amanda started to figure she was moving forward with her life, she was yanked back into the sludge of grief that threatened to suck her down like quicksand.

It was just after five in the morning when Amanda left her room. She took care of business in the bathroom and found Zoe's clothes from last night in there, which she folded. She took them to Lindsey's room, and the smell in the air gave her a clue as to why Zoe might have left this bed. Urine.

She flipped on the light and pulled back the sheets and comforter which Zoe must have laid back over the mattress. It was definitely damp. She wasn't angry at the girl, but at six years old, she should have been past wetting the bed. Maybe the behavior was connected somehow with witnessing her father's murder. She'd have to ask Colleen about it; Amanda wasn't an expert on the topic. A part of Amanda sunk into a quiet desperateness just thinking about how her daughter's bed had been defiled.

If it had been Lindsey who'd peed in the bed, she'd have spoken with her, and they could address what might have caused it to happen. With that thought, she looked at the water glass on the nightstand, thinking she'd failed the girl there, but it hadn't been touched. Really, though, there was no reason to bring this up to Zoe. Her sleeping here wasn't going to be a regular occurrence, and she'd probably just end up making the poor girl feel worse.

Amanda stripped the mattress and found the girl's discarded pajamas on the floor in the process. She'd put them on the side of the bed that didn't face the door. Amanda picked them up and fed them into the washing machine. The bedding would have to wait until the clothes were finished. But that still left the mattress bare for now. She didn't have any spare linens to remake the bed—the set that had been taken off last night and the one that was now wet was all she had. It would probably do the mattress good to air out and dry some anyhow.

She peeked in on Zoe, still peacefully asleep in Amanda's bed. Then she got herself a black coffee and pretty much gulped it back, though she took time to savor that initial mouthful. Nothing came close to touching that first cup of the day.

She parked at the kitchen island with her cell phone and checked her email. She had a few messages. One was from CSI Emma Blair, sent last night, saying that she would have the list of cataloged evidence available by the end of tomorrow—that being today now. No response would have been necessary, but Amanda was curious if, in processing the house, they'd come across the laptop, any backup drives or negatives, the cameras, or Brett's phone. Finding out sooner than later may help the investigation. She flipped back the quick inquiry.

Rideout informed her he was going to conduct the autopsies back-to-back, starting at eleven that morning.

She glanced at the clock in the top left-hand corner of her phone. *5:43 AM.*

It seemed like loads of time between now and then, but given the variables and complexity of this case, it was hard to say where the direction of the day would take her. She acknowledged receipt and said that she and Trent would try to make it up there at some point during the day. She regretted needing to make that concession because being present for autopsies could produce clues and leads. It just wasn't always feasible to attend—depending on the course of an investigation and how occupied one already was in following the evidence.

The next correspondence was from Dr. Colleen Frost confirming that she'd be at Central at ten to speak with Zoe.

Amanda stuck another coffee pod into the machine. It was one of those days when the brew tasted like a gift from the gods, but it probably wouldn't matter how much she drank—she'd still feel like she was half asleep.

She exchanged her phone for her laptop, which she kept in one of the cabinets in the island. It was a relic, but it still worked, if slowly. Someday she'd invest in a new one, but for what she planned to do she'd prefer the larger screen of the computer over the little one of her phone.

If she were at Central, she'd be taking a closer look at the backgrounds on the Parkers, just to see if anything popped for her. But there was something she could do here.

She brought up the internet and searched *Falcon Strategic Technologies* and went to their "About Us" page. She scanned the paragraphs of text that had been provided. It read like a technical manual more than a public-facing promotional piece, but she supposed they didn't really need to impress the public, given what they did. From what she read, Falcon specialized in computer programming for high-end weapons systems, their focus on missiles. They declared themselves as being on the front line in defending America.

She paused her browsing to pop Zoe's clothing into the dryer and the bedding into the washer and was back in the kitchen about to click on Falcon's "Media" page when she heard footsteps shuffling down the hall.

"Well, good morning." Amanda smiled at Zoe, taking in the sight of the tousle-haired little girl in another pair of pink pajamas.

Zoe didn't say anything, just hugged her stuffed dog. The toy clearly meant a lot to her. She'd even slept with it—legs curled up, knees to chest.

Amanda slipped off her stool. "Can I get you anything? Water or…" She stopped there, realizing that it had been so long since she had a child in the house, she didn't have any of the staples, including orange juice. The epiphany also highlighted another problem. She didn't have anything on hand that a child would like to eat. No ingredients to make pancakes, no freezer waffles, no syrup. No colored O's or even berry jam to spread on toast. She had bread but nothing exciting to put on top. She doubted an egg over easy would do the trick, and any cereal she had was meant for grown-ups and chock-full of fiber.

"Do you have juice?" Zoe got up on a stool at the counter next to Amanda.

"I don't, sweetie, but…" She stopped there, a solution coming to her, and looked at the time in the corner of her laptop screen. It was going on eight o'clock. She'd been on Falcon's website longer than she'd realized. Good news was it was no longer an ungodly hour. She could take Zoe to Hannah's Diner for breakfast and as much juice as she wanted. The place was a favorite of Amanda's and owned by Hannah Byrd's mother and named after Hannah. But she couldn't go with Zoe because that would put her at risk. Until they knew more about who was behind the Parkers' murders, Zoe needed to stay out of the public's view. There was another option, though. "I'm going to call my partner, Trent. You remember him from yesterday?"

"Uh-huh."

"I'm going to see if he can pick us up some breakfast. Sound good?"

Zoe nodded. "I love pancakes."

"Pancakes it is, then." She called Trent, and he picked up on the second ring.

"Everything all right?" he asked.

"An interesting way to answer," she said.

"Well, valid right now too, don't you think?"

"Yeah, but everything's fine—except I need you to do something for Zoe."

"Just for Zoe?"

She glanced at her empty mug. Hannah's Diner had the best coffee. "Honestly? For the two of us."

"Name it."

Amanda proceeded to ask for two stacks of pancakes, one for herself and one for Zoe, an apple juice for Zoe, which she preferred to orange, and an extra-large coffee for herself. She also tagged on a side of bacon, justifying to herself that she'd only live once. Trent told her he'd be there with the order as soon as humanly possible.

She set her phone back on the counter and looked at Zoe. "Trent will bring our breakfast soon. In the meantime, do you want some water?"

"Nah." Zoe shook her head, and her eyes blanked over. They had sparked with some life when Amanda was rattling off the order to Trent. Maybe for that brief period in time, Zoe had slipped into another reality where things were normal, like having pancakes for breakfast.

"You know what? Why don't we go into the living room and watch some TV until he gets here?" Amanda led the way to the couch, hearing Zoe's footfalls behind her. "Sit wherever you'd like."

Zoe parked on the couch, and Amanda sat next to her and grabbed the remote from the side table. She flicked through the channels until she found one with cartoons.

"This work?" she asked Zoe.

"Yeah."

Amanda should probably be trying to engage Zoe in conversation, work at drawing her out, but it was still early yet, and she wasn't exactly trained for something like that—not with a child. She thought back to the conversation with Colleen Frost and the delicateness of Zoe's mental state. It was best that Amanda refrained from poking too much.

She watched the screen as two characters bumbled about. Cartoons had really changed since she was younger, and while some of the real-world topics they touched on could be seen as more enlightened, there was something about the cartoons from the late eighties and early nineties that couldn't be rivaled. Even if some people hurled accusations that they solicited outdated mentalities and prejudices.

She glanced over at Zoe, wishing that she could remove the burden she carried—that she could erase all that she had seen and heard. But that was only the beginning. Zoe would be forced to relive it over and over as her mind tried to make sense of it all. And she'd be faced with sharing her experience with Colleen Frost and countless others before healing even had a chance of starting. Then, even when the trial for her parents' murders was said and done, Zoe's life would be changed forever. She'd be an orphan, likely placed in foster care. Maybe Libby Dewinter would be able to step up and adopt her. At least then Zoe wouldn't be thrust into the lives of strangers. But Amanda had to stop analyzing Zoe's situation so much; it was killing her. She had to detach herself emotionally and realize that Zoe was an eyewitness in a double homicide, and beyond that, the girl wasn't her problem. Now if only her heart would listen to her mind.

CHAPTER TWELVE

By nine thirty, Amanda, Zoe, and Trent were all at Central. That put Zoe there in plenty of time for Colleen Frost, who would be arriving for ten o'clock. Amanda took Zoe to the room she had been in last night, gave her a mini carton of milk and told her if she needed anything she'd be right outside the door.

"Thanks," Zoe said to her.

"You're welcome, sweetie." Amanda took a deep breath. It had been one night, and now she could move forward. Even the pair of pajamas Amanda had washed were dried, folded, and back in Zoe's bag. Amanda left the room but found herself standing next to the window watching the girl.

"How are you doing?" It was Trent.

Amanda kept looking at Zoe. The girl was selecting a coloring book and crayons off a shelf.

"Amanda?" Trent prompted.

"I'm fine." She shrugged. "Why wouldn't I be?"

He held eye contact with her and didn't say anything, but she was answering her own question. *Because Hill forced a child on me? A little stranger slept in—and defiled—Lindsey's bed? Zoe is now an orphan, and a part of me feels responsible to ease her grief? Gah*, she needed to let Zoe go; it made the most sense.

"We just need to find out who did this to her parents," she said stiffly.

"We will."

She looked at him, wishing for just a bit of his optimism. She had drive and determination, but sometimes where she fell short was in holding hope for a good outcome. She nodded. When they'd been eating breakfast, she'd updated him on the schedule for the autopsies and that Blair anticipated having the evidence list available for viewing later that day. She also told him that she'd emailed Blair about the laptop, cameras, negatives, backup drives, and Brett's phone. "Today, I say we visit Angela's workplace. We've already spoken with the owner, but Angela's fellow employees might give us other insights into her character and relationships."

"Brett's work?"

"Yeah, we'll go there too. After. I did some digging on Falcon Strategic Technologies, if you want to call it *digging*. They specialize in the computer programming of missiles."

"And he was a programmer…" A flicker of excitement danced in his eyes, and she held up a finger at him.

"Don't get carried away. We can't pigeonhole the investigation and let our imaginations take the lead."

"I know but, come on… even you must see it. We have two bodies and a connection to a Washington defense contractor." He raised his brows and snickered.

"Someone has seen too many movies," she kicked back, but she was amused. When she'd first been partnered with Trent, he'd been quiet and reserved, but that dam had burst quickly, exposing his true personality, which was somewhat spark-plug and unpredictable. "We just have to follow the evidence. If it takes us to some conspiracy theory, then heck, I'll explore it."

"We do have the professional killer."

She nodded. That was something she couldn't ignore. Well, that and someone cracking the security system and probably jamming the cell phone signals. The fact the murders had been premeditated was indisputable. It was just the question of what had drawn the target on the Parkers' backs.

"Detective Steele."

She turned to see Malone coming their way.

"Can we talk a minute in my office?"

"Sure."

Trent started to move with her, but Malone held up a hand. "Just me and Steele."

"I'll follow up on the subpoenas, then," Trent said and turned on his heel.

Amanda was curious what it was Malone wanted to talk to her about. He sounded gruff and irritated, but she couldn't think of anything she'd done overnight that would make him angry with her.

He closed his office door behind them and gestured for her to sit across from his desk. He slipped into his chair and clasped his hands on his desk. "I just heard about…" His cheeks flushed, and his facial expression softened somewhat. "I just heard that you took Zoe home last night."

"Not by choice." Her insides shook just thinking about it again. It had been quite a challenge and a hardship—at least on an emotional level.

"No doubt. I just wanted to check in with you and see how you're doing this morning."

She relaxed and let her shoulders sag. He was concerned about her. Any anger that was emanating from him was likely caused by Hill. "I'm doing all right."

He took a long inhale and let the breath out on a ragged sigh. He sat back in his chair, his gaze going over her, studying her. There was more purpose to his calling her into his office than just checking on her welfare.

"What is it?" she prompted.

He ran a hand over his head. "Obviously you haven't heard yet…"

Whenever he'd start a conversation like that, bad news was coming. "Just hit me." She'd rather know sooner than later what she was dealing with and face it head-on.

He opened a drawer in his desk and pulled out a copy of *Prince William Times*, then handed it to her. She groaned internally because nothing much good came from the media. Every time some "news" surfaced in relation to her or an investigation, it was always a shit-show. She glanced at the headline: DEFENSE CONTRACTOR EMPLOYEE AND WIFE MURDERED.

She angled her head, not sure what to make of the title. She looked at Malone, questioning him with her glance.

"Give it a quick scan."

She did just that. Her redhead temper was beyond the boiling point by the time she'd finished, and she hardly knew where to begin. But she'd start with who was in immediate danger. "They… they…" She couldn't get her mouth to speak the words.

"Yep. The public knows about Zoe."

"Not just that…" She was going to be sick. "The article hints that she may have seen something. Who would… who…?" She was talking in fragments—practically stuttering. She was furious. She tossed the paper back onto Malone's desk. "Hill did that."

"I've spoken with her. Well, *asked* her about it. She is technically my boss. She said she never said such a thing at all."

"She had to have done this. But why mention Zoe and put her in danger?" Amanda felt like she'd been struck from behind and was now being bashed repeatedly.

"She's not telling me."

"Is she dumb as a stick?" Amanda slapped out. "Seriously? Her head isn't screwed on right." With every word she said, Malone's face tightened into a knot. Amanda went on. "Zoe's a six-year-old girl who lost her parents—not just lost them… they were *murdered*. Now she's plastered in the news with a target painted on her back!"

"I'm on your side here."

He used to say, "I've got your back." The words he'd just said were similar, but there was still something a little broken between the two of them that needed time to heal. And the fault was entirely hers as she'd betrayed his faith in her by charging ahead in a case this past April. It was the one that had caused her suspension and Trent's temporary position as a desk jockey. While the investigation itself came to a suitable resolution in Amanda's mind, the brass, namely Sherry Hill, who was a lieutenant at the time, hadn't seen it that way. Hence, the disciplinary action.

Malone continued. "As you already concluded, Zoe may be in more danger than ever now."

The way his voice had softened, it was like he was shifting direction again—taking off the boss cap and putting on the personal one.

"Hill never should have asked that you take Zoe home last night."

"I don't remember her asking," Amanda mumbled.

"It was inappropriate."

"Yeah, you could say that." She was bitter, but not toward Malone—at Hill. Next time she saw her face, it would be a miracle if she didn't punch it.

Malone rubbed his chin, dropped his hand. "With Zoe in danger, Hill has requested that you take the girl in—"

"No. I did it last night. Last minute, once and done." Amanda was shaking her head furiously.

"I had a feeling you'd feel that way."

Amanda scowled. "So you told her no for me?"

"I told her I'd speak with you."

Malone was all about holding up his end in things, and now his conscience would be clear. "Which you've done," she said.

He nodded. "I refuse to order you to take Zoe in, and there's no pressure on you to accept."

"Well, then, no." Her heart was hammering one moment and frozen mid-pump the next.

"Understandable and…"

She didn't hear the rest of what he'd said as she was too angry to listen. She didn't need him to understand her position; he just needed to accept it. Really, no one was in the position to *understand* her feelings on the matter. Not unless they'd lost their little girl.

Malone was still speaking. "… we'll figure something out. But as horrible as it is that Zoe was mentioned in the article, that isn't all. It steers people's attention to Brett Parker's place of employment."

She blinked him into focus. "I picked up on that too. But people are going to think what they want. I'm not going to let what the media says influence me."

"No, but it influences the public's mind," Malone said. "And the PWCPD needs to be prepared to comment on the status of the investigation. The first thing people will want to know is where things stand with—" He picked up the paper, his eyes skimming.

"Falcon Strategic Technologies," she said, figuring that was what he was hunting for.

"Right. So where are we with talking to them?"

"Trent and I are going there today."

"Okay, good. Keep me posted on how you make out with them."

"Did Hill tell the media about Falcon, or how did they find out?" She didn't respond to Malone's request to keep him updated; in her mind, it was a given. She was typically good about doing that.

"You know what the media's like and how sensational they can be. They find out what Brett Parker did for work, and the conspiracy theories write themselves. And all that sells papers."

She wasn't about to admit that she and Trent had briefly entertained some theories themselves. "So Hill didn't plant this in their minds?" Nothing would surprise her about Hill anymore.

"Hill's adamant that was none of her doing."

"All right." Amanda got up. "I'll go fill Trent in on the latest. And please work something else out for Zoe."

"I'll do whatever I can."

"Thank you." Amanda turned to leave, and it felt like the breath had been sucked from her lungs. As much as she wanted to be there for the girl, she just didn't think she had the strength to see it through. She'd focus on what she could do to help Zoe, and that was to find her parents' killer and bring them to justice.

CHAPTER THIRTEEN

Trent was at his desk, nose to the computer screen. Amanda brought him up to speed about the newspaper article. It was surprising that he hadn't read it yet himself, as he'd given her the impression in the past that he stayed up on current news. She left out Malone's request about Zoe, and she purposely didn't swing by the interview room to look in on her before leaving. She had to put some space between her heart and the girl. She couldn't let herself get wrapped up. Zoe was sad collateral damage, but even as Amanda thought that, she realized just how cold it sounded.

Their first stop wasn't going to be Falcon Strategic Technologies; she refused to have her movements bullied by the media or guided by conspiracy nuts. They stopped in at Mind Your Own Business and spoke to Angela's coworkers there. None of them knew of anyone that she might have been seeing romantically on the side or had any inkling that she would even do such a thing to her husband.

Warren Kennedy was at the office, and he provided them with a report from the security system that showed his code entered at 6:07 on Tuesday morning. While he technically could have still committed the murders, he had no apparent motive that gave Amanda and Trent reason to probe his background or finances. The same could be said of Angela's colleagues, and none of them had any idea who would have wanted to kill her and/or her husband.

All that was an hour behind them, and it was going on eleven thirty now. They'd have to get the recap on the autopsies from Rideout. She and Trent were currently in the lobby of Falcon Strategic Technologies in Washington.

The business was housed in a large, three-story warehouse, and the mortgage wouldn't have come cheap. But given Falcon's line of work, and a look around the opulent space, money wasn't an issue.

The receptionist, a fifty-something woman, was a rigid gate-keeper—her attitude matching her tight bun. Her dark hair was pulled back so fiercely, it appeared to tug at her skin. She wasn't impressed that they were the PWCPD or that they wanted an audience with Charles Windsor, the CEO. She scowled and asked, "What is this regarding?"

Amanda would take the question to mean Charles was on the premises. "It's regarding an employee here. Brett Parker."

The woman didn't react to the name, but according to Falcon's website, they employed three thousand people. It wouldn't be feasible that she'd be familiar with all of them.

"If you could let Mr. Windsor know we're here," Amanda prompted.

"Mr. Windsor has an incredibly packed schedule, and unless you have an appointment already…"

"I think you might find that if you paged him, he'd be more than interested in speaking with us." Amanda's mind was on the newspaper and the implication that the Parkers' murders were somehow connected to the defense contractor. She went on. "Mr. Parker and his wife were found murdered yesterday, and the media has hinted that it might have something to do with his employment here."

The woman regarded Amanda with skepticism and then drew her pointed gaze to Trent. "That's absurd."

Amanda hitched her shoulders but remained silent.

The woman huffed but started to click away on her keyboard. "Brett Parker reported to Marcel Hudson. Let me start there. I'm not going to pester the CEO."

Amanda glanced at Trent. The murder of an employee was a *pester*? It was obvious the receptionist hadn't known Brett, but still it seemed she was lacking empathy. Even if a person didn't know the deceased, most showed more emotion than Miss Cyborg here.

She made the call and said into her headset, "Mr. Hudson, there are two detectives at the front who wish to speak with you about Mr. Parker... Uh-huh... Yes. I will do." She tapped a finger to her ear, which must have ended the call. To Amanda and Trent, she said, "Mr. Hudson will see you in Conference Room A. Just go to the elevators"—she pointed past an indoor waterfall—"and up to the third floor. You'll find a reception desk when you unload, and the person there will direct you the rest of the way." She didn't wait for them to respond but put her gaze immediately back on her monitor.

Guess we're excused...

They turned to leave.

"Hey, where are you going?" the woman called out. "Neither of you can go anywhere until I give you these." The woman set two lanyards on the counter with visitor badges attached, along with a tablet and a stylus pen. "You'll also need to sign in."

Amanda and Trent followed the on-screen instructions and put on their lanyards.

"Before you leave the building, you'll need to return the lanyards to me and sign out."

"Will do." Amanda resisted the urge to salute the woman and headed for the elevators.

A minute later, they were off-loading on the third floor and being greeted by another stiff receptionist. "If you'll just have a seat, Mr. Hudson will be out for you shortly."

Amanda acknowledged her with a dip of her head and sat down in one of the chairs. Trent followed her lead.

"Detectives?" A middle-aged man in a tailored business suit came out, hands clasped in front of himself. "I've been told you'd like to discuss Brett Parker?"

Amanda and Trent got to their feet.

"That's right," Amanda said and proceeded with the formal introductions.

"Marcel Hudson. I'm Mr. Parker's manager." He straightened out his posture, squared his shoulders a bit more.

Amanda glanced past him, not sure why he wasn't taking them to Conference Room A as the first receptionist had mentioned. "Is there someplace private that we could talk?"

Marcel regarded her for a few more seconds, slid his gaze to Trent, back at her. "This way." There was just the hint of a smile on his face before he turned to lead them down a hallway. He stopped next to a door with a brass plate that read "Conference Room A" and gestured for them to go in ahead of him.

A mahogany table surrounded by twelve leather swivel chairs took up most of the real estate, but there was a cabinet at the far end of the room. Straight across from the door was a wall of windows, and while it allowed ample sunshine into the room, the view wasn't impressive. There were just other industrial buildings and a parking lot full of vehicles.

"Sit wherever you'd like." Marcel pulled out a chair at the head of the table and sat down.

Amanda sat on his left, and Trent to her right.

Marcel adjusted the lay of his suit jacket and settled his gaze on her. "Why is the Prince William County Police Department interested in Brett Parker?"

"Brett Parker and his wife were found murdered yesterday in their home in Triangle which, you may know, is part of Prince William County." She watched him for any sort of a reaction.

Marcel's well-adjusted and put-together demeanor fell away and was replaced by sagging shoulders and a paled complexion.

He ran a hand over his mouth and jaw. "Murdered?" The word sounded like it had scraped from his throat.

She'd guess *Prince William Times* wasn't at the top of the corporate reading list. "That's right."

"Wow. Well, that explains why I couldn't reach him and why he didn't come into work yesterday or today." He blinked slowly, and his forehead pinched like a headache was forming. "What happened?"

"That's what we're trying to figure out," Trent said. "We're hoping you might be able to aid the investigation."

Marcel cleared his throat and pulled on the collar of his shirt; his necktie seemed to be suffocating him. "I'm not sure how I can help."

"To start, we'd like to know what Mr. Parker did here at Falcon," Amanda said.

"He was a software programmer." Marcel wasn't looking at her or Trent but at the table.

"We were hoping for something more specific," she said gently while still asserting her authority.

Marcel sat back in his chair, and it creaked with the movement. He put his elbows on the arms and clasped his hands across his front. "Brett was one of a team of ten assigned to specific and highly important work on the GMD system."

"And what is that?" Trent asked, beating Amanda to the question.

"Ground-based Mid-course Defense system." Marcel stopped there and must have read the confusion still on their faces. "Its purpose is to protect the US from long-range ballistic missiles in the case of enemy attack."

"I see." Amanda could feel her partner's gaze on her but refused to acknowledge it. "So highly valuable and confidential work?"

"Absolutely."

Trent moved forward on his chair. "Something that a lot of people would be interested in getting their hands on?"

Amanda drilled him with a glare, and he slid back.

"Countries would kill for the information he was working on."

The skin pinched at the back of her neck. *Did Brett's work get him and Angela murdered after all?* "Can you tell us a bit more about his work?" she squeezed out.

"As you might suspect, it was highly sensitive, highly classified. I can give you an overview that anyone could find on the internet, but he was assigned to programming the GFC—that's Ground Fire Control—software. The GFC receives data from various sensors throughout the world."

Amanda held up a hand. "I'm going to stop you there. The world?"

"That's right. America needs to proactively protect its interests on a global scale."

She nodded, supposing that made absolute sense. She'd just never had reason to give it any thought before. "Continue. It receives data…"

"Yes. All this is done through satellite communication. After analysis of the data, planning and launching decisions can be made. This software also keeps tabs on the GBI fleet." Marcel shifted and cleared his throat again. "That's Ground-Based Interceptor. The government loves their acronyms."

"Missiles?" Trent asked.

Marcel nodded. "Due to the scale of the system, it needs to remain protected at all times. But GFC is housed on several computers and has certain inherent technological vulnerabilities."

"It can be hacked," Trent put out with confidence.

Marcel met his gaze. "That's right," he said tightly.

"And this was what Brett was working on?" Amanda asked. "Making the software more secure against attack?"

"Yeah, and he was getting close too."

Not to dramatize it, but if someone knew what Brett was working on, they could have come after him for it. As Marcel had said, countries would kill for it. Countries had budgets for professional hitmen. Goosebumps rose on her arms, and tingles trapezed across the back of her neck and on her shoulders. "Who would know what Brett was working on and its progress?"

"His team."

"I meant outside of Falcon," she countered.

"We have very strict security measures in place."

Amanda remembered that Libby had said Brett brought his work home but had a feeling if he indeed had, it wouldn't be something Marcel or Falcon would approve of. "Would Brett ever have worked on the programming after hours, possibly at home?"

Marcel's cheeks flushed a bright red. "Heavens no."

"So definitely not?"

Marcel squirmed in his chair, suddenly appearing uncomfortable. "If he took his work home, then he violated his contract with us."

"And you don't see him as the type to do that?" Trent asked.

Marcel shook his head. "I don't."

"That doesn't mean that someone hadn't found out what Brett was working on and strong-armed him into sneaking the software out," she said. "Is there any way you could know if he took his work home?"

"I don't see how he could have. We have systems in place to prevent such things." Marcel took a deep breath and leaned forward, placing his elbows and arms on the table. "Every employee consents to being recorded—both audio and video. The only places that are exempt, of course, are the washrooms. Everywhere else in this building is bugged, as you would say."

Amanda recalled reading about this when signing the visitor form, and it should set her at ease that employees were under such surveillance, but it did the opposite. It would only make it necessary for Brett to be clandestine if his intentions were less than favorable. Him taking his work home could also support why he'd been so adamant about creating backups.

Marcel went on. "Everything is recorded and monitored, every keystroke. The files are protected and can't be copied or cut without management authorization—that would be me. All of this makes a data breach highly improbable."

She could point out that Brett's job had been to plug vulnerabilities, which meant first seeing them. He was essentially wired to see the loopholes. "So there's no way he could copy the software and take it off premises?"

Marcel laughed at that. "The software is huge and housed over several servers. There's no way he could."

"What about bits of code?" Trent asked.

"As I said, there's no way the software could be copied—whole or in fragments."

Maybe it was time to let the theory go that Brett's work at Falcon got him and his family murdered, but she thought of one more possibility. "Brett couldn't have copied the information, but could he have keyed code into his personal laptop?"

"I don't see how. Remember everything is videotaped. Seeing him typing into a laptop—something that wasn't Falcon property—that would have raised my suspicions, and I would have confronted him." He stopped speaking and paled. "Thing with Brett, though… he was a genius, and he had an extremely strong eidetic memory—almost photographic."

That raised another scenario. "Brett could have picked up work at home by just remembering where he'd left off, then? Or even worked on new snippets of code and then input them the next day here."

"Suppose so, but why would he put the software at risk like that? I just don't see it."

"People can surprise you." The statement came out sounding critical of humankind, but it could also apply to happy outcomes.

"Do you really think his job somehow got Brett and his wife murdered?"

"It's too early to know for sure, but we'll need to speak with his fellow employees." They could get a feel from them for the type of man that Brett had been. While he might have had his boss fooled, maybe they were aware Brett had taken his work home. They might even have insight into what he'd been like in the days leading up to the vacation. If someone was bullying him to hand over Falcon's software, Brett's personality would have likely shown changes. *Speaking of the random need for a vacation...* "We understand it wasn't usual for Brett to take a vacation. He hadn't in years."

"That's right, but I'm not sure where you're going with that. He just said he needed a break. Thing with programming is you can think you're getting close, but then a glitch arises and you're back to square one."

"How was he in the days leading up to his time off?" she asked.

"Normal. Just hard at work."

She nodded. "He and his family came home early from that vacation—Brett's doing. Would you know why?"

"Not the foggiest."

"As I said, we'll need to speak to the other members of Brett's team," she said with more urgency.

"I can have them brought up here one by one, but I can't let you go to them."

"That's fine."

"I'll also need to be present for the questioning."

She regarded Marcel and interpreted that to mean he was concerned his employees might say something they shouldn't about the software. "That's fine."

"All right, I'll be back shortly." He left the room, and she looked at Trent.

His eyes were wide.

"Don't go down the rabbit hole," she warned him.

"As if you're not just a bit. Admit it, at least a toe."

"Maybe a toe," she admitted, and her mind spun another hypothetical. What if one of Brett's coworkers had set him up for a fall?

CHAPTER FOURTEEN

Amanda checked her email and saw that Emma Blair had messaged. "None of the investigators remember finding a laptop, cameras, negative rolls, or backup drives," she told Trent. "Also no sign of Brett's phone and any attempt at tracing it was unsuccessful."

"So we can assume the shooter was after information, likely a photograph since they took the negatives. Could still be something related to the Falcon software."

She wasn't ruling it out yet, that was for sure. It held a lot of potential for a motive for murder.

A twenty-something in a stiff-looking, navy skirt suit came into the conference room holding a tray with a platter of mini sandwiches, another one of fruit, and a few small plates. She smiled at Amanda and Trent as she set everything on the table, then she proceeded to the credenza, where she pulled out a large pitcher and some glasses.

"All of this is appreciated but not necessary," Amanda said to her.

"I'm just doing what I'm told." The woman smiled again and carried on with what she'd been doing. She filled the pitcher with water from a cooler in the room and set it and the glasses on the table. "Mr. Hudson should be along shortly but, please, go ahead and help yourselves." With that, she reversed out of the room as if she were a server at a fine restaurant and shut the door behind her.

Trent poured himself some water and then held up the glass. "Want some?"

"Ah, sure." What she really wanted was answers not a distraction. Trent filled her glass and slid it over to her. "Here you go."

"Thanks."

"No problem." His gaze dipped to the plate of sandwiches.

"Go ahead if you'd like, but chew quick. The second Hudson and our first guest arrives, it's work time."

Trent snatched what looked like turkey and Swiss on pumpernickel. "I'll be so quick, I won't even dirty a plate." He pushed the triangle into his mouth.

She shook her head. At least her partner was amusing.

There was a robust knock on the door as it swung open. It was Marcel with a new face beside him. Introductions were made, and that man would be the first of nine interviews they'd hold that day. They learned little of substance from the first eight—*Brett was a nice guy; No, they hadn't socialized much; Nothing seemed unusual in his behavior.* Then came the last interview, with a man in his forties called Dale Crawford.

"Why are detectives here asking questions about Brett?" Dale asked, posing the question to Marcel, but something in his eyes belied his ignorance. Even if Marcel hadn't told him about the murders, surely one of his coworkers who'd returned from this room would have.

Amanda introduced herself and Trent and then responded to Dale. "We're investigating the murder of Brett Parker and—"

"His what now?" Dale's eyes widened, and he swiveled to face Marcel. "What happened, Marcel?"

Marcel put a supportive hand on Dale's shoulder. The relationship between these two men was far less formal than had been the case with the previous employees.

"Brett and his wife were…" Marcel's voice fractured, and he looked at Amanda.

"Brett and his wife are dead. They were found murdered in their home yesterday afternoon."

"They were…" Dale swallowed roughly, his Adam's apple bobbing heavily. It would seem this was his first time hearing about the Parkers. "Why? Who?" His gaze flicked from Amanda to Trent, back to her again.

"We're still trying to figure out those answers," Amanda said.

Dale shook his head. "I knew something was wrong when he didn't show up for work. I told you, Marcel."

The manager flushed under the scrutiny. "I just figured he was delayed returning from vacation."

"You should know Brett better than that. And, I mean, I thought maybe he got into a car accident. It never crossed my mind that he was… uh… murdered. Who would have done this?"

"The question is at the top of our list, I assure you," Amanda told him.

"You said that Brett and Angela were… but what about—" His eyes were full of tears. "What about Zoe?"

Amanda wasn't quite sure how to answer the question—not until they knew more about what and *who* they were dealing with. If, and it was probably a *huge* stretch, Dale was somehow involved in the murders, he might want to know Zoe's whereabouts to get to her, to silence her. But the papers had already advertised her survival.

"Please, tell me she's okay," Dale pleaded.

"She's alive."

"Thank God!" he said, flailing his arms in the air.

"Were you and Brett close?" She assumed so for him to inquire about Zoe's well-being in the first place.

"We were friends. Got together from time to time and had beers. We both have young daughters."

"Do you know if Brett ever took his work home with him?" Amanda asked, though she knew she was putting him in a compromising position with Marcel sitting right there. But even if Marcel were out of the room, there was always the surveillance that Falcon could draw from.

Dale seemed hesitant to answer.

"He was probably dedicated to his job," Trent said conversationally. "He rarely took a holiday."

Dale's gaze snapped to Trent's. "He lived and breathed this job."

"So that's a yes, he took work home?"

"Yeah." Dale glanced at Marcel, who flared his nostrils.

"He took confidential data off the premises?" Marcel snarled.

Dale chewed his bottom lip. "Not exactly."

Amanda's mind went back to their earlier conversation with Marcel. "Did he work out code at home on his own laptop?"

Dale nodded, but it was barely perceptible.

"What?" Marcel burst out, his cheeks flaming red. "How could he?"

Dale turned to his boss. "You and I both know how seriously Brett took his work. He would have been careful."

"If he took it seriously, he wouldn't have worked on it outside of these walls. Do you take proprietary information out of this building with you—physically or in here?" Marcel tapped his head and grimaced at his employee.

Dale scrunched up his face. "Of course, it's in my head but, no, I don't key any code or try to work any out after leaving here."

Marcel scoffed. "And I really expect you to tell me if you did? That would be ludicrous."

"I've worked for you for ten years."

"Sure, and Brett worked here for twelve. He knew, just as well as you do, that taking proprietary information from Falcon property is not only a fireable offense but a matter of national security. And you do realize that they"—Marcel splayed a hand across the table, gesturing to Amanda and Trent—"think the software is somehow connected to Brett's murder."

Dale's brow furrowed. "I don't understand."

"We've been told it's extremely sensitive and highly sought after," Amanda said. "People have killed for less. It's possible that someone killed Brett for software code or that he—"

"No," Dale said abruptly. "If you're going to think for one second that Brett was going to sell the software, think again. He was a patriot through and through. His father fought in Vietnam, won more purple hearts than you can count. Brett even served some time in Iraq. Received some military commendations himself."

Amanda scanned Dale's face and took in his body language. It was defensive but not closed off; she'd wager he was telling the truth. Besides, it was easily verifiable, so it wouldn't make sense for him to lie. But Brett Parker being a war hero was news. That didn't reconcile with him suddenly turning against his country to sell secrets, but it still left open the possibility that someone knew about his work and threatened him to deal. When he didn't, they killed him and stole the software code—but would one snippet of code, or even several, be enough to justify such action? "Who all knew that Brett took his work home?" she asked Dale.

"We know it's news to me," Marcel mumbled.

"It's not like he prattled on about it," Dale said. "And I only found out by chance one day."

"Over beers, at a bar?" She was thinking someplace an interested party might overhear.

"No way."

"Then when and how?" She wanted the picture fully filled in.

"Guess it was more I had a hunch what he was doing."

"What led you to suspect he was bringing work home?" Trent asked.

"Ah, just how fast he'd be keying in code when he got to work. Anyway, I ended up confronting him in the parking lot here after work one day, and he admitted to sorting code at home."

Amanda nodded. So Brett had been discreet about taking work home with him. Dale had only figured it out because they'd worked near each other. But with something such as the software under discussion, evil people had a way of slinking out of the darkness. She and Trent would pull the Parkers' financials and see if there was any evidence that Brett was taking money to hand over the technology. But if he had simply been coerced with a threat to his and his family's lives, the trail might not be as easy to follow. "How did Brett seem to you in the days leading up to his vacation? Was his mood different?"

"Maybe a little stressed out, but we'd been putting in long hours," Dale said.

"He wasn't acting out of the ordinary?" she asked.

"I wouldn't say so. Not really. Possibly a little more strained, but I have been lately too. We were getting very close to resolving all the bugs in the software. It was sort of eating him up."

"Seems like an odd time to go away on a vacation," she said, chewing on that. Maybe she was making too much out of the impromptu vacation. It very well might not mean anything, just as the family returning home early might not.

"With Brett, no time is a good time." Dale smiled softly, not seeming to notice referring to him in present tense.

"Did you know that Brett cut his family's vacation short?" she asked.

Dale's face pinched up. "Huh. No idea. I'd say that was like him if he'd come back to work, but he didn't."

And that was another aspect to consider. A workaholic who took a random vacation, cut it short, but didn't return to his job. What had Brett been doing since Thursday? They needed to look closely at his correspondence, just as they needed to look at Angela's. She addressed her next question to Marcel, not having thought of it before now. "When did Brett request the time off? Had he planned it for a while?"

Marcel shook his head. "More last minute."

"Impressive, given where he went," she said. "Usually rentals are booked for months in advance."

"Struck it luck—" Marcel left the rest unsaid because ultimately Brett and his wife—and Zoe, for that matter—had been extremely *un*lucky.

"When did you last see or talk to Brett?" Trent asked Dale.

"Haven't seen or spoken with him since the Friday before he left."

"And that was?" she asked just to verify.

"The twenty-seventh."

She nodded. It was the next day, the Saturday, that Libby Dewinter told them the Parkers had left—the day Zoe had her mother send the picture. "We're sorry for your loss, Mr. Crawford, and thank you for your time." She pulled out her business card. "If you think of anything, even something that might seem inconsequential, please don't hesitate to call me—day or night."

"I will." Dale took her card and left the room.

"Please let me know if you discover that some of the software is out there," Marcel said, giving her his card. "If even a bit of the code gets out, it could have severe repercussions."

Maybe she should tell him about the missing laptop and backup drives, but she wasn't willing to part with that information until they got further along in their investigation. And why bring it up and risk having governmental agencies crawling all over them for no reason? She didn't need anyone tramping on her toes and hindering progress on the Parker case. "I'm sorry for your loss."

She and Trent headed to the front desk. The entire time, elements of the case were swirling together—possible compromised defense software, the Parkers' vacation, the mystery of why it was cut short, and what workaholic Brett had done to occupy his time when he returned home. She was certain the motive for murder lay somewhere in there—but where?

CHAPTER FIFTEEN

Amanda stepped outside Falcon with Trent, and the sun was already setting in the sky. When they'd returned their lanyards and checked out with Little Miss Sunshine, it had been just after five thirty. Now they were walking to the department car. She could really use something solid to eat and another coffee. She'd ended up helping herself to a few sandwich triangles between interviews, but they were long gone.

"Do you think the software got the Parkers killed somehow?" Trent asked, and by the way he looked over at her, she could tell he was just tossing it out there to see if it stuck.

"I admit that it's a possibility."

He smirked.

"But I'm not attached," she amended quickly. "We'll still need to get their financials, see if there are any unexplained deposits." Also worth considering was if Brett had a bank account they didn't know about. But surely if one did exist, they'd eventually uncover it.

"Yeah, makes sense. The guy was a patriot too. Won military honors."

"Something else we may need to confirm. But I'd like to know what Brett did once he returned home. He was painted as a workaholic, but he didn't return to Falcon."

"Yeah, that's a really good question."

"Thinking maybe his correspondence or call history might help us figure that out."

"I'd think the latter should be in by now…" Trent pulled his phone from a pocket in his pants.

"Those providers don't work that quick. We'll be happy to see them this week."

His attention went to his phone, and he moved his finger around the screen. "Yeah, no email yet from the provider, but I'll give them a push."

They reached their vehicle and got in, Trent behind the wheel. He pecked on his phone and proudly announced, "Done."

"Good job." She smirked at him. "But I'm out of gold stars."

"Someone's more witty than normal."

"I'm exhausted. Coffee please."

"I'll hit the first drive-thru."

"All I can ask."

As Trent drove, she checked her messages. She'd turned her phone to silent while at Falcon, and given the lack of ringing on Trent's, he must have too. It was best not to have any distractions during interviews. And it was a good thing she'd muted her phone. There were missed calls, voicemails, and emails.

Trent got them each a coffee and a donut. She munched and sipped while she listened to her voicemail. Four messages. Not as many as she would have thought. They were now on the highway back to Central.

The oldest message was Erica Murphy from Child Protective Services checking in that morning. She said that a Libby Dewinter was requesting to temporarily foster Zoe and the process was being started.

Amanda would have to touch base with Malone, but she'd assume that he'd have worked out a protective detail for Zoe.

The next message was from Colleen Frost at around lunchtime with an update on Zoe. "She's still not talking, but she is starting to draw. She has one that's for your eyes only, and she refuses to share it with me."

Amanda stopped listening and called Colleen. She answered on the third ring.

"It's Detective Steele. Amanda," she amended. "I just got your message about Zoe. Did the rest of the day go any better with her?"

"Unfortunately, no."

Amanda should probably bring up the bed-wetting, but with Trent beside her, she somehow felt like she would be betraying the girl's privacy. "I'd like to talk with you when I get back to Central."

"When will that be?"

"Trent and I are on our way back to the station now. Should be about forty more minutes."

"I'll stay."

"Thank you."

Amanda ended the call and found Trent looking over at her.

"Zoe's still not talking. It looks like she may be going home with Libby tonight." She rushed that last bit out, not wanting to get weighed down in the logistics. She never told him that Malone had asked if she'd take Zoe on. She had a feeling that Trent wouldn't be impressed he'd brought it up, but she'd known Malone's motive—just to do what he'd said he would.

"Well, that's probably a good thing."

Amanda could feel his eyes on her as she looked out the window. "At least she knows Libby, and Malone will have arranged for officers to watch the place," she said. "Zoe will be safe."

"For sure."

She wished she felt as confident. As much as she didn't want Zoe back under her roof—for personal reasons—she was drawn to protect her, and there was an unmistakable bond between them. They'd both been dealt a crappy hand by fate. She easily recalled what it was like in the aftermath of losing Kevin and Lindsey. How hard that had been, and she was an adult, not a six-year-old girl. To Amanda, it had been like she was moving about in a dream world, nothing quite real about it, except for the intense pain that had lodged in her chest. Each breath was shallow, and their deaths were never far away. The strength of her grief ebbed and flowed like waves coming to shore, but it was also ever present.

"Dr. Frost said she'll be there when we get there," she added. "So we can talk to her in person."

"Okay." Trent kept his gaze on her for a little longer before returning it to the road. She was quite sure that he was picking up on her emotionally charged energy, but thankfully, he didn't pick at the scab.

She went back to her voicemail. The next was from her sister, Kristen. "We need to talk. Call me the minute you get this. There's something you need to know." Her message came in around five. Amanda had just missed the call.

Kristen sounded panicked. Did something happen in court with their mother today? Amanda hadn't even fired off so much as a text message to say she was thinking of her. She wouldn't be making daughter of the year anytime soon—or sister. She had one more voicemail. She'd listen to it first, then call Kristen back. Maybe by then she could do so from someplace a little more private than next to Trent.

Her last message was from Malone, left minutes after her sister's. He said that Zoe had gone home with Libby, but not to worry because he had an officer watching over the place.

She hung up but kept her grip tight on her phone. She felt worry and relief—a comingling of two emotions that shouldn't coexist, yet they were. For some reason, she didn't trust anyone except herself to keep Zoe safe, but she was relieved that it technically wasn't her job. Last night really could be relegated to an anomaly, a one-off, and she should just be happy about that. But all she could see was Zoe's blue eyes looking into hers, and Amanda had the strongest desire to wrap the girl in her arms and shield her from harm. But she had to remember that Zoe wasn't hers to protect.

CHAPTER SIXTEEN

Amanda walked into Central, a woman on a mission. She found Colleen Frost in the break room cradling a cup of coffee. She looked wide awake, her eyes alert, her clothes pressed, and not one hair out of place. It was like it was the beginning of the day, and not the end. It was nice of her to wait for them, given that Zoe was already gone. Amanda couldn't exactly put Colleen off any longer to fit in a call to her sister, but she fired off a quick text to Kristen to say she'd be calling soon. That was the best she could do for now.

"Sorry we were so long," Amanda told Colleen as she dropped into a chair across the table from the shrink. "Thank you for waiting."

Colleen offered a polite smile that reached her eyes. "No problem at all."

Amanda looked around for Trent, having expected that he'd sit beside her, but he was across the room hitting up the vending machine. A donut didn't exactly have staying power, but nothing he'd select from the machine would either.

She turned her focus back to Colleen, whose gaze dipped to the table where a few pages where stacked. "Zoe drew all that?"

"Yes, and there's the one for your eyes only that I told you about, but she took that one with her."

Somehow hearing about the drawing a second time made the implication sink in. *Zoe is attached to me.* The thought made the next bit a little harder, and Trent was still within earshot. Not that it truly mattered if he found out. "I probably should have told you something this morning," Amanda began, and it had Colleen looking at her with a blend of curiosity and concern. "Zoe wet the bed last night. I'm sure it has to do with what she's been through…?"

Colleen nodded. "Absolutely. Regression—that is, acting younger than one's age—is completely normal after the trauma she's experienced. It's probably only temporary, but as I said yesterday, I'm quite confident that Zoe witnessed the murder of her father."

Something fell inside the vending machine with a *clunk*. Trent fed more change into the thing, made another selection, and Amanda mindlessly watched the metal curl and release its treasure. When she turned back, she saw that Colleen had moved the top drawing across the table to her.

It showed three stick figures—one man, one woman, one little girl. The woman was holding a book and was next to what could be a bench, and the man was next to water with what could be a camera in his hands. The little girl was behind a tree, only her head and arms showing from around the trunk—the dog in her hand.

Trees and water… possibly a snapshot of when they were on vacation?

Amanda's gaze landed on the words "Love U mommy and daddy" scrawled in red crayon across the top. She blinked away the tears that wanted to fall. Amanda was happy that Trent had joined them just then, giving her a distraction and time to rein in her emotions. He had a mug of black coffee for himself and put one in front of Amanda, and then added a bag of chips.

"Thought you'd be hungry," he said.

"Thanks." But she couldn't think of eating right now. Her stomach was twisted into a knot. "Take a look at this." She pushed the drawing over to Trent, studying it again for herself as she did so.

Each person was holding something. Zoe, the dog she loved so much. Could the same thinking be applied to the items that Brett and Angela held? After all, Libby had said Brett loved photography, and that was evidenced in all the framed photos in the Parker house. Angela must have enjoyed reading.

"I figure this was a memory from their vacation," Colleen said, cutting through Amanda's thoughts.

"I wondered that."

"To me, it almost looks like she's playing hide-and-seek… the way she's peeking around the tree."

Amanda could understand the doctor's interpretation.

Colleen went on. "I asked Zoe if that's what she was doing, but she wasn't talking to me."

"Amanda found her hiding in a storage bench in the bedroom," Trent began. "She could have been playing that night."

Amanda nodded at Trent, turned to Colleen. "It's assumed that the Parkers realized there was an intruder in their home, giving them a few precious minutes to secure Zoe inside the ottoman." After all, one of them would have had to set the cushion so it wasn't off-kilter. Amanda added, "Presenting it to the girl as a game would have been a lot less scary for her." She was just guessing, of course, but it seemed like a logical thought process.

Colleen said, "I agree. Then there's this." She pushed another drawing across the table.

There was a jagged slash drawn in yellow and coming from a black cloud. Underneath, Zoe was pictured with her dog again.

"You may remember that two nights ago, more specifically early morning Tuesday—"

"There was a thunderstorm," Amanda finished. "Sorry, I didn't mean to cut you off."

"Don't worry about it." Colleen was polite in her statement, but something in her eyes communicated she'd appreciate it if interruptions didn't happen often. "I was going to say that I think Zoe did play a sort of 'hide-and-seek' just before the murders. It would support the need for her to draw the storm. It's now linked with what she witnessed that night as well." Colleen got up. "I'll be back tomorrow. If you can find time, Detective Steele, I think it might be very helpful to Zoe if you could join us for a bit." She turned the last drawing over; it was Zoe with a female figure holding something yellow. The word "Friend" was scrawled across the image. Colleen pressed a fingertip to it. "I'm pretty sure that's you and your badge."

With that bomb, Colleen left. Amanda swallowed her emotion. The girl *was* attaching herself to Amanda, which made sense; Amanda had found her, had taken care of her for one night. The night after the worst day of her life. It didn't necessarily mean anything long term. Amanda was just a familiar face and presence, and the girl trusted her. For a minute, Amanda felt guilty for letting her go with Libby. She should have just taken her home again. But she really had enough going on in her life already, and she needed to call her sister back.

She got up and told Trent she had to take care of something really quick, then she'd meet him at their desks.

"You're not going to drink your coffee?" he asked.

She just shook her head, saving herself from having to admit she didn't think it would stay down. She went out to the parking lot, got inside her car, and called Kristen.

Her sister answered before the second ring. "Amanda, about time."

"What's going on? Is Mom okay? Something with the trial?"

"It's, ah, a bit of both." Kristen sniffled and sounded stuffed up.

"Have you been crying? You're making me worry here."

"Let's just say I found out something today and…" She blew her nose.

"Kris," Amanda prompted.

"I was going to just tell you over the phone, but this is probably a better conversation to have in person. Can you come over?"

"I'm in the middle of a—"

"You're always working a case, but I need to talk to you."

Just the stress on the word *need* had Amanda's attention. "Okay, let me see what I can do, and I'll be there as soon as I can."

"Okay." Kristen hung up, and Amanda was left holding her phone out and staring at it.

What the hell?

Amanda had failed to be there for her family when she was going through her own grief, and she had the opportunity to make up for that now. But she was drawn to seeking justice for Zoe and her parents. She'd go back in and see Trent, knock some things off the to-do list, then head to her sister's.

When Amanda approached Trent at his desk, he looked at her but didn't inquire as to how she was. He seemed rather grim himself, but she'd return the favor and not poke him as to why.

She cleared her throat. "Where are we?"

"Well, you know I followed up with the cell phone and internet provider. I just got started on the subpoena for the Parkers' financials. Saw an email from Rideout, too, about the autopsies."

She'd been so focused on the voicemails that she hadn't checked her emails. She sat at her desk and opened Rideout's message, leaving Trent to carry on with what he'd been doing.

In his message, Rideout said he'd missed her and Trent but expressed understanding, and he'd attached his reports on the Parkers.

She opened the one for Brett Parker and read:

Time of death confirmed between 4:03 AM and 5:30 AM
.22 cal bullets—retrieved fragments to send to the lab for ballistics

*Cause of death—first bullet hit the heart and would have
resulted in instant death*
No sign of defensive wounds

Next, she opened the report on Angela, and it read much the same.

She closed both reports and stared at her screen, her heart leaden with all the loss. At least Zoe had Libby Dewinter, someone who truly cared about her. Maybe the family friend would be able to adopt Zoe and give her a permanent home. Being with a familiar person would make the road ahead a little easier for Zoe.

Amanda then remembered that Libby was a teacher at Dumfries Elementary; Amanda's niece had gone there. She made a mental note to ask Ava about Libby. Perhaps Ava knew of her, maybe even had her as a teacher at one time and could provide some insight. Amanda would probably see her tonight when she went over to talk with Kristen.

Thinking of her sister and what she might have to say, Amanda was having a hard time focusing on work. "Trent," she said, and he lifted his head. His eyes just reached over the partition between them. "There's something I need to do. Can I leave everything with you? Not sure if I'll be back tonight or not." Given the way that Kristen had sounded, Amanda wasn't about to make any promises she might not be able to keep.

"Of course. Everything okay?"

She could brush him off, but she had the nudge to just be honest. "I don't know. Doesn't sound like it. Something to do with my sister and my mother's trial."

Trent glanced away, just briefly.

It didn't escape her notice. "What?"

"I got a voicemail from Ken Moss today."

He was the assistant district attorney.

"And?"

"They need me in court tomorrow morning."

"All right. Well, we knew the day would come."

"Doesn't make it easier."

She respected his loyalty toward her, but he had his pledge to his badge to uphold, and that should come before anything else. "You just do your job, Trent. That's all this is."

"It's your mother and—"

"Yeah, you could send her to the big house." She smirked, not even sure how she was making light of this conversation, but it was probably a way of preserving her sanity.

Trent's face contorted. "I don't really want to do that."

"Your job is to present the facts in the case. I was just joking about sending her to the big house. That's on the jury."

"You're sure that if she's found guilty, our partnership won't change?"

"I'm sure." She didn't even need to give it thought, because she'd done a lot of thinking on the subject already in the past few months.

"Okay."

She'd love to pry him for details—if he even had any to give on how the case was looking—but it wouldn't be ethical for him to share backdoor trial information with her. There was someone who was free to speak about the trial, though—her sister. She got up and said, "Just leave me notes about where you leave off on the Parker case so I'll have them for the morning—if I don't get back here tonight."

"Will do." He smiled at her.

She returned the smile and recalled how she'd initially fought Malone on being paired with a partner, a new detective at that, but she was happy she hadn't won that particular battle.

CHAPTER SEVENTEEN

Amanda had filled Malone in on how she and Trent made out at Falcon Strategic Technologies before she left the station, and it had chewed up more time than she would have liked. She was knocking on Kristen's door around nine thirty.

"Come in," her sister called out, then feet padded toward the door.

Amanda let herself inside. "You know you really should lock your door."

Kristen dismissed her with a shake of a hand, and Amanda shouldn't have expected anything else. The conversation was an old one. Her sister lived in Woodbridge, not far from the station, and having been a small-town girl all her life, she'd fallen into the belief that she was somehow secure and sheltered from the evil of the world. It was interesting that their father being a police chief hadn't been enough to instill some awareness in her.

Amanda slipped out of her shoes and hung her light jacket inside the closet. Her sister looked amazing even for this time of night—something else that wasn't a surprise. Kristen was two years younger than Amanda, at thirty-four, and some people might mistake her for vain, but that would be those who judged her by appearance only. Her sister had dark-red hair that fell just over her shoulders, and she always wore it down and in large curls. Amanda didn't recall ever seeing her with it back in a ponytail. Maybe when she was little.

"I'm so glad you came over." Kristen hugged Amanda and tapped a kiss on her cheek. "You look exhausted."

"You have no idea." She scanned her sister's eyes, curious as to what was going on. When Kristen had called earlier, she'd sounded urgent and upset. Now she was a semblance of calm. "What's up?"

"Right… *that*." Kristen turned and walked toward the back of the house where the kitchen was. "I'll put on the kettle."

Her family and tea… "I'd prefer a coffee."

"No problem. Help yourself. You know where it all is."

Amanda followed her into the kitchen and couldn't shake the way Kristen had basically spat the word *that*. What was she talking about? Amanda wished she'd just come out with it; she'd never been good with waiting. Besides, bad news was best delivered swiftly.

Kristen flicked on the kettle and grabbed two cups from the cupboard. She handed one to Amanda.

"You going to tell me what had you so anxious?"

"Not until I have tea in a cup."

Her sister could be a tad dramatic and was prone to sensationalism, but Amanda also knew how hard-headed she could be. So if she'd decided she wasn't going to talk until she had tea, there'd be no fighting it—or no *winning* anyway. Amanda grabbed a coffee pod from a drawer and set the machine to brewing.

Kristen sat at the kitchen table, and Amanda plopped into a chair across from her. She studied her sister's face.

"Don't do that," Kristen said and averted her eyes.

"Don't do what?"

"What you always do. You try to figure out what I'm thinking, and you convince yourself you know and can read my mind. I hate it."

"You hate it because I'm usually right." Amanda smiled when her sister finally looked her way again.

"Well…" Kristen sighed. "I don't think you could ever guess what I have to say tonight."

"Hey, Aunt Amanda." Ava, Kristen's thirteen-year-old daughter, came into the room and hugged Amanda over the back of the chair and kissed her cheek.

"Hey, sweetie. How's it going?"

"Ah, don't get me started." Ava rolled her eyes in exaggerated teenager fashion. "I'm never going to finish my homework tonight."

"That's because you need to get off your phone for long enough to do it." Kristen regarded her daughter with seriousness, but Amanda had a hard time fighting her amusement. Her sister was a great procrastinator herself, and she'd never turned her homework in on time in all of high school. It was amazing she'd graduated and even gone on to finish college. Not that she'd put her business degree to use. She'd gotten married and pregnant straight out of college, and her husband, Erik, had become the sole breadwinner.

"Very funny, Mom." Ava shook her head and sneered, her back to her mother, but facing Amanda so she could see.

Amanda bit her bottom lip to stop herself from giggling. Ava was such a cute kid, though she'd object to the term *kid* at her age. Probably *cute* too, as if the phrase should strictly apply to a child. But Ava was cute, and to Amanda, she'd always be a kid. Ava had long, brown hair, which she got from her father, and wore it straight. Her eyes sparkled with life, and she had the most endearing dimples in her cheeks when she smiled. A family trait that Lindsey had picked up too.

"And don't you start." Kristen shook a finger at Amanda.

"I never…" Amanda covered her mouth, but the laughter exploded through her fingers. "I'm sorry."

Ava left the room, rolling her eyes. The kettle clicked, and Kristen finally was able to make her tea. Amanda retrieved her brewed coffee and returned to the table.

"Erik's not home tonight?" Amanda asked. There was an unsettling energy in the room, and it was hard to navigate. What her sister was going to tell her was significant. On rethinking her question, she wished she could reel it back in. What if her sister and Erik were having marriage problems? She quickly dismissed that idea, recalling Kristen saying it had something to do with the trial and their mother.

"Oh, yeah, he's home." Kristen bobbed her teabag by its string, up and down in her cup. Then she tossed it in the garbage and sat at the table. The water was hardly colored. "He's in his room doing whatever it is he does."

"Playing video games?"

"Uh-huh. Thirty-eight, a grown-ass man, and he plays games at night. And he wears this thing…" She mimed with a hand sweeping over her head and coming down over her ear to her mouth.

"A headset?" Her sister was never great at charades, but somehow Amanda could figure out what Kristen was going for.

"Yep, and he talks to people he plays with. He tells me he's being social." Her sister paused there and crossed her eyes. "Also says I should be happy because at least I know where my husband is. Anyway…"

"People need to do what helps them relax at the end of the day."

Kristen scoffed. "Is that you dishing out advice on relaxation? You look tense as hell. Your shoulders reach your earlobes."

"I'm working a double homicide."

"The one in Triangle?"

Amanda nodded.

"I saw the news article."

Amanda sipped her coffee and crossed her legs at the ankles. "So what is it? What couldn't wait?"

Her sister's eyes darkened, and her lips twitched like she was fending off crying.

Amanda reached across the table and put her hand on her sister's arm. "Talk to me."

"It's…" A tear rolled down her cheek, and her sister was quick to wipe it away. "Dad cheated on Mom."

Amanda felt herself go cold and numb. She idolized her father, and even though she knew he wasn't perfect, she wanted to go on believing that he was. Her mind was filling with images and question marks. She recalled that her father hadn't always been the ideal husband. He put in long hours on the job when he was on the force, and he went through a period when the bottle was one of his best friends. She remembered her parents fighting despite them doing a good job of trying to hide it from Amanda and her five siblings. But what couple didn't have arguments or squabbles? "He… ah… when? With whom?"

Kristen licked her lips and drank some tea. Her eyes were filling with more tears. "It was a while ago." She sniffled.

Amanda was trying to make sense of all this. She'd always seen her family as somewhat idyllic, not dysfunctional like everyone else's. That image was starting to crack. "Okay. When? I guess I don't understand. Why is this coming up now? And you made it sound like it had something to do with Mom's trial."

Kristen met her gaze, her face dark shadows. "Dad's mistress was Emma Blair."

Did I hear her correctly?

"Emma?" Amanda squeezed out and rubbed the back of her neck. The image of that perfect family was now completely shattered.

"That's why Hannah moved to have her testimony revoked."

"She would have just been presenting forensic evidence." Amanda heard her defense of the CSI come from her mouth and hardly believed it, but it was easier to fall into cop mode than daughter mode right now. The former made it easier to detach and see the situation objectively. Blair's testimony would be crucial for the prosecution's case against her mother, and her mother deserved to pay for what she had done. At least that was what the cop in her was preaching, but as the daughter, she didn't want to hear it. She felt relief and a glimmer of hope for her mother's future.

"You heard me, Amanda? She had sex with Dad. And more than once."

Amanda slowly met her sister's gaze again. "So you think she tainted the evidence to hurt Mom?"

Kristen shrugged. "It's possible, right? Obviously it's enough to put doubt in the jury's minds. That's how Hannah was able to get her testimony removed."

"And all this came out in court today?" *In public?* Amanda was feeling mortified for herself, her siblings, her parents. Even a little for Emma Blair, but now she had her answer as to why the woman seemed to despise her. Nathan Steele had ultimately chosen Amanda's mother, not Emma Blair. No doubt there was years of resentment there—even though Emma had married. But was that before or after the affair?

"Yesterday. After you left, the judge demanded a reason to remove Emma."

"And you're telling me now?" Amanda snapped.

"Don't get mad at me. I thought Mom should tell you, but when I asked her today, she said she would get to it. Probably at Sunday dinner."

Every Sunday, the family shared a meal at their parents' place.

"Speaking of which, who knows if that's even going to happen?" Amanda sighed and stared up at the ceiling. "The trial could be over before then, and Mom in prison."

"I know, and that's why I decided if Mom wasn't going to tell you sooner, then I would."

"I should call Mom."

"No." Kristen held up her hand. "Just leave it for now. She's under enough stress with the trial."

Amanda hesitated, considered. "I just can't believe it."

"A real shocker, isn't it?" Kristen got up, snatched a tissue box from the counter and returned with it to the table.

"Yeah, you could say that."

"You look like I must have when I first heard. Shell-shocked, in a trance."

"Like it's not even real," Amanda admitted. "And I'm in some sort of nightmare. Mom and Dad don't have a perfect marriage, but I thought it was solid."

"Me too." Kristen took Amanda's hand and squeezed.

"You never said when they'd slept together. Just that it was a while ago."

"Mom said I was eight and that the affair had been brief. She wants us to forgive Dad, because she has."

Amanda did the quick math. It had been twenty-six years ago. Her father would have been drinking in those days, but that was no excuse for cheating on her mother. And was adultery something a person could truly forgive, especially when forgiveness was so often linked to forgetting? Surely the affair must have been lurking in the back of her mother's mind all these years. Maybe it wasn't just the grief of losing her granddaughter and son-in-law—and also Amanda, who'd decided to pull away from her family for five years after the accident—that had led her mother's mind to murder. Maybe it had also been the hell brewing in the background, screaming that she wasn't enough to hold her own husband.

Now Amanda no longer had to carry the guilt for her mother's actions by herself; she could share this with her father and Emma Blair. She clenched her jaw, fueled with rage. How dare that woman treat her with disdain when she'd slept with a married man—possibly even married herself!

Her phone rang, and caller ID said it was Penny Anderson.

"Don't answer that, Amanda, please."

Penny… The name sounded familiar, then Amanda's mind cleared. That was Libby's girlfriend. She answered, and her sister groaned. "Detective Steele."

"It's Penny. I need you to…" She sobbed, and the hairs rose on Amanda's arms.

"Is Zoe okay? Libby?"

"Someone… someone came into the house from the backyard, and they—"

"Did they take her, hurt her?" Amanda jumped to her feet and headed to the front door, her sister trailing her.

"No. Libby was able to stop them, but Libby was… uh, shot." She broke down and spoke through crying. "There's so much blood."

"Hold on. I'll be right there and get help on the way." Amanda whooshed out the door with one quick glance at her sister, to whom she mouthed an apology. Every nerve ending in Amanda's body was screaming. The shooter had come for Zoe, and he'd gotten Libby.

She jumped into her car, disconnected with Penny, and called dispatch. She requested a response team for Libby Dewinter's residence. She informed them of the gunshot wound, that the assailant should be considered armed and dangerous and was a suspect in a double homicide. "He may still be in the area. You'll need to look up the address and tell me where it is too." She'd forgotten to ask Penny.

The woman came back with the address. Amanda gunned the gas. She was about to see just how fast her Honda Civic could take her from Woodbridge to Dumfries.

CHAPTER EIGHTEEN

Amanda made sure dispatch notified responding officers that she and Trent would be on scene. She didn't want a bullet in her back from one of her own while she was out looking for the person who'd likely killed the Parkers and now shot Libby. She didn't really want a bullet in the back, period.

Her heart was racing, and the guilt was immense. She never should have let Zoe go with Libby. She should have told Malone she'd take care of the girl, no matter how uncomfortable it was. Now someone had come for the child and had almost succeeded in their efforts. The officer charged with watching over the residence had been completely clueless about the home invasion as it was taking place. She called Trent on the way, and he agreed to meet her about a block from the house.

"We approach this like the shooter might still be in the area," she told him, hoping that was the case. She'd love nothing more than to apprehend him and secure Zoe's future.

She'd just parked when Trent pulled up. She could hear approaching sirens and felt a sickening dread tug at her stomach. She wanted to check on Libby and Zoe, but the responders would take care of Libby, and Penny would attend to Zoe. The best use of Amanda's and Trent's time was to see if they could find the shooter.

Ahead of them, the officer who had been posted on the street was out of his car, standing next to it and watching them approach. She signaled to him, and he acknowledged that he was aware of their presence. She wanted to confront him and ask why he'd had no idea what was going on in the house, but Penny had said the shooter came from the backyard.

Police cruisers and an ambulance raced past them, stopping in front of Libby's house. It was a single-story home with neighbors on both sides and, from the map in Amanda's head, in the back. Most of the properties in that area weren't fenced, and she was quite sure that was the case with Libby's yard and the one in the rear. The shooter would have free access to go anywhere after fleeing the house.

But why leave Libby alive, and why not take Zoe?

The questions fired through her mind so quickly, she could barely grasp hold of them.

Assuming the shooter was still around, she and Trent could go to the back street and cut him off, smoke him out. But he could flee to the front, the home's facing street, and with the ambulance there, that wouldn't be the smartest option.

She looked over at Trent. "We're going to split up. You go around the left side of Libby's house, and I'll go right. If the perp's still here, hopefully we'll wedge him in the middle."

They popped communication buds into their ears, got on the same frequency as the rest of the responders, and proceeded with the plan of action. They both drew their guns so they'd be at the ready if they needed to fire. She stopped at the back corner and listened. Nothing but her labored breathing.

She peeked her head around the corner. A shadow on the move. Male. "Prince William County PD," she shouted and stepped out.

The flash of a muzzle. A thunderous crack.

A stinging burn in the top of her right arm.

Shit! She'd been hit. She quickly looked down and concluded it was just a graze, but it still hurt like a son of a bitch.

"Shots fired! I repeat, shots fired!" she echoed over the comms. She aimed her gun on the man and squeezed her trigger. He ran toward the house behind Libby's. "Suspect is on the run! I repeat, on the run!"

The figure turned and fired again, lighting up the night. She ducked behind a shed for cover. Trent joined her there.

Another report rang out, but then all went silent except for the voices transmitting over the comms.

"He's running to High Street," she said as she ducked out to see his retreating figure and started after him. The thought that she was insane ran through her mind on ticker tape. Sane people didn't run toward gunfire; they ran away. But she kept on the move, her breath exhaling in puffs of white in the cool night air.

"Stop! Prince William County PD!" Trent yelled, keeping stride next to her in the pursuit.

She carefully took in her surroundings as she moved. Nothing. She stepped out onto the road. "Where the hell did he go?"

Suddenly, headlights were coming straight for her. She could hear the car's engine rev as it sped up, and she knew immediately she was the target—the vehicle did not waver in its bead on her. She stood there, frozen in place, her gun held high, and she squeezed off three rounds.

The windshield exploded. Two pings sounded against metal— the bullets must have penetrated the hood. But the vehicle wasn't slowing down.

She continued watching the lights get closer and closer, brighter and brighter.

"Amanda!" Trent lunged at her, and air whooshed from her lungs.

But just as he was barreling her over, she saw the driver's face. A man, blond hair, cropped short and spiky, with a high brow ridge, defined jawline, and piercing eyes. He was holding a gun toward the passenger window, but he never fired.

"Move, Trent!" She shoved him off and held her gun poised to fire, aiming for a tire, but she couldn't bring herself to pull the trigger. She no longer had a good line of fire. The risk was too high.

What if her bullet went astray and injured an innocent… or worse, killed one? But she caught the car's color, make and model, and license plate. "Write this down!" She told him it was a dark-blue Dodge Charger and gave him the license number.

"Got it," he screamed back, needing to speak over cop cars that now zoomed past them, sirens screeching in the night.

Her comm was alive with voices and updates, but for now, she and Trent weren't going anywhere. They'd never be able to catch up to the pursuit, so she had to trust the officers who were already on the perp's tail.

She wiped the seat of her pants; it was wet from the damp grass. "We need to run the plate." She started toward the department car Trent had driven, cradling her injured arm. When she pulled her hand away, it was red with blood.

"Amanda!" Trent hustled toward her. "You're shot! Crap, crap, crap!" He spoke into the comms and requested a paramedic. "Cop hit. Need medical—"

"One more word and…" She eyed him with seriousness, hoping to squash his would-be hero moment.

He stopped speaking but was doing something on his phone.

She pulled her comm piece and said to him, "It's just a graze."

"Let a doctor take a look and determine if—" He snapped his mouth shut at her glare.

"Just call Crime Scene and run the plate. Please." She added the last bit to soften the request. He had just been showing concern, but her mind stuck on *Crime Scene*—more specifically homewrecker Emma Blair. "I'm going to check on Zoe and Penny, find out Libby's condition."

"You really think that's a good idea?" He swept a hand up and down, emphasizing her torso, specifically the blood leaking from the sleeve of her jacket.

She took a deep breath. He was right. She couldn't see Zoe like this. She had to get cleaned up first. They got to the car, and the pain that had started off mild bloomed into searing agony. Her adrenaline was wearing off. She winced. So much for the myth that bullet grazes didn't hurt.

Trent didn't say another word about her injury and did what she'd asked him to. Her phone rang.

"Amanda, are you okay?" It was Malone.

"I'm fine, or will be fine." She wished that everyone would stop making a fuss about her. Being shot was a risk she'd assumed when she donned the badge, but maybe she should have listened to that little voice that tried to caution her that sane people ran *away* from gunfire.

"You were shot."

The PWCPD's rumor mill worked fast... And she suspected the culprit at the helm of this one was standing next to her. Trent must have texted Malone when she'd seen him fiddling with his phone a moment ago.

"Grazed. And Trent should know the difference." She passed a sideways glance at her partner, who shook his head and smirked. At least he'd picked up her jab. As a young and eager officer assisting the FBI years ago, Trent had gotten himself shot twice by a serial killer.

"Don't make light of this," Malone said. "I want you to go to the hospital and get it taken care of."

"How about a compromise? I get cleaned up by medics on scene and go on about my life?"

There was silence on the other end of the line. She'd wait it out. It was like a staring contest, but instead of who would blink first, it was whoever *spoke* first lost.

Seconds ticked off on clocks everywhere.

There was a large sigh on Malone's end, then, "Fine."

She smiled, taking the small victory, but her mood soured quickly. There was something she needed to do—whether it was for her good or not remained to be determined. "I'll be taking Zoe home with me."

Trent was on a phone call, but apparently he had caught her words. He looked at her with wide eyes. Malone remained silent.

She persisted, "She's not safe staying with anyone who doesn't have a badge and a gun."

"I can find someone else."

"No. I'll take her."

"I don't know if that's a good idea, Amanda."

"It's the best offer on the table. I know kids, and the girl likes me. I'm sure I can get her to talk. I can certainly protect her. Two birds, one stone."

"Ha, the stone being you, Ms. Stubborn." He was attempting to lighten the conversation, but there was a lack of mirth in his voice.

"Come on, Sergeant." She pulled out his title for extra emphasis. "I wouldn't say I could handle this if I couldn't."

"Yes, you would."

She had nothing to say to that.

"Just earlier today you didn't want to take her in, and now you do."

"Well, things change."

There was a brief pause on his end, which she'd label as hesitation.

Eventually, he said, "I'll contact Murphy with child services and apprise her of the situation. But you get medical attention before you go to the girl."

"I saw his face," she blurted out.

Another pause, probably trying to register what she'd just said. "Good enough to work with a sketch artist?" he asked.

"Maybe. Also got his license plate. Trent's checking on it now. Don't know anything about it yet."

"Keep me posted. We'll get an all-points bulletin out on the car, and I'll get a sketch artist to the station for first thing in the morning."

Her memory could be hazy by then, but there wasn't really another option. The artists weren't typically on call. Besides, tonight she had Zoe to think about, and the hour was already getting late. She'd write down the man's facial characteristics before going to bed. "Okay," was all she said and then ended the call.

Trent pocketed his phone and bridged the distance between them. "I should know the difference between a gunshot wound and a graze? Nice." He narrowed his eyes, but a smirk played on his lips.

"Well…" She shrugged her shoulders. "Have they caught up with the perp?"

He shook his head and kicked the toe of his shoe into the grass. "They lost him. We'll put all hospitals and medical centers on alert for men coming in with a GSW, in case one of us got lucky and hit the guy."

"We can always try, but I don't think the man would seek treatment at the usual places. He's a professional, remember?"

"Part of an organization, though? Or a standalone hired gun?"

"At the moment, I'm a little torn on that. The Parkers were executed, yet Libby gets shot and is left alive, Zoe wasn't hit, and the shooter fled? In some ways, that doesn't sound like the same person who took the Parkers out in cold blood."

"Have to agree with you there. And why not kill Zoe? That's if his interest in her is to silence a potential eyewitness to the murders."

She had this horrible gnawing in the pit of her stomach. They were missing something. "I don't know."

"But it has to be related to the murder. I mean, otherwise, why come for Zoe at all?"

"Exactly, but I keep coming back to why did he leave without taking care of her? What made him leave—or retreat anyway? Guess he was hanging around. Maybe he was going to try again?"

"He could have had that intention. Originally he could have gotten spooked by something."

"I'd say sure, but a professional wouldn't panic, and they wouldn't screw up. And when he drove past us, he was looking right at me. He had his gun drawn, but he didn't fire. Makes no sense either. I don't know what's going on here, but it's not adding up."

"That is strange. But I'm happy he didn't pull the trigger," Trent added quickly.

"Aw, shucks."

Sirens were now approaching. An ambulance for her. She shook her head at the overkill. Lights would have been sufficient; it's not like she was bleeding to death. Though she did feel a touch lightheaded. Maybe she was losing more blood than she realized. Or she had high blood pressure thanks to recent events, including learning of her father's affair. With Emma Blair, no less.

"Do you think he'll be back for Zoe?"

She nodded. "I do, and that's why I'm taking her home with me." She paused there, giving Trent the opportunity to insert his two cents about why it was a bad idea, but he didn't. She went on. "And when he does return, I'll be ready."

"You mean *we'll* be ready?"

"Isn't that what I said?" she tossed back and turned away toward the approaching ambulance. The sirens were off now, but the vehicle's strobing lights danced off windows like a giant disco ball.

When the paramedic came over to her, Amanda said, "Let's get this over with."

The man chuckled and helped her into the back of the vehicle. "It takes the time it takes."

She grumbled internally. Of all the times to have to deal with someone so calm and laid back. All her cylinders were firing. She was ready to catch the asshole who likely killed the Parkers, shot Libby, terrified a little girl, and took a bite out of her own flesh. Amanda was starting to think that the Bible's code for justice was onto something with the whole "an eye for an eye" thing.

CHAPTER NINETEEN

Last night was like a bad nightmare that had turned into a horrid hangover. Her father and Emma Blair. Libby being shot. Zoe coming home with Amanda. She hadn't had time to switch the sheets and comforter to the dryer and had nothing for Lindsey's bed. She'd ended up putting king-size sheets on the twin. She still couldn't bring herself to address the bed-wetting with Zoe, but her sleeping here wasn't permanent, so why bother the girl with it? She seemed like she was folding in on herself even more than before, the evening's events shaking her something fierce.

At least the doctors were positive that Libby would pull through. Gracefully, the bullet had done minimal damage, and surgery to remove it had been a success. Small miracle considering an otherwise hellish day.

The license plate was a dead end. It hadn't been a valid number, but they had the APB issued on the Dodge Charger with a description—newer model, dark-blue, windshield blown out.

Trent wouldn't be in until at least noon, as he had court testimony this morning. Amanda wished that she could be there to support him and her mother, but with everything going on, she couldn't get away. Hopefully, Trent would be able to stay awake. He'd been at the Dewinter residence questioning Penny Anderson until late. According to her, she and Libby had been watching TV when they heard the back patio door slide open. They'd gone to investigate when they should have informed the officer out front.

The perp held them at gunpoint and told them to take him to the girl. Both women refused, and when he made a move to search the house, Libby had stepped in front of him to thwart his plan. That was when she was shot.

Penny said the man's eyes had enlarged, and he looked all around like he was cagey, then ran out the back door. She was too frozen to follow, but placed the call to Amanda instead.

One small mercy from the whole thing was that Zoe had been upstairs and hadn't witnessed this shooting. And while the man might have run out the back, he hadn't gone far. He'd been in the yard when Amanda and Trent had shown up. Had he been trying to build up his courage to go back inside? Though that didn't fit with a professional hitman and trying to align the inconsistencies was giving her a headache.

Currently, Amanda was sitting at Central. It was about eight in the morning, and she was across from the sketch artist, while Zoe was in the interview room eating her breakfast and coloring. She'd stayed in Lindsey's room the entire night, but from the look of her bloodshot eyes, she hadn't slept much. Again, Amanda wished she could piece the girl together and heal her, but that was a journey that Zoe ultimately had to make for herself.

"And his forehead, Detective?" Tobias Villa, the sketch artist, prompted her. He had green eyes and a full head of silver hair, but she'd guess him to be no older than forty.

"Ah, he had a high brow ridge."

Tobias started drawing, and she held out her hand to stop him.

"I don't know. Never mind. Maybe I'm not remembering correctly. This was probably a bad idea." She kept going back and forth like this with almost every feature, second-guessing herself. But it had been dark, and it had been for a fleeting moment in time. She laid a palm over her arm where the bullet had grazed her, a mindless touch made on instinct, and dropped her hand. It still stung and probably would for a while. She wondered if the pain came from the abrasion alone or was aided along by her troubled memories.

Tobias was patient and meticulous—probably two traits strongly required in his line of work. But he was also particularly skilled at asking the right questions, which helped her to concentrate and conjure up what she had seen. Sadly, it didn't stop the doubts. "It's okay, Detective. Things like this take time. I'm not going anywhere."

She smiled… or at least tried to form the expression. "How about a break?"

He winced. "I don't recommend that now that we've started."

Tobias had already stressed how important it was that she stick with the image and didn't let her mind wander too much. But that was a tall feat to master, especially when her thoughts kept skipping all over the place, constantly returning to her father and Emma Blair's affair. How could her father hurt her mother like this? She wanted to give him a piece of her mind for putting her through the pain; even if it was an old wound, surely the recent situation had tugged on the scab. But Amanda had more pressing issues to deal with. A killer to catch, for one.

"Detective?" Given the way Tobias's face was all scrunched up, he must have been trying to get her attention for a while.

"Oh. Sorry, my mind drifted."

He gestured to the sketch, drawing attention to the brow line. "What about that?"

She hesitated, considered, then nodded. "Looks right." *Though, is it? Gah!*

For the next hour, she watched the minutes pass on the clock while she worked—and reworked—through the different facial features with Tobias. She drank the last of the water from her bottle, her throat dry from all the talking.

"All right, I think we're finished here." Tobias sounded proud as he sat back and made sure the sketch was at an angle to afford her a good view.

As soon as her gaze met the eyes in the drawing, she knew. "That's him." She wasn't about to lavish praise on the man before her, but the artist had done an incredible job recreating the perp's image based on nothing but answers to his probing questions.

"Glad to hear that I did this justice. I'll email a digital copy over to you immediately."

"Thanks," she said, handing him her business card. "My email address is on there."

She got up, feeling a little lost. Now that they had the picture, what was the plan? She had to assume it would be hitting the news media—print, television, and internet. Then, there was the other bit… Zoe should be shown the sketch to see if she recognized the man as the one who had killed her parents. And along those lines, it truly made no sense why he had let Zoe live. As she'd told Trent last night, she was fairly sure they hadn't seen the last of their shooter.

Amanda knocked on Malone's door, though the blinds were open, and she could see that he was sitting at his desk working on paperwork. Knowing the man like she did, he wasn't a huge fan of paper shuffling.

He waved her in.

She entered, shut the door behind her, and sat across from him.

"I take it you're finished with the sketch artist?"

"Uh-huh. What's your plan from here? Wide distribution of this guy's face to every media outlet?" She typically wasn't a fan of news reporters and their ilk, but they could serve a purpose, such as the case here. The more people who saw this guy's face, the higher probability of someone recognizing him and turning him in. She'd already sent the sketch to Penny Anderson, and she confirmed that was the man who broke into their house, shot Libby, and demanded to be taken to Zoe. Amanda shared this with Malone.

"Good. Though the likelihood of someone else lurking around in their yard was slim to none."

"How I feel."

"You need to show the sketch to the girl, that's if you haven't already."

She knew it was necessary even if she wasn't entirely comfortable stirring up bad memories for Zoe. She'd just have to focus on the bigger picture—the more she could pry from Zoe, the faster they'd catch her parents' killer and Libby's shooter, and the faster Zoe could start to heal.

"Amanda?" he prompted.

She shook her head. "I haven't yet, but I understand it needs to be done." She could always hand this over to Colleen Frost to broach with the girl. She was the one experienced in dealing with trauma victims. She surfaced from her thoughts and realized he was studying her. "What?"

He leaned back in his chair, swiveled a little. "There's always more than one way of looking at something."

"Uh-huh." She had no idea where he was headed with his statement.

"We could go the route of making his face public. It could net a solid lead, an identity."

"That's what we want, right?"

"You've already made it clear that you believe a professional is behind the murders. Most likely that applies to the person responsible for last night's events too. One and the same? Not sure, but if we put his picture in the papers, he may just slink off, and we'll never find him."

"No, I don't believe that. He came for Zoe once. He'll be back. Or…" Her next thought sank in her gut. "Someone else might come in his place."

"Someone else? You make it sound like there's a whole organization behind this now."

"I'm not entirely sure what's going on."

"This have to do with Brett Parker's work?"

She shook her head and shrugged her shoulders. "I don't know. Maybe. Maybe not. We're still looking into Brett's life."

"You might want to get on it faster."

"Not like we haven't been trying," she flipped back, her body tensing. She took offense at his comment. She'd gone above and beyond with this case by taking Zoe into her home, into Lindsey's room, her bed. She took a deep breath and went on. "If we make his face public, we could send him into hiding, sure, but more likely it will result in a lead. We take what we can get."

Malone mumbled something, not that it was coherent enough she could make it out. "Let me think about this."

Obviously his primary intention for the sketch had been to show it to Zoe, not to plaster it everywhere.

"About leads, I've heard from CSI Blair. As you know, Crime Scene scoured Dewinter's yard and the neighbors' and recovered some bullet casings. They even found a bullet lodged into wood trim on the house next door."

"Probably the one that just missed me."

"Did it really miss you, though?" His gaze drifted to her injured arm, and he flicked a finger toward it. "How is the injury?"

"Barely a scratch." It had required stitches, but Malone didn't need to know everything, and the wound was safe and sound behind a bandage under her sleeve. There'd be no peek-see for Malone to make a dispute of her claim that it was just a *scratch*.

"I'm sure it's more than that, but I'm glad you're gonna live." He smirked at her, but then his expression went serious. "The bullet was a twenty-two."

"Just like the caliber used on the Parkers. Then again, it's a popular caliber."

"Am I sensing you don't think the perp from last night was the one who killed the Parkers now?"

"There are just some things that aren't adding up for me. Obviously, the intruder at Libby's home is involved on some level."

"Give me a clue here."

She told him about the way he'd acted at Dewinter's. Jumpy, and how he could have shot her and her girlfriend dead, but he hadn't. He'd only struck Libby once, not three times, as was the case with the Parkers.

"Huh. Really, though, the chances of this being an unconnected event are slim to none."

"Yep, a mystery to solve, to be sure." She realized how she was always stressing to Trent that he keep an open mind and remain objective. Maybe she was failing to do that here. There could be one way to know for sure. "I assume a ballistics comparison will be made between the bullets used on the Parkers and Libby Dewinter to see if the rounds came from the same gun?" But then again if they were looking at a professional, he could have used a different weapon.

"Of course, and I've requested that be rushed along."

"Good. And any prints left at the scene?" She highly doubted that the perp had time to collect his brass in the hail of gunfire as he fled the area but didn't figure there'd be prints on them. The gunman probably would have loaded his magazines with gloved hands.

"There were. On the casings left behind."

Not so professional… "Surprising. Let's hope it leads somewhere. The sooner we can get this closed, the better for Zoe. She deserves justice for her parents and to be able to move on with her life."

Malone didn't say anything, but his eyes did. There was concern in them, as if he suspected her desire to want to close the case was personal, to make it easier on herself. And his mouth kept gaping open, shut, open, shut—like he wanted to say something but couldn't spit it out. She had a hunch this conversation was going from business to personal. He was well aware of the similarity between her and Zoe—how they'd both lost family.

"Yes, I have an idea what she's going through," she volunteered. "I also know that life is often up in the air, or it's as if the ground will give way at any moment."

"As they say, control is an illusion."

"Yeah, and I hate that." Her mind slipped to her mother's trial, to what had surfaced about her father's affair, and she regarded the man across from her. He was a good friend of her father's—had been for years. Had he known about the affair and played a role in keeping it secret? Even worse, had he condoned and justified her father's actions? She wasn't sure how to bring it up or whether she even wanted to.

"No one likes feeling they don't have control, but kiddo, it's a fact of life."

Not one that you need to tell me... He didn't pull out "kiddo" very often; it was reserved for rare personal interactions between them. She should bring up her father's affair, but if Malone had been aware of it, she wasn't sure if she could forgive him. "I should get back to work." She stood and headed for the door.

"Detective." There was the hint of playfulness in his tone of voice.

She faced him. "Yeah."

"If you could stay out of the path of bullets today, that'd be great." He chuckled, but she caught sight of the person outside his door. Police Chief Hill was about to come in.

"Why do I have a feeling it's too late for that?"

CHAPTER TWENTY

Amanda tried to bypass Hill and get to the hallway, but the woman stood in the doorway like a barricade, blocking Amanda's freedom.

"You're just who I'm looking for," Hill said and let her eyes trace over Amanda's shoulder to Malone. "Both of you. Please." She gestured for Amanda to back up, and the inference was there for her to take a seat.

Amanda wasn't fooled by her use of a pleasantry. Hill was just biding her time to lash out; Amanda could feel it radiating from her. Was the woman ever in a good mood? Regardless, the next few minutes might go better if she did sit down. It would be far more difficult to strike Hill in her big fat piehole if she wasn't standing next to her. Amanda reluctantly sat.

Hill closed the door behind her and slinked into the room in her high heels and tight-fitting pencil-skirt and jacket. She'd always fit the image of a bureaucrat well. It was the heart of a cop that she lacked.

"What is it, Chief?" Malone asked. His voice wasn't laced with complete disdain, but it was still there.

"I've been informed this morning that there was an exchange of gunfire last night in a Dumfries residential neighborhood. Said to have involved the PWCPD." She slid her reptile eyes toward Amanda, just briefly.

"Sure, and a fleeing perp suspected in a shooting," Malone clarified.

"I see," Hill dragged out and slithered around the room. "So we know that the person running away was the gunman?"

"He was in Dewinter's backyard—" Amanda clamped her mouth shut when Malone raised his hand as if to tell her to let him do the talking.

"The suspect was found in Dewinter's backyard, but he was also the one to open fire on PWCPD officers first." Malone angled his head and clasped his hands in his lap, presenting a solid front.

"I see."

Amanda wanted to take the chief's *I see* and stuff it down her throat. This woman's attitude was unbelievable. The way she was always attacking their efforts made it feel like she was playing for the other team—that being whoever was in opposition to the PWCPD at any given time.

No one said anything for a few seconds. Hill broke the silence—the quiet obviously being a tool she wielded for her advantage.

"The thing is…" Hill paused there as if to insert dramatic effect. "We can't just have officers running through neighborhoods firing their weapons."

"Every one of my detectives' bullets have been accounted for," Malone said.

This was something else Amanda had taken care of last night before crawling into bed—writing up a report for firing her weapon. Trent would have too. Procedure dictated that anytime a cop even *pulled* his or her weapon, it needed to be accounted for.

Hill's lips curved in a tight smirk. "So because a suspect is seen running, opens fire, it excuses putting the lives of innocent people at risk?"

"No one was at risk," Amanda spat, not able to sit quiet any longer. "It was equal force."

Hill burned her gaze through Amanda's forehead.

Amanda went on. "You do know that when a suspect resists arrest as police we have the right to meet that resistance with equal force?"

Hill grimaced, but Amanda found pleasure in the expression because it meant she was getting to the woman. Though she'd never get *through* to her.

"That means if they are shooting at us, we can—"

"Yes, I know what it means." Hill rolled her eyes and sighed. "I thought your suspension would have given you time to think through your actions so you could make better decisions in the future, yet here you are firing your gun in a residential neighborhood. It doesn't seem like you did any self-reflection in your time away."

Hill made it sound like the thirty-day suspension Amanda received back in April had been a vacation request. It had been painful to hand in her badge and gun and step away from all she'd known in her adult life. Days had passed before she didn't feel like she was simply flitting about without purpose, but she'd used the time to get closer to her family.

"I don't think this is necessary, Hill," Malone inserted and received a glare from the chief for his trouble.

"I disagree." Hill crossed her arms.

"You make it sound like I went cowboy," Amanda pushed out, but the moment she did, she wished she could reel her words back in. She had resurrected Hill's tirade.

"Cowboy, cowgirl… whatever. You didn't consider that someone could have gotten hurt."

Someone's about to get hurt! Amanda clenched her hands into fists. "Someone did get hurt," she ended up saying. "Libby Dewinter is in the hospital recovering from surgery. She was trying to protect Zoe from the shooter."

Hill met Amanda's gaze. "Another thing, and thank you for bringing it up. If the girl had been with you as I'd requested in the first place, maybe none of this would have happened. Have you thought of that?"

"I…" Amanda couldn't talk. Her throat was constricted from anger and guilt. She'd thought the same thing herself, but Hill had no right to make that sort of demand of her.

"Detective Steele's job is to solve murders for the PWCPD, Chief," Malone said firmly. "It's not to take in eyewitnesses. For her to do so is going above and beyond."

Hill looked at Malone, and Amanda noted the fire in her eyes.

"Well, from this moment," Hill began, "I want that girl to be under Detective Steele's care so that there's not a repeat of last night's events."

"You can't insist that she—"

"It's all right, Sergeant," Amanda cut in. "I'll take care of Zoe Parker's welfare, but not because the Chief has requested it. It's because I want to."

Hill faced her, and her shoulders lowered just slightly. By volunteering, Amanda had taken the chief's power and her pleasure in trying to force Amanda to do something.

"Oh, okay, very good." She leaned against a filing credenza. "But did anything good come from your exploits last night? The guy wasn't caught. I heard that much."

"I saw his face," Amanda offered stiffly.

"Is that so?"

"Detective Steele just finished working with a sketch artist."

"Can I see?" Hill slipped off the cabinet and came over to Amanda.

She pulled out her phone, brought up the drawing, and held her screen so Hill could view it. Hill took it, her long, slender fingers wrapping around the phone.

"He looks like a Joe Schmoe." Hill gave the phone back to Amanda.

"Guess so," Amanda said.

"Well, there's nothing extraordinary that I see about him." Hill shrugged nonchalantly. "It's unlikely anyone would come forward, even if we plastered his face everywhere."

"Someone knows him," Amanda said coolly. "And he's far from 'nothing extraordinary.' He is the man who shot a woman, likely intended to kill a little girl, and he's probably the same man who shot the Parkers."

"Sounds like a lot of uncertainty. And if this man was there for the girl, it makes no sense that she's still alive. You might want to consider this a separate incident altogether."

"We have reason to believe otherwise," Amanda said.

"What would that be?"

There was something predatory in Hill's eyes, and Amanda didn't care for it—at all.

"Detective?" She raised her brows.

"Before she was shot, the perp had asked to be taken to Zoe Parker."

"Says who?"

"Libby Dewinter, the victim here. Also her girlfriend, Penny Anderson, attests to this. It was when Libby refused to let the man get to Zoe that she was shot." Amanda would tell her no more. Something was feeling a little off with Hill's swelling interest in the case.

"I see." Hill scanned Amanda's face. "Well, it's all the more important that we protect that girl, isn't it?" Hill then spun on her high heels and saw herself out. Amanda stayed put.

"I'm sorry about all that," Malone offered.

"She's just a witch. Plain and simple." She met her sergeant's eyes.

"I can't disagree with you there."

"There's something else I think she is. Corrupt."

"I don't think I'd go that far."

"You wouldn't? I'd like to know why the police chief is so interested in this case. Could just be its high-profile nature—a double homicide, in which one victim was an employee of a defense contractor, and a little girl caught in the fray—but I think there's something else going on here." Not that she had any idea what, exactly.

Malone regarded her thoughtfully. "One suggestion, if I may make it again. Stay out of the path of bullets today."

Amanda understood the enclosed message this time was more metaphorical. She needed to watch her step. "Will do my best."

"All I can ask."

She left Malone's office, a part of her wondering if finding justice was worth all this stress and struggle, but her heart answered for her. It absolutely was.

CHAPTER TWENTY-ONE

Amanda detoured to the break room before going to check on Zoe. She needed to calm down a bit for one thing. She wouldn't want Zoe to feel her stress and take it on herself as children tended to do. Lindsey had always seemed to pick up on Amanda's and Kevin's moods and imitate them.

Amanda was probably letting her hate for Hill color her perspective. After all, Malone didn't seem to think she was corrupt or working her own agenda, but he really should know better. Hill—even if it wasn't illegal—was always working her own agenda.

She went to the vending machine and had her fingers poised over the first digit in a string of three that would send a bag of cheese puffs pummeling to their destiny, but she stopped short. She should probably pick something a little healthier for Zoe. Amanda went for a package of crackers and peanut butter—a guaranteed hit with every kid unless they were allergic to nuts. Something she should have asked about before now. She ended up getting the chips, too, just in case.

She approached the interview room and peeked in the window. Zoe was at the table, her stuffed dog tucked under her right arm and a purple crayon in her left hand. Colleen was sitting across from her, and Amanda's shadow must have caught her eye. The doctor said something to Zoe, then got up and headed toward the door. Zoe looked up and saw Amanda, and her eyes lit.

Don't get attached, she coached herself.

Colleen stepped outside of the room.

"How's it going in there today?" Amanda asked.

Colleen crossed her arms and shook her head. "She's still too traumatized to say much, but in the little she has said, she asked for you."

Amanda's heart softened at that. Impulsively, she wanted to rush into the room, but sensed Colleen had more to say.

"She hasn't shown me that drawing yet, the one for you, even though I asked nicely." Colleen smiled at the last word.

"Well, I'll see if she'll share that with me today," Amanda said. "I also have a drawing to share with her. It's a sketch of the man who shot Libby Dewinter last night. I'd like to know if Zoe recognizes him." Earlier that day, before Amanda had sat with the artist, she'd brought Colleen up to speed about last night's events.

Colleen unfolded her arms and stuck one of her hands into a pocket of her pressed pants. "I'd recommend that you introduce the picture with care. Her psyche is certainly very fragile, even more so after knowing that her friend was hurt."

Amanda had explained as delicately as possible to Zoe last night why she was going home with her again. Part of that involved telling her that Libby had been hurt. Amanda wanted to sugarcoat it with something like Libby wasn't feeling well instead, but it wouldn't do the girl any favors in the long run, and kids weren't stupid. "So you don't think I should show her the sketch?"

"I don't think you have much choice but to show it to her, but just be patient enough to wait until the right time."

"How will I know when that is?"

"You'll know."

"I'll be sensitive to her situation."

"I know you will be." Colleen smiled kindly. "You're really good with her. Do you have children, Detective?"

Amanda wished this conversation hadn't gone down this path, but she responded with a quiet, "I had a daughter."

Colleen's gaze softened as did her voice when she spoke. "I'm sorry for your loss."

"Thank you. Well, I should get in there."

The doctor nodded and said, "Good luck."

Amanda entered the room. "Hi, Zoe."

The girl stopped doodling, the pink crayon she was now holding suspended in the air over her page, but she didn't turn to look at Amanda or say anything. It was reminiscent of that morning—the two of them orbiting each other, but universes apart.

"I hope you like peanut butter and crackers," Amanda said, taking a seat beside Zoe. "Lindsey used to love them." She went to set the package in front of Zoe but remembered she had to ask something first. "Are you allergic to nuts?"

Zoe shook her head.

"Any allergies at all, do you know?" Amanda asked.

"No."

Amanda put the snack on the table, and Zoe set her crayon down but didn't reach for the offering. "What are you drawing?" Amanda leaned over to look, but Zoe pushed the page aside and pulled another one out of her bag.

"This one is for you."

It had to be the special drawing Colleen Frost had mentioned. "Oh? Can I see it?"

Zoe put the paper on the table and sat back to let her see. Amanda's first reaction was to gasp out loud. A stick-figure man was lying on the ground surrounded by a pool of red. Behind him was what could be a bed. A girl was next to the body with a dog dangling from her hand.

Amanda glanced up at the window, seeking out Colleen, but she was nowhere in sight. This was more the psychologist's area of expertise. She so feared doing or saying something that might hurt Zoe's healing process.

The child touched Amanda's injured arm, and Amanda let out a hiss and drew back.

"I'm sor—" Zoe's lips quivered, and Amanda rushed to comfort her.

"No, no, it's not your fault."

"I hurt you." Her eyes were full of tears.

"No, honey, I hurt my arm last night. Nothing to do with you, I promise." She'd been careful about keeping her wound covered and out of Zoe's line of sight. When she'd redressed the bandage this morning, she'd locked the bathroom door. Amanda suddenly got the sense Zoe was assuming guilt for more than the present moment. "Honey, it's not your fault *anyone* was hurt."

A fat tear fell down her cheek. "Lucky saw."

"And who's Lucky?" Amanda had a feeling it was the stuffed dog, and that was confirmed when Zoe pushed a fingertip into its head. "Lucky saw what?"

"He sees everything."

Amanda broke eye contact with Zoe for the briefest of moments to glance back at the picture. She noted the dog in the girl's hand—both of them standing near the body. "Did Lucky see the person who shot your dad?"

Zoe traced a fingertip around the circle of red on the page but remained silent.

"It must have been awfully scary, Zoe—for you and Lucky—but you're both safe now, and you can talk to me."

She paused movement. "Daddy loved my drawings."

"I can… uh… see why." At least when they depicted peaceful scenery like the one she'd seen the other day.

"Daddy took nice pictures." Pride was in her voice as she looked up at Amanda. "The man wanted them, but Daddy said no."

"He wanted your dad's pictures?" she asked, just to confirm.

"Uh-huh."

The skin tightened on the back of Amanda's neck, and goose-bumps raised on her arms. The absence of photo negatives and cameras that should have been somewhere in the Parkers' home. Also Brett's missing phone. Was it something that Brett had captured in a photograph that got him and his wife killed? She and Trent had considered that already, but now it seemed even more likely. "And what man was this, sweetie?" Amanda wanted to hear it from Zoe.

Zoe picked up a black crayon and began to draw. Amanda waited for the image to emerge, and her heart hammered once it did. A stick figure to the other side of the body, all black, including a black jacket, black pants, and black boots. There was something black in his hand in the shape of the letter L, held tip out. *A gun!*

"And you saw this man?" Zoe's eyes met Amanda's, and she amended her question. "I mean, Lucky saw him?" Amanda touched the dog's ear, which the girl was clutching.

"Uh-huh." Zoe accompanied her answer with a bob of her head and hugged Lucky tighter to her body.

Amanda pressed a finger to the shooter. "He's the one who wanted your dad's photos?" She just wanted to be sure.

Zoe bobbed her head.

Colleen said that Amanda would know when the time was right to show the artist's rendering to Zoe. That time was now. She took out her phone and pulled up the image. "I need to show Lucky something. Will that be okay?"

"Yeah." Zoe bit her bottom lip, her big eyes meeting Amanda's again.

She held the screen so that both the girl and the dog could see it. "Mr. Lucky—"

Zoe giggled. "He's not a mister!"

Amanda smiled, struck by the girl's massive shift in mood. "He's a girl?"

"No." She gave Amanda a goofy look and shook her head.

"Okay, then how should I address him?"

"*Sir* Lucky." She chuckled. "That's what Daddy called him."

"All right, then. *Sir* Lucky, have you seen this man before?" Amanda indicated the sketch on her screen.

Zoe bobbed the dog's head up and down. "Woof."

Okay, this could be interesting… "Is this that man?" She pointed to the figure with the gun that Zoe had just drawn.

Zoe strangled the dog by twisting his head left and right.

No? But Zoe had recognized the man's face from the artist's sketch… "Does Lucky know the name of the man on my phone?"

More twisting of the dog's head. "Did you ever see him with Zoe's daddy before?"

The dog's head was at risk of being ripped off.

So Zoe definitely recognized the man from the artist's sketch, but she didn't know his name, and he wasn't the one with the gun in her drawing. Then who was this man who'd shot Libby and fired on Amanda and Trent? "And never with her mommy?"

The dog's head was twisted side to side yet again.

Amanda replayed the conversation to this point. The man in the sketch was a stranger to Zoe, and presumably the Parkers. But what about the man in Zoe's drawing? Amanda pointed to him. "Did he say what his name was?"

No reaction from Zoe or Lucky.

Amanda decided to try a different approach but still spoke to Lucky. "Zoe mentioned this man wanted her dad's photos." She tapped a fingertip over the gunman in the drawing again. "Is that right?"

"Woof."

Yes. "Did he say why?"

"No, but he was mean. He yelled."

"Why did he do that?"

"Daddy wouldn't give him his pictures." Zoe had shifted from her dog's perspective. "And he got meaner and louder, then…"

She dropped her chin to her chest. At first, Amanda thought she was miming death, but then she heard the sobs.

"Oh, sweetie." Amanda rubbed her back, but the girl jumped up from her chair.

"Lucky's mad. Very mad!" She pursed her lips in a scowl. "He couldn't help Daddy." She sniffled.

"Sir Lucky did the right thing, Zoe. So did you. You both stayed in hiding. If you hadn't, you both could have been hurt."

"But Daddy got hurt. Mommy got hurt." She burrowed her face in Lucky's "fur."

"Sometimes…" Was she really going to give Zoe the spiel that sometimes bad things happen? She wished she could shield this little girl from that fact of life, but it was far too late. "I'm so sorry, Zoe. Things happen that can really hurt us. I know that sort of pain."

Zoe lifted her head and looked right in Amanda's eyes. "Lindsey and her daddy."

Amanda nodded and bit her bottom lip, quelling the urge to also tell her about the unborn baby she'd lost. Of course she wouldn't. That would be too much. Besides, only Amanda and her doctor knew that truth, and she preferred to keep it that way.

"Did you lose someone else too?"

This girl is sharp! "Let's just say, I am here for you."

Zoe fell against Amanda, wrapping her small arms around her. As Amanda reciprocated, she had to wonder who this was healing more—Zoe or herself. She let the girl stay in the embrace until she wanted to end it, and it was a good long while. Amanda needed to revisit the artist's sketch and see how that man fit into what happened at the Parkers'—assuming he did at all. The mother in her just wanted to let the matter go for now and come back to this unpleasant task another time, but the cop in her knew that as unfortunate as it all was, Zoe was an eyewitness in a double homicide.

"There's one more thing I need to ask Sir Lucky," Amanda began. Her heart was fracturing just thinking about putting Zoe through more questioning. "Would he be willing to answer one more question?"

Zoe looked down at Lucky and made the dog nod. She sat back in her chair.

"Okay, then." Amanda unlocked her phone, and the sketch was showing again. She needed to get some clarity. The man in the artist's sketch was recognized, but a stranger, and not the one with the gun that Zoe had drawn. "You're sure this wasn't the man who shot Zoe's father?"

A rogue tear fell down Zoe's cheek as she twisted the dog's head left and right. *No.*

"Her mother?"

"Lucky never saw."

"Was this man there?"

Zoe sat back in her chair and picked up the black crayon again. Amanda waited her out in silence. Eventually, Zoe let the crayon drop and pushed the paper over to Amanda.

The girl had drawn another stick figure standing next to a door. She pressed a finger to the image. "Sir Lucky says that's him."

Amanda's gaze bounced between the two men she had drawn, one with the gun and one near the door. "There were two men?"

"Woof." Zoe made Lucky's head nod *yes.*

CHAPTER TWENTY-TWO

Amanda thanked Lucky and Zoe and praised their courage, and when she left the room, Zoe had begun to eat her snack. Colleen was standing in the hallway, waiting. Trent approached then, looking like he was just getting in from court. He was wearing a light jacket and had a bag strapped over his shoulder. "Come with me," Amanda said to the two of them and proceeded to lead the way to her cubicle. "The man from last night didn't shoot the Parkers, but he was there."

Trent set his bag down on his desk and joined the women in Amanda's area. "There was more than one person?"

"Yep. Two men."

"So she did see," Colleen whispered.

Amanda nodded. "The drawing she had for me was quite macabre. It was her father dead in a pool of blood."

"Poor thing," Trent empathized, showing his first real crack in his armor for the girl. Amanda had never really considered him as the father type. Then again, you didn't have to be a father to have empathy for a child who had witnessed something horrific.

"You can say that many times over. But as we spoke"—Amanda looked at the doctor—"actually, as I spoke with her stuffed dog, I learned quite a bit."

"Transference," Colleen said. "It's sometimes easier to project experiences to a third party. It's a defense mechanism, the mind's way of protecting itself."

"Well, to get more out of her in the future, you might try talking to the dog. Sir Lucky is its formal name. Maybe you can let her know that I told you about him."

Colleen's brow tightened. "I wouldn't put it that way because Zoe could feel betrayed and stop talking to you too."

Amanda hadn't thought of that. "Good point, but I'm sure you can figure out how to handle it. I just wanted you in the loop."

"I appreciate that." Colleen smiled pleasantly. "Is there anything else I should know?"

"Something both of you should know. She heard the shooter ask Brett for his pictures."

Trent met her gaze. "Huh. We thought the shooter might have been after a picture. Did he say anything more specific? What he might have been looking for a photo of?"

Amanda shook her head, but Trent's questions got her thinking. "Sir Luck— Zoe said that the man just asked for the pictures. Brett refused, and that apparently only made the man angrier and louder and— Well, we know the rest."

"Brett Parker knew what the man wanted," Trent concluded.

"I think he did."

"And they probably got what they were after in the end," Trent said. "No negative rolls or backup drives in the home."

"Wow. It sounds like you guys have some work ahead of you," Colleen said and jacked a thumb over a shoulder. "And so do I."

"Just take it easy on her this afternoon," Amanda blurted out, and added, "Please."

"Always, Detective." Colleen dipped her head and left.

Amanda turned back to Trent.

"Two perps," he said incredulously.

"Yeah. The guy from last night probably searched the house while the other one went straight to the Parkers' bedroom."

"Likely to see if Brett would hand over whatever photos they were after willingly."

"I don't think the Parkers were ever going to walk away alive."

"What picture or pictures got a couple killed?"

"Question of the day. Let's see if we can find the answer." Their eyes locked, and she wanted to ask how the trial was going, but there was also a part of her that didn't want to poke at that topic. But it was her mother. "How did things go this morning?"

He wet his lips, glanced away, then back at her. "I did my job. That's all I can do."

"Not sure what that's supposed to mean."

"It means I presented the facts as I know them."

"Right… which I'd expect you to do. But what's the feel in the courtroom?"

"I'm not sure what you're really asking."

"Is it looking good for my mother or not?"

"Her defense attorney did a good job of knocking my testimony." Shadows danced across his features, and a glint of what Amanda would peg as anger showed in his eyes.

"That's her job."

"It is." He was becoming sullen and moody, and he went to his desk.

She'd take from his words and reaction that her mother might actually get off. She felt relief, then confused by that relief. Amanda's life had been dedicated to the justice system, and that meant locking up killers.

But… this was also her mother.

"All right. Some good news." Trent looked at her over the partition. He was already seated at his desk. "I have the Parkers' financials and their phone records."

"Access to their cloud storage?"

"Not yet."

"All right. We work with what we have."

"Uh-huh, and now we know the shooter and his accomplice were after pictures. Brett must have seen something he shouldn't have, photographed it, and they—whoever *they* are—found out."

"Right." Amanda paced.

"Maybe when the family was on vacation?" Trent's eyes enlarged. "I mean, maybe we've been looking at this wrong. They could have just taken a vacation because they needed a break—nothing more. But then they came home early…"

"Dewinter said that Brett had made that decision and wouldn't give Angela a real reason why. She hadn't believed it had to do with avoiding traffic."

"Uh-huh. So did Brett see something in Lake Chesdin, and that's why he rushed his family home? Maybe he thought if he got his family back to Triangle, they would be safe."

"But they weren't. And then he refused to hand some pictures over. Of what, and why refuse? He could have used them to save his family. Not that I think it would have done any good."

"So what did he see? And if this took place in the Lake Chesdin area, how did those men know where to find him? We know they're professionals."

"Hmph. Not sure I'd go quite that far. The man who shot the Parkers… yes, I believe he was, but the man from last night? Not so much. He sure wasn't cool under pressure. He's certainly no good at aiming. To my benefit—and yours."

"Moving targets are harder to hit," Trent offered.

She shook her head. "Wouldn't make a difference to a skilled gunman."

"So he was… what, a professional hitman in training?" Trent smirked.

"You make fun, but it is possible. Everyone needs to start somewhere." She was only half serious. "Zoe didn't draw a gun in his hand, but had one in the hand of the man who killed her dad."

"Maybe she didn't get that far."

"Possible." She walked a few steps, spun back. "We'll work with what we have," she said, repeating her earlier words. "Dewinter said that Brett took both old-school pictures and digital ones—had backups of all of them. Also had film rolls, which he probably got developed…" She paused to see if Trent was following her, but he seemed lost. "We have the Parkers' financials. Maybe it will tell us where he normally got his pictures developed. We could see if he got any printed recently."

"Yeah, but I just thought of something else. What if Brett got rid of the pictures altogether? Could be why he didn't hand them over and try to negotiate for his family's safety."

"Crap, you could be right." She swept a hand through her hair. "Whatever he saw was a big deal. It got them killed, and it was quite possibly responsible for the rushed return home."

"But he didn't come forward to the police either."

Amanda nodded. "Out of fear maybe? But sticking with this scenario, a patriot like Brett Parker, someone wired to do right, would ensure he had backups, possibly multiple copies so that he could use them if he had to or wanted to in the future."

"All right, I can see that."

"And maybe he kept the photos somewhere else, off premises."

"Like in a safe-deposit box?" Trent suggested.

"Why not? We need to see if any keys were found that could have belonged to one. You see the evidence list from CSI Blair yet?"

Trent shook his head.

"Me neither." Blair had said they should have had it the end of yesterday. Amanda pulled out her phone, called the crime lab, and got put through to CSI Blair. "It's Detective Steele," she rushed out. If she didn't just get to the point of why she'd called, she might get lost in other thoughts—about Emma sleeping with her dad. And now wasn't the time to get into that sordid topic. "Regarding the Parker investigation, were any keys recovered at their house that could have belonged to a safe-deposit box?"

"I'll speak to the investigators who processed the home."

"And get back to me?" Amanda shoved out.

"Yes," Blair hissed.

"Thanks." Amanda ended the call without a goodbye but figured she'd done good showing a crumb of gratitude. And she could have brought up the fact she should have the promised list by now, but she hadn't. She also could have brought up that Blair hadn't sent Angela's emails from her phone over either. But she wasn't going to get into it right now. Amanda thought instead about the facts they had and where they were leading the investigation. They probably wouldn't even need to look at the Parkers' financials. The pictures, it would seem, were a different animal than a conspiracy theory involving a payday for Brett Parker due to software secrets. What that was—the different animal—remained to be seen.

"Just run through this again for me," Trent said. "The shooter asked Brett to give him his photos. Did Zoe get any more specific than that?"

"No. She did well to get that much out. What she's been through…" She stopped there, feeling herself getting worked up in defense of Zoe.

"I'm not saying the girl hasn't been amazing considering all this. I was just asking, Amanda."

"No. She didn't have anything else to say. Maybe I could get more out of her, but I'm leaving her alone for now. Let Colleen work with her."

The way that Trent was gazing at her, she could tell he suspected she was getting attached.

"She's an eyewitness," she said, "but she's also a child."

Trent didn't say anything.

"Do we have access to the cloud yet for the Parkers' files?" She just had to direct the conversation from Zoe.

He quirked an eyebrow. "We didn't five minutes ago. Just a second…" He went back to his cubicle and clicked his mouse a couple of times. "Yep, we're in."

"Great." She walked around and perched on his desk. "Log in and let's take a look-see."

Trent entered the username and password. "Oh."

"What?"

"There is a ton of data here. You might want to pull up a chair."

"Actually, is there a way to sort by date? We're suspecting that he saw something last week on vacation."

"There is…" He clicked, and the list of files rearranged so the most recent was at the top. "There's only one folder that was created last week."

"Open it."

Trent smirked at her. "In a hurry much?"

"Just open it." She smiled and shook her head.

The folder was full of thumbnail images.

"JPEGs," she said. "Select one and expand it."

Trent did so, and a picture of a lake came up. He smiled at her. "I'd say these are the photos Brett took last week on vacation."

"Bingo. Let's look through every single one and see if anything pops as a motive for murder."

"Sure. There are…" Trent leaned in and looked at the bottom left-hand corner of his screen. "Three hundred and fifty photos."

"Hmm. Brett Parker was a real shutterbug. There must be some way of narrowing them down. Are they date stamped?"

"Yeah, every time you take a digital photo, the time and date are added to the metadata."

"Are there any from Thursday, the day the Parkers left Lake Chesdin?" She scooted off his desk and came up beside him to get a better look at the screen.

He changed the view to Details and sorted the files by date with the most recent at the top. "There you go."

"Open them."

Trent turned to face her and leaned back in his chair. "You think Brett saw something just before rushing home on Thursday?"

"Yep."

He spun back around and started clicking picture after picture. Lots of landscapes, some goofy family shots. Zoe in a lot of them, Lucky never out of reach except for when she was in the lake. There were shots of the water, blue skies, not a cloud in sight. Brett had a gift for capturing a feeling, and it would appear the family was having a fun, relaxing time. But there was nothing nefarious here, just boring old vacation photos. Certainly nothing to necessitate an urgent return home or provide motive for murder.

"Well, that's disappointing," Trent said, pulling from her thoughts.

"Keep going."

And that's what they did for at least an hour. It was one in the afternoon by the time they'd finished, and they were no further ahead.

"There is absolutely nothing here. We've looked at all the pictures." Trent closed the viewing window. "Did he do something else with the photos? Are we jumping ahead of ourselves? Maybe Zoe was confused or didn't understand—"

"No, she knew what she heard," Amanda said in defense of the girl.

"Well, right now it seems we're at a dead end."

She was staring at the screen, begging it to give up its secrets. Then her gaze landed on the file sizes. Most were about the same size, but some were quite large. "Trent, why are some of these JPEGs so much larger?"

He leaned in as if he needed glasses. He was probably just eye-strained like she was by this point. "I don't know."

"Bet I know someone who might." Detective Jacob Briggs in Digital Crimes was brilliant with computers. Usually he worked the night shift, but this couldn't wait. She pulled out her phone and brought up his mobile number. She hoped he'd forgive her for contacting him when he was off duty, but she was relying on their friendship and his love for his job to make him cooperative. And if that failed, she'd tell him about the little girl who lost her family and witnessed her father's murder.

Jacob answered on the third ring. "Amanda. To what do I owe the pleasure?"

She smiled. The man was a saint. "I know you're not at work, but I think you're the man for this particular job."

"Flattery, as they say, will get you everywhere." Jacob laughed.

"Then it worked." She chuckled but turned serious rather quickly. The grim flash of imagining Zoe holed up in that bench at the end of the bed, seeing what she had, snuck in with a chokehold. She went on to tell him about the case and what had led them to the victim's cloud drive. "There are some unusually large JPEG files."

"Come on over. Right now. I'll do whatever I can to help."

"You sure?"

"See you in five? My house? You know where it is?"

"Of course. How about ten? Maybe fifteen?" She was starving and could use a coffee.

"See you then." Jacob beat her to hanging up.

"Jacob's going to help us." She got to her feet. "Log out of the drive, and make sure you bring the login information with you. We're going to his place now."

Trent scrambled to do what she'd asked while she watched. She just hoped that Jacob could not only help them understand what the files were but, more importantly, get them closer to the shooters.

CHAPTER TWENTY-THREE

Amanda had Trent hit Hannah's Diner for coffees and a sandwich on the way to Jacob Briggs's house. She got a coffee for Jacob, too, and a half dozen cookies.

Jacob greeted them with a contagious smile when he opened his door. He was middle-aged with a full head of brown hair and average looks except for that winning grin. With that alone, he probably got his way often.

"You didn't need to do that." Jacob referred to the tray of coffees and the brown bag.

"Cookies are always a good idea, and this is the least I could do," she said.

He let them in and showed them to his home office. It was also a graveyard for old computers and related paraphernalia. Keyboards, towers, cables, cordless mice, a few old scanners, and some items Amanda didn't recognize. All these were stacked in every corner and along the walls.

Also in the space was a piece of plywood supported on three sawhorses—a do-it-yourself quick fix for a desk. There were three decent-sized monitors on the "desk" and a couple of keyboards. Underneath the plywood were more CPUs.

Jacob went off with Trent and fetched a couple of chairs from the dining room.

"You sure you can help us?" she asked Jacob with a wink when they returned.

"I'm quite sure that I can. Here you go, my lady." He smiled as he slipped in a chair behind her.

"Thanks."

"All right, so what have we got?"

"The login for the cloud drive," Trent said.

Jacob flicked on all three monitors and braced his hands over his keyboard. "Let me have it."

Trent rattled off the information, and Jacob typed it just as quickly.

"I'm in. So what am I looking for?"

Amanda should probably direct him to the large image files first, as it seemed that the killers were after photos, but she wanted him to check for something quickly—even if it was to rule it out. "Are you seeing any coding files?"

"Something specific?"

"Brett Parker was a computer programmer and worked for Falcon Strategic Technologies. He would sort out code at home on occasion." She realized he could have brought the code home in his head, but if he was meticulous about backup as he worked, then there might be snippets to find.

"The defense contractor from Washington?" He raised his brows.

"That's the one."

"Let me look." He started doing just that by running searches for files with certain extensions. After a few moments, he shook his head. "Nothing here, and honestly it would be incredibly stupid to put files of such a sensitive nature on a cloud server."

"I suppose that's true." Amanda realized Jacob didn't know the details of Brett's focus but would understand anything related to the company was likely sensitive. But just because Brett didn't back up to an off-site server didn't mean the code was safe. It could be on the laptop or the hard drives that were missing. If so, did the shooters have the code or even know what to do with it... or what

THE SILENT WITNESS 167

it was for? Probably unlikely, but a sliver of doubt moved in. What if Zoe had remembered wrong and the shooter hadn't asked for her father's photos? What if they had been after defense software coding? She shook the doubt aside. Even she had defended Zoe's recollection earlier; Amanda was getting carried away.

"When you called, you said something about large JPEG files," Jacob prompted.

"Yes. They're our main interest. We think the victim, Brett Parker, captured a picture of something he shouldn't have, and the wrong people found out and came after him."

"But we looked through the pictures," Trent added, "and didn't see anything that stood out about them."

"Except for these large ones you mentioned?" Jacob faced Amanda.

"That's right."

"Where can I find them?"

She told him, and he opened the folder.

"Huh. Interesting. You said this guy was a programmer?"

"Yes…?" She wasn't sure where he was going.

"Well, the next time you come to see me, bring a bottle of eighteen-year-old Glenlivet. It's my favorite."

Pricey Scotch if she remembered correctly. "All right… why?"

"Because I'm about to earn it." He was grinning.

"So I take it the large file sizes mean something?" she asked, getting a little excited by Jacob's reaction.

"Oh yeah, it means something. It's called digital steganography."

"What now?" She always knew that Jacob was super intelligent, but he was blowing her mind right now. She was far from being a Luddite, but she wasn't a tech wizard either.

Jacob laughed. "I assume by the look on both your faces that neither of you have run into this before."

"Good assumption," Trent said, beating Amanda to the admission.

"Digital steganography is when hidden code is embedded within a file, such as images or videos. In this case, it's obvious to me just based on file size that the large ones here contain code. It could be text or an image within the image."

Amanda shifted forward on her chair, realizing briefly that she hadn't even sipped her coffee since she'd arrived. "Could it take a lot of time to do this, assuming he had?"

"It could, depending on how complex he got. Why?" Jacob studied her face, and Trent was also looking at her.

"There's just some time unaccounted for after the family returned from vacation," she began and turned to Trent. "We were trying to figure out what he was doing after returning home. It could be he was busy with this."

Trent nodded.

She returned her attention to Jacob. "Can you decode them?"

"Good thing for you, I can." Jacob beamed. "And I'm quite good at it. I'll start with the oldest and work my way to the most recent." He proceeded to do just that.

The first image was of Zoe going down a slide in a park with a blue sky and trees and the lake in the background—a photo she'd seen at Central on Trent's computer.

"Now, this picture probably exists elsewhere in this folder, taken at another time, and it was just one that the victim chose to embed other data within."

"Yeah, we saw it when working through the pictures," she said on behalf of herself and Trent.

Jacob set about opening a program and clicking here and there. He didn't share his process in narrative as he went along. Then the image popped over to his second monitor, and he enlarged it to the size of the screen. "Now watch as I pull back the curtains."

She wouldn't believe it if she wasn't seeing this with her own eyes. The picture transformed from day to night, and Zoe and the slide disappeared. The lake was there, but the focus of the shot was a motorboat on the water.

She sank into her chair, disappointment causing her bones to ache. "But that's nothing. Why would Brett go to the trouble of hiding this photo inside of another? Why would anyone kill him and his wife over this?"

"The point of this picture might not be obvious yet, but it could still make sense overall. Remember, there are more encoded photos. I'll decode each one, and we'll see where we end up."

Trent rummaged in the bag from the diner, pulled out a cookie, and chomped down. "What?" he said when Amanda looked over at him. "I eat when I'm anxious."

"Just watch the crumbs," Jacob said with a grin.

The smell of the chocolate chip cookie had Amanda's tummy rumbling. She helped herself to one and chewed away.

Jacob decoded the next image and unveiled another photo of the same motorboat, but in this image, there was a figure on the boat.

Jacob proceeded to the next file, and the hidden graphic revealed a close-up shot of the figure on the boat. It was a man, bald, solidly built, and tall, probably about six foot three.

"These all appear to be taken in sequence," Amanda concluded. "Like he was out at night—"

"Five in the morning on Thursday, according to encoded timestamps," Jacob interjected.

"Okay, so in the morning, Brett's up before his family, and he's got his camera and is looking out over the lake." She began the brainstorming.

Trent added to the narrative. "He took quite an interest in the boat."

"Yes," she agreed, "and kept with it, snapping numerous pictures." She turned to Jacob. "What's next?"

"Let's find out."

It was another shot of the motorboat. This time there were two more men, making three in total. One of the men's arms were behind his back.

"He's tied up?" she asked, leaning in.

"I'd say so," Trent responded. "And is that a gun in Baldie's hand?"

She looked closer, but it was hard to make out.

Jacob decoded the next image. It was zoomed in closer than any of the others. The bald man had a wrinkled face like a bulldog, and the man who was bound was a redhead with a pale complexion. But it was the third face—the one belonging to the man who was guiding the redhead. *Blond hair, a high brow ridge, square jaw…*

"That's the man who shot Libby and tried to shoot me."

"Tried or succeeded?" Trent countered.

"Ha."

"You were shot?" Jacob's eyes enlarged.

"It was a graze. Anyway, that's him, and Zoe also ID'd him as being in her parents' room with the man who killed her father."

"Maybe the bald man from the boat was who shot the Parkers?" Trent suggested.

Amanda went cold, but it was very possible.

"What are they doing?" Trent nudged his head toward the displayed image.

The montage of images was starting to form a coherent picture in her mind—one that would be motive for murder. But she'd reserve comment for now. She asked that Jacob continue.

In each progressive picture, the bound man was getting closer and closer to the bow. And the bald man lifted his arm. The subsequent image completed the story. A flash of light.

"Gunfire," Amanda said. "It *was* a gun in the bald man's hand."

The next photo showed the redhead in the process of going overboard with the help of the blond man. Brett would have been clicking like mad when he'd figured out what he was seeing.

They continued working through the rest of the pictures. The last one was even more chilling to witness than the shooting itself had been. The bald man was looking through binoculars, pointed in Brett's direction.

"Guess we know what got Brett and his wife killed," Amanda said. "He witnessed a murder, and the killers witnessed him."

CHAPTER TWENTY-FOUR

Amanda and Trent rushed from Jacob's house with lots of gratitude *and* with the promise of bringing him that bottle of Scotch. They had their motive for murder and photos of both men likely involved in the Parkers' home invasion and deaths. The one man—the blond with the high brow—had been identified by Zoe, and the other was now a prime suspect as the shooter in the Parker case. They'd have to show the bald man's face to Zoe to confirm, but they were running on that assumption. And regardless, that man had unquestionably killed the redheaded man in the photos. But they were also coming away with the boat's registration number, which had been in plain sight.

Trent pecked the number into the onboard laptop in the department car, and he was paling in front of her eyes.

"What is it?"

Instead of answering her, he moved the screen so she could see. "Eugene Davis… or should I say *Congressman* Davis."

"Also brother-in-law to our newly appointed police chief, Sherry Hill." She was going to be sick. Anyone in law enforcement who valued their badge didn't make accusations against someone like a congressman—not unless the evidence was mounted sky-high and bulletproof. They certainly weren't there yet. Sure, they had a guy getting murdered on the congressman's boat, but there was no picture of Eugene Davis himself. Maybe the shooters had stolen his watercraft?

There could be a simple explanation. There had to be. But it wasn't like they could just go to his door and start asking questions—at least not accusatory ones based on an assumption that he knew what had transpired on his boat.

And if all that wasn't enough to step back and regroup, there was Hill. She'd suspended Amanda and had Trent briefly riding a desk. If the two of them went after her brother-in-law without a solid case, they'd be lucky if they both didn't lose their badges for good.

"Amanda?" Trent prompted.

"Do you think…" She studied his face, not sure whether to bring up her suspicions about Hill. Could she somehow be involved in the whole sordid mess and that was the real reason she was so interested in this case? Was she trying to protect her family and herself?

"What is it?"

"Never mind for now."

"Should we talk to the congressman?"

"Oh, we will, but not until we have everything in order." She leveled a serious gaze at him. "We can't attack him; we can't even whisper a word that might be construed as an accusation."

"I understand. This is a nightmare."

"You can say that again, but we're not without options. We get the case together, then at the right time, we seek an audience with the congressman from the standpoint of giving him the benefit of the doubt. In other words, *his boat was stolen* type of approach."

Trent nodded. "I get that."

Her mind was racing as she considered their next steps. She wanted to check property records in the area and see if any belonged to the congressman, but she didn't want the search to come back and haunt her. They did need to dig into something that couldn't wait, though. "We need to find out the identities of all the men on that boat. Thanks to Brett and Jacob, we've got their faces, and the quality looks good to me. We'll have the crime lab run them through facial recognition software."

Jacob had made them copies of the decoded photos and put them on a data stick for Amanda and Trent to take with them.

"We could try Missing Persons, too, for the redhead who was shot and tossed overboard."

She snapped her seat belt into place. "But we don't have anything to really go on. We know nothing about him. No idea where he's from, how old he is, whether he's married or not. Needle in a haystack."

"And which haystack?" Trent kicked back.

"Exactly. Let's get back to Central."

He put the car in drive, and they pulled away from Jacob's home. "For all we know he was a criminal too," Trent said. "He could have worked with those guys at one point and crossed them."

"Good point. He might not be that innocent himself." Her mind went right to the congressman with those words. Did Eugene Davis present a false front to the world while he was really the money and power behind an underworld criminal organization of some kind?

"Let's just hope at least one of 'em *pops* in facial rec. He could lead us to the others."

She was trying to muster optimism but failing greatly. Unfortunately, facial rec databases weren't the magic pill they were often depicted to be on television. "We also need to get divers in that lake. Thanks to this"—she held up the data stick—"we have justifiable reason to do so. There also has to be someone who can triangulate where that boat was when the man was shot and shoved overboard."

"Not to be a pessimist here, but what's to say the body even sank to the bottom? It could have floated away in the currents."

"Ever hear of cement shoes?" She glanced over at him, her words an attempt at joviality, but the complexity of this case and its direction made her ill. "We'll search the lake. First, we'll brief Malone on everything—even about the congressman. He needs to be kept in that loop. And we'll rope in the local law enforcement from the area. Someone was murdered on Lake Chesdin, and we have photographic proof." She sank back in her seat, looking at the passing scenery, her mind spewing out the cliché that a picture was worth a thousand words. Well, the ones that Brett Parker had taken were worth far more than that. And the registration number on the boat, the tie to Eugene Davis... The fact that Zoe wasn't shot at Libby's house...

Her head went dizzy, and she swallowed a mouthful of bile as her mind assembled the pieces. The first time she'd met Davis had been earlier in the year—January, specifically. She'd been working a murder case and, during the investigation, had uncovered a sex-trafficking ring. She'd been haunted by the ring ever since. In the months following, she realized it operated and branded its girls with the letters DC. It was uncertain whether that represented the initials of a person or stood for DC, as in District of Columbia, but they were operating in Prince William County. That made Amanda suspect there was more to the name than a location.

Their first lead to the ring had come from a data chip hidden in the clasp of a silver link bracelet. It contained a catalog of young girls—bought and sold—and bank transfer records.

When she'd met Eugene Davis, the congressman had shown up at Central to express his gratitude for her efforts in working to expose the ring. But when she had shaken his hand, she'd noticed a bracelet, just like the one that had surfaced in the case, around his wrist. A whisper of suspicion had fluttered through her back then, but she had dismissed it.

Then in the murder case she'd worked in April, the sex-trafficking ring had raised its ugly head again and ended up bringing forward two people who were turning state's evidence. They didn't know the leader of the ring but suspected it was someone powerful—probably a person in law enforcement or politics. Did the DC in the ring's name represent a politician? Could that be Congressman Davis?

It would seem he wasn't as innocent as one might think. She and Trent had just looked at photographs showing a murder on the congressman's boat.

All these things couldn't be a coincidence. There was too much stacking up against him. Her entire body was tingling and alerting her distinctly to the fact Congressman Davis may, in fact, be a very evil man. Possibly the head of a sex-trafficking ring.

Then it hit her with a thud. What if the perp from the other night hadn't killed Zoe, not just because he hadn't gotten to her, but because he never planned to kill her? Could his intention have been to turn her over to the ring?

Amanda and Trent reached Central and were headed to their desks. Her phone pinged with a text from Emma Blair. There was no sign of a key for a safe-deposit box. No sign of an evidence list yet either… "Too little, too late," she mumbled.

"You say something?" Trent looked over at her.

"Yeah, but no. Don't worry about it. I want us organized before we go in with Malone. Now, I'm guessing you're with me that the shooting was witnessed from the cabin rental property?"

"I'd say so, given the other photos taken at roughly the same time showing the cabin and comparable surroundings."

"Right. Now we need to know exactly where the Parkers stayed. Seems their financials and messages might come in handy after all. You look at their bank and credit card statements and see if there are any charges from last week that can point us to the rental, and I'll see if Brett's or Angela's phone history lends us any clues. Though I'll start with Brett's as it sounded like he'd booked the vacation."

"You got it." Trent sat at his desk and got to work. She did the same at hers.

She looked at Brett's text messages and call logs with an eye for area codes linked to the Lake Chesdin area. She'd been at it for about an hour and had come up empty. She looked over at Trent's cubicle. "How you making out over there?"

"They had several credit cards and a few bank accounts, but I think I just might have found something…" Trent clicked on his keyboard. "Yep. There's a rental company called By the Lake that manages a few properties in the Lake Chesdin area."

"Okay, call them, get the address where the Parkers stayed."

"Will do." He dialed, and she listened to his side of the conversation for a little while but began tuning it out. Her mind was on Zoe. She wanted to go to her, but she couldn't risk getting roped in right now. There was another loose end she could quickly take care of, though. She called Marcel Hudson from Falcon Strategic Technologies, and he answered his extension on the third ring.

"Detective Steele," he said warily. "I was hoping I wouldn't hear from you."

She didn't take his reaction personally and went on to tell him about Brett's missing laptop and backup drives. "Now, I don't know if there's any proprietary code out there, but it is possible."

Marcel's end of the line was silent.

"Are you there?"

"I can't believe this is happening." Marcel sounded like he was on the verge of having a panic attack. His breath was coming over the line in gasping heaves.

"We don't know for sure that it is." She felt for his predicament, but this was where she backed away. "I just wanted to inform you."

Marcel hung up on her without another word.

"You're welcome," she said to the dead line.

Trent replaced his phone receiver in its cradle. "All right. I know where the Parkers stayed. As Libby told us, it was in Sutherland,

and I have the exact address, but I also found out more. I assume you heard me on the phone?"

She shook her head. "I called Marcel at Falcon just to let him know that Brett's laptop is gone along with any backup drives he had. Due to that, it is possible that there are bits of company code out there."

"Oh." Trent winced. "How did he take that?"

"He hung up on me."

"At least you told him. All right, well, you know how we were wondering how the shooters found the Parkers? We now know that Brett was spotted on the rental property, so I asked some questions of the office. Like if anyone had called them, curious about who had been staying there—maybe in an inconspicuous manner with some sob story or other."

"And?" She was thinking her partner was rather a genius at the moment.

"Marilyn, that's the manager at By the Lake, said that no one had called the office to inquire about the cabin or the Parkers. But I kept her talking, and eventually it came out that last Friday morning when she got in, one of the windows in the office was broken. She didn't report it to police because nothing appeared to be missing, and she just dismissed it. But when I asked her to check the files for the Parkers' rental agreement, she couldn't put her hands on it. She suggested that a summer temp may have misfiled it."

Two questions were rolling through her mind right now. She'd start with one. "All right, if the agreement is gone, how did she know the cabin's address?"

"The contracts are keyed into a computer, and check-in is done through software. The paper is just the legal stuff that gets filed away."

"And obviously this agreement has the renter's home address?" Not her original second question, but a necessary one.

"Yep."

Now for her second question. "How did the perps know which agreement belonged to the cabin? You know what I mean?"

"I do, and Marilyn said the contracts are filed behind cabin address tabs."

"That made it too easy. I'd say it's clear that our perps took the agreement to track down the Parkers."

"I'd say so."

"Now we know where the Parkers had been staying and how the perps found them. Great job." She got up. "Time to talk to Malone."

"This is unbelievable." Malone sat back in his office chair, and it moaned under the movement.

Amanda and Trent had just laid out everything they'd uncovered at Jacob Briggs's house, including the decoded photographs.

"It gets worse from here," Amanda said, warranting a side-glance from Trent.

"Worse than murder?"

"Maybe equally bad. The pictures very clearly show a registration number on the boat, and it's owned by Eugene Davis." She stopped there and waited to see if Malone recognized the name. A few seconds passed, then he spoke.

"The congressman? Yeah, that's worse. You can't be rushing into his office and accusing him of being involved in a murder."

"And he's the police chief's brother-in-law," she added.

"That's right. I can't stress this enough: Tread carefully. I want every step you're about to take run past me."

"We completely understand the delicacy of the situation. Trust me."

"Precisely. Every step. Past me," he reiterated.

She nodded. "We'll need to get divers in Lake Chesdin as soon as possible. But first we'll need someone who can triangulate where the boat was on the water based on the photos."

"That might be trickier than ya think. I used to scuba dive a bit when I was younger. There's a saying that if 'you miss by an inch, you miss by a mile.'"

"I appreciate that, but we've got to try. Trent and I figure the photographs were taken from the property the Parkers rented. They were in Sutherland, part of Dinwiddie County, and the photos were taken across the water, so I figure the boat may have been in the vicinity of Chesdin Landing."

"I believe that's another county. Chester-something…"

"Chesterfield County," she said. What she didn't want to point out was that Chesdin Landing, a prestigious neighborhood in the town of Chesterfield, catered to the wealthy. Something that would be within the congressman's reach.

Malone sighed. "Two police departments will need a heads-up before we move in."

"Technically, one PD and one sheriff's office," Trent corrected.

Malone shifted his glance to him for a second, then back to Amanda. "I guess you're looking for my permission to go on a little road trip?"

She nodded. "I don't see any way around it, and I'd also like to be there when the body's pulled up." That sounded far more macabre when spoken aloud than it had in her head.

"All right. Well, a road trip never hurt anyone. Let me make the call to the local cops. Though I'm sure once they see the pictures you have and find out about the connection to our double homicide in Prince William County, they'll be cooperative."

Amanda gave him a pressed-lip smile. Malone, even though he was in his fifties and had served all his life, held his fellow officers in high esteem. It took a lot to knock them off the pedestal he had them on. And that apparently included Hill, given his response to Amanda's accusation that she may be corrupt. "I'd like the dive to happen tomorrow. Would that be possible?" Her father inculcated into her that "you don't get what you don't ask for."

"I'll push for it."

"Thank you."

"I'll do my best, but if you go up first thing tomorrow, see if you can figure out where exactly Mr. Parker had taken the photos from on that rental property. That will give everyone a better starting point to figure out where to send the divers."

She nodded. "There's something else I think we might want to do." She glanced at Trent; they hadn't discussed what she was about to say, but it was something that hit her just now, while sitting in Malone's office. "We have the images of the perps and the man who was murdered on the boat. Could we publicize the victim's picture? See if someone comes forward." She knew he wasn't keen on doing so with the bad guys, but maybe it would be different with the victim. But there was also the victim's loved ones to consider. "Of course, we wouldn't say he was dead, just a person of interest maybe?"

"Let's see if we get a body first."

"We really don't need a body. You saw the murder with your own eyes. The man is dead, and if he has family out there, they're missing him and want answers. Even if it's not the one they want to hear."

"I saw the murder in photographs—*manipulated* ones."

Amanda bristled. "Now you're dismissing their value?"

"I never said that. But if I made his face public, where would we even begin? We don't know where he's from."

"Ahem." Trent cleared his throat and held up a finger like he was raising a hand in class. "That's the great thing about the internet, Sarge. It's global."

"So you want me to post his picture on the internet?"

"Why not?" Amanda said. "You could start with the PWCPD website or Facebook page, but even if you contacted the papers within a few hours of Sutherland in each direction, that would give the photo a lot of publicity and coverage." As she spoke, she was thinking about the repercussions. As the saying goes, she'd love to be a fly on the wall in the room with the shooters and the congressman, too, if he was involved, when the picture went live. "As I suggested, we go with 'person of interest, last seen on Lake Chesdin.' Or something like that."

Malone seemed to consider her proposal, and eventually he nodded. "We could spin it further. 'This man was last seen near Lake Chesdin, and it's believed he may have gone missing in a boating accident.' That would also explain the presence of divers."

"Sure. However you want to present it, I'm on board. I just think his picture needs to be out there," Amanda said. She looked at Trent, who nodded.

"I'll get it done," Malone said. "In the meantime, make sure to get the images of these men run through facial rec. If these guys are the professionals you think they are, they should have a record."

She didn't even want to consider that they didn't have a record because they were so good at what they did, they always evaded capture. She just wanted to find justice—for the mystery man from Lake Chesdin, the Parkers, and those who grieved them. Also for Libby's suffering from being shot. All this brought her thoughts to Zoe. Amanda had another picture to show the girl—the shooter from the boat.

CHAPTER TWENTY-FIVE

"Trent." Amanda hustled close to her partner's side as they walked down the halls of Central to their desks. "Could you get the pictures to Forensics for running through facial rec? I'd like to check in with Colleen and Zoe."

"Sure." He took the turn toward the warren of cubicles, and she headed in the opposite direction.

Amanda approached the interview room and watched Colleen in there with Zoe. The doctor got up when she saw Amanda through the window and stepped out.

"She's not really saying much more than she already told you, though that was a huge step forward."

Amanda glanced past Colleen into the room. She had more faces to show Zoe—the shooter from the boat and the victim—as it was possible that Zoe knew the man who'd been tossed overboard too. Amanda met Colleen's gaze. "We've uncovered a huge lead in the case today, and we think we know what got the Parkers killed."

"That's fantastic. Any leads on suspects?"

Amanda nodded. "We have pictures of them." The question whether she should show them to Zoe wasn't said yet, but the doctor was already wincing.

"May I suggest that you leave the matter for today? I think that if you don't, she might retreat again, maybe completely, maybe for a long time."

Amanda nodded. She wanted answers but not at the expense of the child. "I understand."

"She was asking about Libby today. I wouldn't suggest taking her to the hospital to see her, but maybe she could talk to her on the phone?"

"I should be able to arrange that."

"Good. Otherwise, Zoe just really needs a night off to experience as much normal as possible. It will help her to relax and heal. It will also put her in a more receptive place tomorrow."

Normal, relax, heal... Amanda caught the time on a clock on the wall. It was just after five. Right on the mark for dinner by a child's standards. "Okay, I'll wait. Did she eat today?"

"Just those peanut butter and crackers you got her, which she pecked away at all day. She could do with a home-cooked meal." Colleen offered up a gentle smile.

Amanda thought about one of Lindsey's favorite meals, and she had all the ingredients at home. There'd be no need to stop for groceries and expose Zoe. "I know exactly what to make her."

"Good. Just take her home and relax with her." Colleen dipped her head and placed an encouraging hand briefly on Amanda's shoulder.

"You'll be back in the morning?" Amanda asked.

"Yes, at nine."

Amanda had hoped to get an earlier start and be in Sutherland by that time, but she had Zoe to consider. It really wasn't feasible to leave before the break of dawn. "See you then."

Colleen went back into the room, collected her things, and said goodbye to Zoe.

Amanda entered, and Zoe got up from her chair, hugging her dog to her chest. "Can we go to your home?"

We... home? Amanda's mind plucked out those two key words. She really had to watch her heart before she lost it to this girl. "We can. How does spaghetti and meatballs for dinner sound?"

A touch of light brightened her eyes, and she nodded.

"All right, then. Let's go." Amanda turned to lead the way from the room, and Zoe caught up and slipped her hand into Amanda's.

Before heading home, Amanda updated Trent and told him to be ready to hit the road with her for Sutherland tomorrow morning at nine. She explained that was when she could pass Zoe over to Colleen. It wouldn't get them to Sutherland until closer to eleven, but maybe she could shave some time off the trip if she drove. She tended to press a little heavier on the gas than her partner. The local departments would also be in possession of the photos and maybe even get started on triangulating where to begin the dive ahead of their arrival.

Back at the house, Zoe got comfortable on the couch in front of the TV. Amanda went down the hall to her bedroom and made a quick call to Penny Anderson.

"Hello?" There was obvious confusion in Penny's voice, but Amanda's phone wouldn't show caller ID because it was tied to the PWCPD.

"It's Amanda— Detective Steele," she amended.

"Oh, hi." Sadness was now the dominant inflection in her tone.

"Is everything all right? Libby still on the mend?" Amanda added a smile to instill some optimism—for herself—hoping there would be a reason for it.

"She is. The doctor said she'll make a full recovery, but he just wants to keep her for a couple more days."

"That's great news. Well, I'm calling because Zoe has been asking about her. She's not in a good place to go to the hospital, as seeing Libby right now might send her spiraling, but maybe she could talk to her on the phone tonight?"

"Ah, yeah, sure. I'd have to check with the nurses and call you back with a good time."

"Even a text will work… with the direct number to her hospital room or her extension."

"Will do." There was a pocket of silence, then Penny added, "Did you, ah, catch the guy who did this to her?" She sniffled.

"Not yet, but we're getting closer." Maybe she shouldn't have said that, but she wanted to provide some good news.

"Excellent. He deserves to go to prison."

"We're in agreement. Okay, so text me?"

"Yep."

They both said goodbye, and Amanda went to the kitchen and got to work on dinner.

The pot was starting to boil, and Amanda was just getting ready to dump the noodles into the water when there was a knock at the front door.

Zoe scurried from the living room and wrapped her arms around Amanda's legs.

Who could that— Ohhh. She knew exactly who it was and had forgotten all about their arrangement.

"It's okay, Zoe. It's just a friend of mine." Amanda patted the girl's back and tried to pry her loose, but Zoe wasn't having it. Who could blame her for fearing strangers when two had killed her parents and hurt Libby? "Okay, we'll get the door together." They walked hand in hand, and Amanda peered out the window just to confirm it was who she suspected—and it was. With everything going on with the investigation, her mother's trial, finding out about her father's affair, Logan had been the last person on her mind, as horrible as that might sound.

She opened the door, and he smiled at the sight of her, but his expression faded as his gaze went down and took in Zoe. He cocked his head to the side, evidently confused.

"I didn't know you had company," he said and grinned at Zoe, seeming to have recovered from his initial shock.

"Zoe, this is my friend Logan."

Zoe hugged Lucky to her face and mumbled a hello.

Back to Logan, Amanda said, "I'm so sorry. I forgot we'd made plans."

"I should probably go. It's obvious you have your hands full." He made the offer but didn't make any move to leave.

"Come in. It's fine." She wasn't sure how she felt about his presence right now, but she didn't feel like she could exactly send him away either. "I'm just in the middle of making dinner and—" She heard the pot boiling over. She rushed into the kitchen and turned the burner down, then called out to Zoe, "Go back to your show, sweetie. Dinner will be ready soon."

"We're having spag and balls," Zoe said to Logan.

"Well, it smells delicious," he responded.

Spag and balls… Amanda chuckled at that. She wasn't even a teenager, and she was abbreviating her language.

The noodles and the sauce would have to wait. At least the meatballs were staying warm in the oven. She went to return to the entry, but when she spun, Logan was standing in front of her—just inches between them. She could feel the heat from his body; the chemistry between them had never been an issue. It sizzled hotter than the garlic she'd sauteed earlier.

"It's feeling a bit like the twilight zone in here." His gaze drifted to the living room.

"It's been a crazy week."

He swept a strand of her hair behind an ear. "I can see that, and you have your mother's trial too."

"Yeah, but don't even get me started on that."

"You're doing all right, though?"

"Depends on your definition of all right."

"Can you tell me about…" He nudged his head in Zoe's direction.

She didn't want to shut him out, but she wasn't about to mention the murder of Zoe's parents with her in the next room. "I can, but not this minute. Let me at least get the noodles started." She turned the burner back up to get the boil going again.

She didn't hear him close the distance between them, but she felt his arms wrap around her waist and the warmth of his breath on the side of her neck. She twisted in his arms, holding the lengths of spaghetti between them as some sort of weapon of defense, conscious of the fact Zoe was in the next room. "Logan," she cautioned.

"What?" He looked over his shoulder. "She's not watching." He planted a kiss on Amanda's lips. A display of affection he apparently wanted to stretch out, given the fact his body moved closer to hers.

She pulled back. "Do behave." She winked at him, wishing they could carry on.

"No fun… But I understand."

She dropped the pasta into the pot of water and waved for him to come down the hall with her.

"Yes, I like the way you think." He pinned her to the wall and nuzzled into her neck.

She laughed but tried to keep it quiet. "Not why I asked you to follow me."

"Dang."

"I want to fill you in on—" She angled her head toward the living room to indicate Zoe. "I'm basically serving as her protection," she said, barely above a whisper. "Her parents were murdered and—"

Logan gasped, and Amanda pressed a finger to his lips.
"Shh."

"Sorry," he whispered. "Wow, a crazy week for sure. Rough."

Logan knew about her history and how she'd lost her husband and daughter, and the way he was looking at her now made her think that wasn't far from his mind.

"It's been a little tough having her here. I'm not going to lie."

"I bet it has." He looked at her with tender eyes.

His face was one that was becoming familiar and comforting, and she found herself wanting to sink into his arms to melt away her stress. But she couldn't allow herself that indulgence, that weakness—could she? There'd be no recovery for her heart if something happened to him after, well, losing Kevin. She was past due for a happy ending but wasn't sure such a thing existed. It would, in some ways, just be easier to cut ties with all people and barricade her heart. Then again, she'd tried that in the years after the accident, and it hadn't worked out so well for her either.

He pulled her into an embrace and, in the process, rubbed against her injured arm. She drew back with a loud wince, and he held up his hands. "What...?"

"I was struck by a bullet the other night, but it's not a big deal," she rushed to say.

"Not a big deal? I'd beg to differ." He looked angry now. Brow furrowed, his eyes glazed over to steel.

"Shh. Keep it down." She glanced down the hall in the direction of the living room. Her concern was Zoe overhearing any of this. She didn't need the girl worried about her.

"Keep it—" He put a hand over his mouth, drew it down around his chin.

"It just grazed me. I'm fine. I'm gonna live." She attempted a smile to lighten the tension between them, but it failed.

He was scowling. "Your job isn't exactly a safe one."

"You're just figuring that out?" she snapped back and instantly regretted saying what she had. Back in April, he'd been taken and held hostage by a serial killer.

"I should go."

"I shouldn't have said that. Logan, I'm sorry. It's just that everything's tense at the moment."

A lot was being said in his eyes, and they reflected a conversation he and Amanda seemed to circle around. It had to do with what he'd experienced and how it had affected him. He refused to talk about it, and she couldn't force him to. There were times it felt like they worked at their relationship more than existed within it. Like they were struggling to find common ground but were each lost in their own world. But now wasn't the time to get into it. She needed to think about Zoe above all else. "I have to get back to dinner."

"Yeah." His jaw was tight, and his gaze piercing.

"We'll talk, but not right now." Her phone pinged with a text message.

"I'm gonna go," he said and left without a kiss or goodbye or even a promise to be in touch.

As she watched him retreat down the hall, and then heard the front door open and close, she stiffened, suddenly feeling cold, isolated, and alone, but she had more to think about than herself. She returned to the kitchen and finished cooking dinner.

Zoe was all "ymms" while she ate, so Amanda took that to mean she'd done a good job with the meal. By the time the girl was finished, she had red sauce on her cheeks and chin, a little on her shirt. It took Amanda back in time to how Lindsey would wear her food. Kevin used to say the messier the food, the better. She smiled at the memory as she helped Zoe get cleaned up, then went on to do the dishes, which Zoe offered to do with her.

Amanda pulled a step stool over in front of the sink and let the girl wash.

Lindsey had loved being involved with anything and everything she could. She'd found it hard to accept when she bumped against her limits with jobs she wasn't quite ready to undertake.

Amanda and Zoe finished up, and Amanda thanked her, which earned her a "thank you" in return.

"You're very welcome." Amanda checked her phone to finally read the text message that had come in when she was with Logan. It was Penny saying that seven thirty would be a good time to call Libby, and she provided a number to reach her. It was 7:27 PM now. "Would you like to watch more TV or talk to Aunt Libby?"

Zoe's eyes widened. "Auntie Libby."

"All right, then. Let's go in the living room and give her a call."

"Okay." Zoe bounded ahead to the couch, and Amanda placed the call. She put it on speaker so she could listen to the conversation in case anything came up that might help the investigation. Otherwise, she'd just let Zoe have her time with Libby.

It was apparent the two did share a close bond and that Libby really cared about Zoe. Hopefully, when everything got sorted out, the two of them could be together. They spoke for about thirty minutes before Libby had to hang up because she needed rest.

"Love you, Libby," Zoe said, and the expression melted Amanda's heart.

She recalled clearly hearing Lindsey's sweet little voice saying that to her, and whenever that happened, it was like time stood still.

After the phone call, Amanda and Zoe watched some TV. Zoe was starting to nod off around eight thirty.

Amanda nudged her. "All right, time to head off to dreamland. It's a fun and magical place where anything wonderful can happen." She smiled at the girl, recalling how she'd use the same tack with Lindsey, presenting bedtime as an adventure. If she didn't, Lindsey would resist terribly.

Zoe hopped off the couch, and Amanda muted the volume on the television. She'd be up for a bit yet, but she probably wouldn't be too far behind Zoe tonight. She rarely got to bed early, and it felt like the perfect time to take advantage of the opportunity.

It took about thirty minutes to get Zoe ready and tucked under the covers. Amanda flicked on the star-projection light and backed out of the room. She was pleased to hear Zoe's deep breathing by the time she'd reached the door.

Zoe might have lived through hell—was still wading through its flames—but at least Amanda was able to offer her some solace. That was one thing that would bring sleep for her when she did get into bed.

CHAPTER TWENTY-SIX

The dawning of a new day, and with it, new problems. They had begun around three in the morning when Zoe woke up screaming at the top of her lungs. It had wrested Amanda from a dream she'd been having, but the violent awakening was enough to stifle any recollection as to what it had been about. She was left with this cloying feeling that it had been more nightmare than a playful romp. Zoe's was certainly a nightmare, and Amanda had moved Zoe into her bed. Eventually she was able to soothe the girl enough that she fell back asleep. Snuggled against Amanda's side and under her arm, no less. Amanda had woken up with her limb all pins and needles, but the soft snores of the child beside her had been enough to make her sacrifice worth it.

But all of that was hours—and miles—in the rearview mirror, as was dropping Zoe at Central and handing her over to Colleen. Amanda had also provided the doctor with pictures of the three men from the boat and asked that Colleen present them to Zoe. They hadn't filled the doctor in on which men they suspected so it wouldn't inadvertently affect her subtle tells and influence Zoe's reaction.

Amanda and Trent were currently in Sutherland at the rental property where the Parkers had stayed. They were standing on the dock, listening to the water lap against the pilings and the shoreline, and had already determined it would have been from this vantage point that Brett had taken the photos.

Now they were just waiting on the Dinwiddie County Sheriff and one of his deputies to arrive. Malone said they were to meet them there at noon, and it was a few minutes past at this point. The Chesterfield PD wasn't going to come out unless evidence recovered from the basin of Lake Chesdin implicated one of their residents. Then they wanted to be involved in the proceedings and the arrest.

Amanda had just finished gulping down the largest coffee she'd ever seen—risking the need to pee a million times. It had been her fourth coffee of the day, and the caffeine still didn't seem to be penetrating her fuzzy mind. Strange, too, because she could usually function quite well on little sleep, and she had gotten to bed by ten—quite early for her. The disturbance in the wee hours must have messed up her sleeping cycle. And she hadn't returned to a deep sleep. She was obsessed with Zoe's anguish. Again, Amanda was burdened with the desire to suck all the poisonous hurt from the girl's wounds and heal her. If only it worked that way. There was also the matter of her father's affair and Logan's abrupt departure keeping her mind whirling.

The property here was stunning, and the surrounding nature breathtaking. The subtle breeze off the lake was cool and carried the foretelling of fall, just as the leaves on the trees that were starting to turn. One could easily get lost in thought here and fool themselves into believing they existed in complete and utter isolation.

She closed her eyes for a few seconds, the rims of them burning from exhaustion, and inhaled the fresh air deeply.

The sound of a vehicle's engine sliced through the tranquility and could be heard over the lapping of the water against the dock. Then came the distinctive slams of two doors. She and Trent turned and bridged the gap between themselves and the new arrivals.

Both men were dressed in tan uniforms complete with a hat and a gold star on the chest. One man was in his fifties and the other probably about the same age as Trent, so a few years younger than Amanda's thirty-six. It was easy to determine who the sheriff was.

"Howdy, there," the sheriff said. "I'm assuming you're the detectives from the Prince William County PD."

"That's us," Amanda replied and introduced herself and Trent.

"I'm Sheriff Mick Henry, and this here is Deputy Tom Whalen."

"Good day, ma'am." Tom dipped his hat at her. "Seems you and I have a little in common." He flashed a bright smile her way, but she found it hard to reciprocate because of confusion. "You said your last name is Steele. The origin's Irish, just like Whalen."

The sheriff rolled his eyes and sighed heavily, then said, "You'll have to excuse *the Whale* here; he likes to go carrying on about things no one else gives a rat's buttocks about."

Now Amanda smirked, and Tom's amusement faded from his expression and his eyes. *Sorry, Tom.* She felt a little bad for any slight toward the deputy, but they weren't there to make friends. "My partner and I," she started, "believe we found where one of our victims, a Mr. Parker, had taken the incriminating photos." She stepped toward the dock, and the men followed her. She spoke over her shoulder. "I'm sure that our sergeant stressed the urgency of this case with you?" She posed it as a question though she was confident that Malone would have made that aspect clear.

"Oh, yes, he did. A possible related double homicide. Tough break."

"More so for their young daughter who witnessed it," she tossed back.

"Ouch." The sheriff's face fractured, and he shook his head. "That's really tough goin'."

Amanda stood where she and Trent had determined Brett had taken the pictures from and said as much to the sheriff and deputy.

"All right, and do you have those pictures on you?" Mick put his hands on his hips and regarded her. She turned to Trent, who pulled out a colored print from a file folder.

Trent handed the photo over to Mick and said, "It's the trees that give it away. See?" He pointed out the branch on the fringe

of the frame. "That looks like it would be this one right here."
Trent hopped off the dock and went over to an oak tree and laid
his flat palm against it.

Mick divided his gaze—a few seconds looking at the photo,
then a few at the tree, repeat. "Uh-huh, I'd say so too. It shouldn't
be hard to figure out then where to dive from here."

"You can do that yourselves or…?" Amanda let her voice fade
off. She was aware that the county was rather small—though she'd
been surprised to discover the sheriff's office had fifty full-time
deputies—and she assumed they'd have limited resources. She
expected they might even call in the state police, or someone from
outside who specialized in this type of thing.

"The Whale here is mighty smart when it comes to math and
figuring things like this out." The sheriff smiled, pride reaching
his eyes, causing the skin around them to wrinkle.

This was the second time Amanda had noted the sheriff's
assumed nickname for his deputy, but Tom didn't seem to mind
it. Then again, one insinuation of being called a whale could only
swell a man's pride. She shoved that imagery out of her mind as
quickly as possible. Tom Whalen didn't have the makings of a
hunky cowboy found in romance novels for a few reasons. His
hair was thinning on top of his head, and his teeth were stained
yellow and crooked. Then there was the matter of his strange
affinity for presenting factoids like a walking encyclopedia, at least
according to the sheriff. Though Tom seemed harmless enough,
kind and polite, Amanda couldn't imagine the ladies were banging
down his door.

Tom pulled out a laser measuring tool and recorded some
numbers.

"He'll have this sorted in no time," Mick assured them again.
"Would be nice to get those divers in the water ASAP."

"I agree," Amanda said.

A few minutes later, Tom was tucking his measure away and smiling. "Got all I need here, but I should head back to the SUV and bring up the file for the photo, do some more calculations."

"Sure." Amanda smiled at the deputy, and they all followed him to the vehicle.

He pulled out a laptop from the back and brought up a program that Amanda wasn't familiar with. He also took out a notepad and a pen and scribbled away. As he wrote, his mouth set askew, and his lips moved as if he were talking in an undertone. Shortly after, he entered some figures into the program and was standing back with both arms open in the air like he was waiting to receive a hug. He exclaimed, "*Voila!*"

"You got it that quick?" Trent asked, disbelief in his voice.

"Yes siree Bob."

"Get the coordinates to the divers," the sheriff directed Tom, who proceeded to take out his phone.

It would just be a matter of minutes now, more practically hours, but the time was drawing to an end. Soon they should have more proof that Brett Parker had, in fact, witnessed a murder—the body itself.

CHAPTER TWENTY-SEVEN

The sheriff had insisted on taking Amanda and Trent to lunch at his favorite watering hole, a place comically called the Dinghy's Wharf. "Brightens people's day, makes 'em smile," Mick had said. Tom "the Whale" Whalen joined them. But given that it was early afternoon, and everyone was working, it was iced teas all around and orders of fish and chips.

"They make 'em better than anywhere else," Mick declared and tapped his belly, which was flat as a board. If he indulged, she'd guess it wasn't that often, or he was just one of those people blessed with a fast metabolism.

"Someone sounds a bit like you with Hannah's coffee." Trent glanced at her.

"Hannah's coffee?" Tom repeated, sounding confused.

"A diner in Dumfries," Amanda said, then looked at Trent. "And they do have the best coffee."

"Oh, I'll challenge that." Mick popped a fry in his mouth, chewed, swallowed. "My sister Pearl serves the best around here. We can hit her up after lunch if ya like."

"Sounds good." And she meant that. Today was one of those days where not enough coffee existed. "But to go."

"Absolutely."

They passed the entire meal making light-hearted banter, but Amanda found the perfect spot to work in an inquiry, only she did her best not to make it sound like one. She started with sincere flattery. "It's so incredibly beautiful around here."

"Sure is." Mick whistled. "Attracts all sorts of tourists."

"I bet. My parents took me and my siblings here some summers when we were kids," she told him.

"Ideal location." Mick grinned, like he took the credit for the county being the way it was.

"And there's some really nice neighborhoods along the water-front," she said, inching closer toward where she wanted to direct the conversation.

"Sure are. Chesdin Landing's one of the best."

"Luxury," Tom added with a grin and popped a piece of fish into his mouth.

Speaking of fish, she'd baited her hook and was hoping for a specific nibble. "It must attract wealthy people, *influential* people."

"Ah, quite sure we get a few celebrities every year." The sheriff pointed to a wall in the pub that Amanda hadn't really paid a lot of attention to beyond just noting the faces of well-known actors. "Every one of them has been in here. Mary Sue, that's the beautiful creature who owns the place…" Mick's gaze seemed to search the woman out. "Anyway, she'll go in her office, print out their picture, and get them to sign it."

"So actors and singers? What about high-profile politicians? You're not too far from Washington."

"Yeah, uh-huh, sure, not that Mary Sue's gettin' them to sign anything. Now maybe if the commander in chief himself passed through." He winked at Amanda.

"But diplomats?" She hitched her shoulders. "Congressmen?"

"Yep. That's right. We get a few of them."

"Oh, really?" She feigned excitement and could feel Trent staring at her profile. He must have figured out what she was doing. "Who?"

Mick gave them a few names, then, "Oh, there's also Eugene Davis. He's a congressman. He owns a place in Chesdin Landing. He's only mostly around in the summer, though."

I knew it! "Huh."

"That's cool," Trent inserted and passed her a smile.

"Yeah, it's a pretty cool place around here." Mick bobbed his head, then glanced over at his deputy, whose cheeks were bulged full.

"Which place does Congressman Davis own in Chesdin Landing?" Amanda asked.

Mick told her where Davis's home was by means of gesturing fingers and a bunch of turn lefts here, rights there. "We better settle up and get on the road, see how the divers are making out." He signaled for the check and was promptly presented with it—and a smile. "Thanks, Mary Sue."

"Don't mention it, Sheriff." The woman was in her late forties, but given the blush to her cheeks, she either had an unfulfilled crush or the two of them were involved. It was apparent he had a thing for her too.

There was no ring on the sheriff's finger or Mary Sue's, so it was hard to say. Not that the wedding band seemed to mean much to some people. It obviously hadn't meant anything to her father when he was sleeping with Emma Blair. The thought had her temperature rising.

They left the Dinghy's Wharf, swung by Mick's sister's restaurant to grab four coffees to go, and headed around to Chesdin Landing. It was a half-hour drive, and it was on the north side of the lake where the divers were going to moor the boat when they were finished. The residents in that affluent neighborhood probably wouldn't take too kindly to the police presence, but it couldn't be avoided. Murder investigations weren't pleasant for anyone.

It had been a couple of hours since Tom had called in the coordinates, and there hadn't been a single word with an update on the divers' progress. At least not that Amanda and Trent had been made aware of. Maybe news had come in to the sheriff on the drive, but they'd find out once they arrived as they were tailing the sheriff in the PWCPD department car.

He pulled into the lot of a marina, parked, and got out of his SUV. Mick and Tom looked like twins when they both hoisted up their pants in unison.

"Ever feel like you've dropped into another universe?" Trent chuckled and glanced over at her.

"Let's just say it's been an interesting day so far." She smiled, holding back more expressive comments, but, yes, it had certainly been an entertaining day at the lake. She just hoped their reason for venturing out there in the first place paid off greatly in the end. They'd already netted that Congressman Davis had a place out there.

She and Trent got out of their car and met up with Mick and Tom. She gazed past them to the water where it looked like there was some activity on the divers' boat.

"So am I right? Pearl serves up the best coffee ever?" Mick was grinning, but she was about to dull the expression.

"It was good coffee…"

"See, I told you."

"But… Hannah's Diner's is still better."

"Well, then, guess I'll need to try it someday."

She smiled and nodded.

"So we just got a call on the way here," Tom began, "and the divers have got something."

"A body?" Amanda asked.

Tom winced. "Not exactly. There's been no sign of one, and they even expanded the diving area by a significant amount."

How was it possible that they hadn't found a body? Could it be that currents swept it away? The pictures showed the man being pushed overboard. Yes, Brett had embedded a photo within a photo, but had he doctored them too? She dismissed the thought.

After all, there had to have been a murder on this lake. It was without a doubt what had gotten the Parkers killed—at least in her opinion. Definitely the best lead they had thus far.

"What did they find?" Trent asked.

"There's a lot of junk down there," Tom said and added, "People are pigs. Want to talk about climate change? Let's talk about taking care of our lakes and oceans—"

"Tom," Mick said sharply, roping his deputy back on topic.

"They found a phone," Tom laid out without any sort of emphasis or enthusiasm.

Sure, the SIM card or serial number could lead to the owner, but after what he'd just pointed out about the litter on the lake's floor, what were the chances this phone belonged to the man who had been shot on Davis's boat and pushed overboard?

"Obviously, we'll take a look at it," she said, trying to muster some excitement, but she was drained dry.

"Well, the good news is it was found in the sweet spot of the search area. It very well may belong to that man shown in the photos." Tom gave her a pressed-lip smile, trying to infuse some spark within her. But she wasn't getting her hopes up yet. It was far too soon for that.

There was another fissure cracking through her thinking… If the man was captured by those two assailants, wouldn't they have unarmed him—if that applied—and taken his phone from him? But that was her filling in a fictional narrative. They could have just as easily picked him up, taken him out on the lake, popped him, and pushed him overboard—phone and all.

"Now, something else you should be made aware of," Tom said, slipping back into a cautious tone. "There are spots in the lake that are quite deep, including in the vicinity of the search grid. It is possible the body is out of the divers' reach."

Yet he believes they have the victim's phone… "Okay, well, tell them to bring in the phone, and we'll have a look at it," she said.

"Both the sheriff and I thought you'd feel that way, so I told them to wrap it up."

She glanced out at the lake and could see the boat coming toward them. She had wanted desperately for the body to be recovered—hard, tangible proof—but it didn't seem that was going to happen. But she'd take what she could get. If only they could get the man's ID, then they'd have a trail to follow to their bad guys. Somewhere other than to Congressman Davis's door? Only time would tell.

CHAPTER TWENTY-EIGHT

"It's an Android, fairly new, good condition except for its swim in the lake." One of the divers, a man by the name of Kane, handed the phone they'd recovered over to Amanda. It was sealed in a plastic bag.

"Had mine fall in the toilet once," Tom began, "and I put it in a bag with some rice, dried the thing right out. It's still ticking." He pulled his cell phone from his pocket as if to give credence to his story, but all Amanda could think about was it had been in the toilet. *Yuck!*

"I'm thinking if we just get the serial number and the SIM card, either one or both should lead us to whomever the phone belonged to." She unzipped the bag, retrieved the phone, and snapped its back off. She rattled off the number to Trent, and he recorded every digit in his notepad. "You want to make the call or…?"

"Sure, I'll do it." Trent stepped aside, his phone to an ear.

"Anything else you found down there that stood out?" she asked Kane.

"Not really, or I would have mentioned it. As I said to Tom, it's like a junkyard on the lakebed. The fact I didn't find more than one phone is a miracle. Now whether it leads you anywhere, well, only God could know."

She nodded. "I understand."

A few minutes later, Trent blurted out, "Got a name."

"That was mighty fast," the sheriff said.

"Who does it belong to?" She wasn't getting excited unless the name matched the face of the victim in their photo.

"Larry Steinbeck from Dumfries."

Her hometown. Suddenly the world felt like it had shrunk around her. "His picture?"

She and Trent hustled to their department car. She could hear the sheriff's and deputy's shoes scuffling along the gravel behind them. Trent got into the front and keyed into the onboard computer. Mere seconds later, a familiar face was looking back at them—it belonged to the man who'd been shot on the boat. "We have our John Doe," she declared.

"Good for you guys," Mick said. "At least this wasn't an entire waste."

Amanda glanced over a shoulder at him. He and his deputy's optimism was something she could handle stuffing into a jar and taking with her. Right now, they had a phone, not a body. Maybe if they could verify this Larry guy's movements, go from there, they could prove without a doubt the guy was dead—something aside from the photos. A skilled defense attorney could argue the pictures were manipulated and get them dismissed. Even a phone at the bottom of the lake truly meant nothing else other than it had fallen in. They needed to speak to those closest to the man and see if they could build a timeline, then a connection to the shooters and motive from there. "Is Steinbeck married?" she asked Trent.

He clicked away on the laptop, pulling up a simple background. "No criminal record, and yes, he's married to a Denise Steinbeck."

"We've got to get back to Dumfries, have a talk with her." Without a body, they'd have to handle things with Mrs. Steinbeck diplomatically. Approach it more as if they were simply looking for him, and did she happen to know where he was. It would have to be improvised in the moment. But there was one other thing she was immediately curious about. Was Larry Steinbeck somehow

connected to Brett Parker and Falcon Strategic Technologies?
"Where did Steinbeck work?"

"He was the manager at Sunny Motel in Woodbridge."

"Sunny…" The rest of it died on her lips. Back in April, an
investigation into Sunny Motel by Sex Crimes, headed up by
Amanda's friend Patty Glover, revealed that the owner of the
place was taking payoffs to facilitate sex crimes. Namely the
prostitution of underaged girls roped into a sex-trafficking ring.
This owner was one of two who were turning state's evidence
and had hinted that the leader of the ring was someone who had
power and influence.

"They probably have new ownership considering…" Trent said.
"So were the new owners bought off too?"

"I take it this Sunny Motel means somethin' to ya?" The sheriff
hoisted up his pants again, a mannerism he didn't even seem to
notice he had. He'd probably been doing it since he was a rookie
and just hadn't stopped.

Amanda nodded and said, "It does."

"And," he dragged out, "I'm taking it that it's not something
you wanted to hear?"

She was aware he was looking at her, waiting for an answer,
even though his question was rather more rhetorical in nature.
She was busy processing everything. Congressman Davis's close
proximity to those they'd arrested from the ring back in January…
The familiar style of bracelet that she'd seen on the politician's wrist.
It was all there, slapping her in the face. "We've got to go, Trent."
She would discuss all this in the car with him, but she wasn't about
to open up in the presence of the sheriff, deputy, and Kane. And
who knew how immersed the congressman was in the waterfront
communities surrounding Lake Chesdin? People like him became
powerful, not due to pure skill. She was never naive enough to
believe that. No, the powerful became such because they put fear
into other people and used it to control them.

She turned to the sheriff, holding out a hand. "Thank you for your help, your cooperation." She shook his hand, let the compliment pass to Tom and took his. Then she thanked the diver for his time and his team's.

She got into the passenger seat of the department car, Trent behind the wheel. The vehicle kicked up dust in the rearview mirror as Trent pressed the gas a little heavier than he normally did.

The clock on the dash read 3:35 PM. It would take them the better part of two hours to get back to Dumfries this time of day. That would put them there for just past five thirty, about the time Zoe should be taken home to relax for the night. "I hate to say it, but I think we need to put Denise off until tomorrow," she began. "I need to think of Zoe."

"I could go myself..." Trent looked over at her and arched an eyebrow.

She winced, because she wanted to be there when they spoke to Denise Steinbeck. Right now, she felt jammed into a corner with a difficult choice to make—that of caring for a young girl or following a lead in the case.

"Okay, so that's a no?" he asked.

"I'd like to be there." Denise Steinbeck needed to be asked about her husband as soon as possible, but they hadn't even looked to see if she'd filed a missing person report. They probably should do that first. They also needed to bring Malone up to speed on today's findings—the congressman owning property on the lake, the phone, Larry Steinbeck, and where he worked. All of this couldn't just be a coincidence, could it?

And those poor children suffering the way they did every single day... Her chest tightened, and she leaned back, gasping for breath.

"Amanda?" Trent prompted.

She tapped her chest, took a long inhale and exhale, and faced him. "What if Congressman Davis isn't just behind the commission of a murder—or murders, if we extend that to the Parkers? What if he's the leader of the DC sex-trafficking ring?" She was going to be sick. Her stomach swirled and lurched. Why couldn't it just be some run-of-the-mill monster at the reins? Why did it have to be someone who held such an esteemed position, a seemingly untouchable post?

"You really think he's into that?" Trent briefly met her gaze and turned back to the road.

"Things are starting to pile up." She looked over at his profile, in this moment very much appreciating his calm and grounded energy and his silence while he waited on her to elaborate. "Trent, you remember when I brought down Davis's aide?"

"Yeah, of course."

"Well, I was called to Hill's office, and the congressman was there."

"Why?"

"He wanted to thank me personally for helping him clean up his office, or so I thought. Now, I'm thinking he wanted to feel out his enemy—that being me. He also wanted to put me off my guard, but I saw something that day. I can't unsee it now, though I had set it aside a long time ago."

"What was it?"

"He was wearing a bracelet that was much like the one that led to the discovery of the ring in the first place."

"The one that had the hidden data chip in the clasp?"

"The very one."

"So you believe the congressman is behind the ring? That the bracelet he wore that day was a replacement for the silver one that surfaced in the investigation?"

"Yep. One hundred percent. That's what my gut is telling me anyway."

"Shit."

"Yeah, shit. Especially if I'm right. But we have Sunny Motel coming up again, the previous owner's claim that the leader of the ring was someone powerful, either in politics or law enforcement. And now, photos that show a murder happening on Davis's own boat." She stopped there, considering whether she should pull the police chief into her conversation with Trent or not. "I want to tell you something that we'll keep to ourselves."

"Lips are sealed."

And she trusted Trent to keep that promise. "I didn't understand why Sherry Hill was so interested in the Parker investigation, but now I'm really starting to think it has nothing to do with her wanting to be the front woman for the media. I bet she's out to not only protect her brother-in-law's back but also her own."

The car swerved toward the outside line.

"Trent!" she blurted out.

"Sorry." He righted the vehicle. "The police chief, corrupt and part of the sex-trafficking ring?"

"Why not?"

"Wow. Now I see the real reason you reacted so strongly to his name coming up with the boat registration."

"Uh-huh."

At that point the conversation just sort of ebbed away, as if it followed its natural course, but there really was so much more that could be said. For Amanda, it was more a matter of where to even begin. She rummaged through her chats with Patty Glover, her new friend from Sex Crimes. Last she knew, Patty was still working on tracking the source of the money deposited into the Sunny Motel's bank account. As far as Amanda knew that was still at a dead end, but it never hurt to follow up. She pulled out her phone. "Calling Patty," she said to Trent when he glanced over at her, curiosity marking his expression.

"Hey, Amanda," Patty answered on the second ring; she obviously had Amanda in as a contact. But there was always something a little disconcerting when a person you called answered in this manner. It threw Amanda for a few seconds.

"Hey." She took in a deep breath.

"What's wrong? Don't tell me that you've run into the ring again?" Patty had a sense about her that was somewhat clairvoyant. Most would probably just say she had excellent detective and deduction skills, and that was probably all it was, but sometimes it felt like more.

"I think I might know who's behind the entire thing."

Trent looked over at her with wide eyes as if to say, *You're going to tell her about Davis?*

Patty gasped. "Now you've got to tell me who and what led you to them."

Amanda recoiled. She'd spoken on impulse and revealed her hand too soon. It was time to backpedal. "I can't give you any names. Yet."

"Okay," Patty dragged out.

"But the reason I'm calling is to see if you've made any progress on narrowing in on the account holder's information—the one who sent the money to Sunny Motel in Woodbridge and Ritter Motel in Dumfries. Even who received money in payment for the girls who were sold to an end-user scumbag." The latter statement really had the fish from lunch wanting to make a repeat appearance.

"Some, yes."

"Some," Amanda repeated and sat straighter. "You have a person that you're getting ready to move in on?"

"Not quite yet." The wince infected Patty's voice and traveled the line. "But I've followed the money outside of the country, which I believe I already told you."

"To Canada."

"I've kept following, and it's led me back to the States, specifically Amelia County, Virginia."

"Amel…" She swallowed roughly.

"Amanda? What's going on?" Concern lit her tone.

"Amelia County," Amanda squeezed out. "That's near Lake Chesdin, right?"

"Yes. Please tell me what's going on."

"There's so much to tell, I'm not even sure where to start. But I am going to give you a name. It's one you're going to keep entirely to yourself. You promise me that?"

"Absolutely."

"I mean don't tell *anyone*. Not your bosses, other detectives in the department. *No one.*"

"Promise. Now tell me."

"Congressman Eugene Davis," Amanda pushed out.

"A congressman?"

"Yes, I think he's behind the DC ring."

"What makes you think that?"

"I can't get into all of it right now. I'm still working to put everything Trent and I are discovering with our current investigation into perspective. But remember you said the people from Sunny Motel and Ritter Motel thought the person in charge was someone in a position of power?"

"Like a politician," Patty said, speaking slowly.

"Uh-huh, or in law enforcement. I'm not saying anything has pointed us right to her, but Sherry Hill is Davis's sister-in-law."

"Yeah… I'm well aware."

"So you can understand? Not a word to *anyone*." She stressed the last word. "Not without concrete evidence."

"Wow."

"Right?" Amanda stopped there, realizing how she sounded like Trent. Was he rubbing off on her? Guess it was bound to happen when she spent several hours a day with him. She went on. "I'm working things on my end, but I wanted to touch base with you. See if you had any updates on the banking. Turns out it's a good thing I called."

"Yes and no."

Amanda hadn't known Patty for long, but one thing she knew was the woman was unstoppable. She was a powerhouse who didn't really give the impression she'd cower to anyone. But the news that Amanda had just given her had obviously rattled her—and understandably so. Amanda gave Trent another glance. "We just follow the evidence to wherever it leads without being swayed or bullied."

Trent smiled at her, and she returned the expression.

"You're right, Amanda," Patty said. "Of course, you're right. And I'll keep this tight to my chest as I work away." There was a span of silence, then she added, "You reacted strongly when I mentioned Amelia County. Can you at least tell me why that was?"

Amanda told her about the witnessed murder and the boat's registration tying back to Davis.

"Holy mother of—"

"Uh-huh. So, to yourself."

"You got it."

The two of them wished each other good luck in their endeavors and ended the call.

"I take it that she had something?" Trent said.

"Oh, yeah." She told him how the money related to the ring led Patty to Amelia County.

"Not a far drive from Chesdin Landing."

"Nope. There's a little distance there, but it's still rather close to home."

"Maybe he doesn't like his money too far out of reach."

"Maybe," she replied. She was thinking, though, that he had ensured the money trail took a wild and long path out of the country, back again, and to who knows where before it landed back in Virginia. What really pained her was knowing she needed to stick a pin in the investigation for at least the night. Tonight, she'd make arrangements for Zoe's care tomorrow so she could pursue the leads they'd uncovered today, starting with Denise Steinbeck.

It would be wonderful if she could just take the weekend off and treat Zoe to the aquarium in Washington. But with dangerous—and unpredictable—people after her, going out in public was far too risky. Amanda's options were either to stay at home with Zoe or hand her over to someone she trusted with her own life. The first person to come to mind was her sergeant, Scott Malone. Would he and his wife, Ida, be willing to take Zoe for a day? They had two grown sons, but it had been several years since they'd cared for a kid. The second was Becky Tulson, Amanda's best friend since kindergarten. As an officer with the Dumfries PD, she was more than capable of protecting Zoe, but she'd never had children. She did live alone, though, so taking on Zoe wouldn't be a decision she'd have to share with a significant other.

If neither would take her, Amanda might have to let Trent talk to Denise by himself. Zoe came first. As the thought hit, she realized how good it felt to be concerned with someone else's well-being after all these years. Actually, not only concerned, but filled with a sense of responsibility toward another person, a child, a little individual who was counting on her to make it all okay. But she hated that no matter what she did for Zoe, it would only be temporary. Her parents were gone, and once this case was tried and over, Zoe would become part of the system or sent to live with Libby Dewinter. And while the girl had just entered Amanda's life three days ago, the thought of letting her go pained her.

CHAPTER TWENTY-NINE

Amanda had called Colleen from the road to give her their ETA, and Trent pulled into the lot for Central just fifteen minutes later at five fifty. Trent headed to Malone's office, while Amanda went to catch up with Colleen. She told Amanda that she wasn't scheduled to work this weekend, but another psychologist could come talk with Zoe if it was deemed necessary. Colleen recommended, though, that some time and separation from being questioned might do Zoe some good.

"She's still young, grade one," Colleen said.

"That's right," Amanda replied, not sure where Colleen was going.

"Part of the path to healing after a trauma like Zoe has experienced is to insert some normalcy back into her life as soon as possible."

Amanda bristled at that. She'd heard the same advice from a shrink she'd seen for a brief time after Kevin and Lindsey had died. There'd be no return to normal—at least not the one that had existed before the world flipped on its head.

Colleen went on. "And, as you know, the school year started this week, and she's only missed a few days, but it might not be a bad idea to arrange for her to attend—"

"Back to school with the killers still out there?" Amanda snapped, and retracted. "I just… She's in danger."

"I'm not saying we send her out with no protection. I'd certainly recommend that she has an officer with her at all times."

Then how is that a return to "normal"? The thought raced through Amanda's mind, but she kept her mouth shut. She didn't need to make an enemy of this woman. The real enemy sat behind a desk at the Capitol Building and declared himself a leader and a patriot—all the while he was selling and exploiting children. She knew it in her bones, same as she had this strong feeling that Chief Hill was bad news, but she needed to gather indisputable proof. She considered Zoe and her education. There was no sense having her fall too far behind. "I'll speak with Sergeant Malone about this."

"Good."

"Did you show her those pictures I left with you?"

"I did, and she recognized two of the men." Colleen produced the printed photos from a folder she held. "These two," she said as she indicated the blond man and the one with the bald head.

"Those are our suspects," Amanda confirmed.

"Good news, but are you any closer to getting them?"

Amanda shook her head. "But it's one step at a time."

"That's life." Colleen smiled kindly. "I'll be back on Monday at four o'clock with the assumption she'll be in class during the day. If that changes, let me know."

"Will do."

Colleen left, and Amanda headed toward Malone's office to catch up with him and Trent.

She found them staring blankly at each other and wondered how much Trent had already told Malone. The sergeant's face was ashen and full of concern.

"Trent hasn't told me much, but he's told me enough. We really think the congressman is behind the DC sex-trafficking ring?"

"It sure looks that way." She dropped herself in another chair beside Trent and proceeded to fill Malone in on their day and all their finds—everything from what the divers found, to the recovered phone belonging to Larry Steinbeck of Dumfries, and then back to the congressman.

"That saves me the trouble of getting Steinbeck's face on the PWCPD website then," Malone said with a shrug. "I hadn't had a chance to forward it on yet."

She continued. "I spoke with Sex Crimes, and payoffs in the trafficking ring are going into a bank account in Amelia County. That's near Lake Chesdin. That can't be a coincidence."

"We need solid proof that Davis is up to no good, or we have to consider that it is all coincidence."

The whole "innocent until proven guilty" adage, but she wasn't feeling it at the moment. She imagined herself storming into whatever mansion the congressman had himself holed up in and slapping cuffs on him. But if he was outside of Prince William County, her hands were tied anyway; he'd be out of her jurisdiction. At best, she'd have to settle for a joint endeavor and being a face in the background that led to his arrest. Yes, she was getting ahead of herself. And sadly, as Patty was always reminding her, more people would slither forward to take over and reorganize. In this case, possibly Sherry Hill. Or was she just paid to watch over her brother-in-law's interests? Either way, her hands were dirty.

Amanda felt tremors of disgust curdle through her. Sure, it was a possibility that Sherry Hill had no idea the type of man Eugene was. He very well could have her fooled along with so many others. Amanda wondered how far back his misdeeds went. And Malone's whole "view it as a coincidence" made her keep silent about Hill. She'd already tried to get Malone to consider that Hill was corrupt, and he'd shot the suggestion down.

Malone leaned back in his chair, swiveled, and steepled his fingers under his chin. "All I can say is continue doing what you're doing, get the evidence—indisputable proof—and then you know I'll have your back to go after the man."

"But we have a boat registered to him that was used in the commission of a murder." The appeal came out, a sad attempt at gaining some leeway, but her thoughts had been down this path before. The congressman could dispute he had any knowledge of this or claim that his boat had been stolen. He'd likely have the perfect alibi and system in place. She could imagine him arguing that he couldn't control what was going on at his part-time residence and therefore his boat.

"It's not enough, and we all know that." Malone massaged his forehead.

"All right. I guess that's it, then." Trent got up to leave the office but stopped when he realized Amanda wasn't joining him.

"I'll catch up with you in a minute," she told him, and he left.

"What is it?" Malone asked.

"I was just speaking with Colleen, and she thinks it's a good idea for Zoe to go back to school on Monday."

"I'm taking it you disagree?"

"Yes and no. I worry about Zoe's welfare. I definitely need you to have an officer watching over her."

"Shouldn't be a problem at all; that goes without saying." He seemed to pause there as if he had more to say but hesitated. The way he kept looking at her made it seem like he was concerned about Amanda's emotional well-being, and she had a strong feeling she knew what it was in regard to. But if he wasn't bringing it up, neither was she—even if the silence tempted her. "I think we might need to clear the air about something." He swallowed roughly, and he appeared upset.

"About?" She bit her bottom lip.

"I, ah, heard some things come back from your mother's trial."

Suddenly she wondered if a verdict had been given, but she would have been notified. She reined her panic back in, as hard as that was to do. "What?"

"Well, it's still plugging along, but… I assume you know?"

"About?" She was making him work for this, especially if he was going to confess to knowing about her father's affair and keeping it from her mother years ago.

Malone rubbed his face. "Your father's affair with CSI Emma Blair." He cleared his throat. "I just wanted you to know that I had no idea. He did a good job of hiding it."

"You were close friends with him," she countered, feeling her core heat. "I find that hard to believe."

"I have never lied to you, Amanda, and I'm not starting now." His voice was firm but tinged with anger.

"Okay."

"Okay," he parroted. "Just a bit more business to attend to before you go. I spoke with Colleen myself, and as of right now, no one is scheduled to come in and speak with Zoe this weekend. You've got all these leads to follow up in the case. Have you considered what you're going to do with Zoe?"

"Actually…"

"Oh, no, I see it in your eyes. I can't do it, Amanda. Ida has this weekend all mapped out for me. Apparently, I'm painting the furnace room. Wahoo," he tagged on, lacking all enthusiasm.

Amanda chuckled. "Yeah, you've never been a painter."

"As far as I'm concerned, that's one job that should be hired out, but Ida has it in her head that would be a waste of money. And you know the saying, the husband is the head, and the wife is the neck, and wherever the neck turns the head follows."

Amanda chuckled. "So you don't have much choice."

"Not if I want a happy wife, happy life."

"And you do."

"I do."

Amanda smiled. Malone might complain, but he still wanted to please his wife. She used to think that his marriage and that of her parents were ones to aspire to, but finding out about her father's affair had flipped all that on its head.

"What about getting Becky to watch Zoe?" he suggested. "She's got a badge and a gun and could take care of her."

"I thought of her."

"It's a great idea if she's up for it. Of course, I'd clear this with Erica Murphy from child services."

"I'll call her right now." She pulled out her phone and stood.

"You might want to check with Becky first."

"Ah, good thinking." Amanda called her friend as she left Malone's office and headed for her desk. Becky answered right away.

"Tell me you're calling for a girls' night out *tonight*."

"I wasn't, but…" She let that percolate. She had Zoe and couldn't exactly go out for dinner, but if Becky was going to sit with Zoe tomorrow, they had to meet. There was no reason why that couldn't involve some fun. "Possibly…"

"Great." Her friend sounded like she'd had a rough day and needed to unwind.

"Everything all right?"

"Yeah, don't worry about me. It's just the new sergeant is riding me. What's up?"

New was debatable, but Sergeant Lisa Greer was new to the Dumfries PD this year, and she could be a bit of a micromanager. "Yikes. Sorry to hear that."

"Hey, you have Hill."

"Glad I'm here to make you feel better." Amanda laughed, then turned serious. "I need to ask you for a favor."

"Shoot."

"This case I'm working is a little more complicated than some others." *Is that what Zoe is—a complication?* Amanda knew the answer the instant the question struck. Zoe was a *huge* complication in many ways. She cleared her throat. "I've been entrusted with the care of a young girl named Zoe."

"The Parkers' girl? How did you end up—"

"Never mind that. The point is I have to make sure she's protected."

"Okay?"

"Some leads have come up in the case, and I need to follow them tomorrow. The psychiatrist that she's been working with won't be coming in. I can't exactly just drop her off at Central and leave." She paused there, wondering if her friend would piece together the direction in which this conversation was headed. If she had, she wasn't volunteering that information. "I was wondering if I could leave her in your care. Before you say anything, you should know that she saw her father murdered. She'll be a key witness when the case goes to trial."

"And right now, she's a huge liability," Becky inserted. "As far as the killer's concerned."

"Two."

"Two, what?"

"At least two killers." There was the one pictured in Zoe's drawing with the gun—the same one who shot Steinbeck on the boat—and the one that went for Zoe and shot Libby and Amanda. As she put that out there, she realized if Eugene Davis had two on his payroll to do his dirty work, it was entirely possible he had many more. Possibly a network. She wasn't going to get into the congressman with Becky—at least not over the phone. "There is something else you should know. The woman who found the Parkers, the family friend… not sure if you heard, but she was shot the other day when a man attempted to get to Zoe."

"Oh my God. No, I hadn't heard. That poor kid."

"And poor woman."

"Well, yeah, but…"

"Would you be able to watch Zoe during the day? Just for tomorrow? I'd want you to be with her at my house because she's used to it."

"Yeah, uh, I could, but I haven't even met her."

Amanda reached her cubicle and sat at her desk. "See, that's where tonight comes in."

"Ha. So not really a girls' night out."

"We're all girls," Amanda said with a smile. "But we can't go out. Too much risk."

"What do you have in mind?"

"Pizza and movies at my place. My treat."

"Cartoon movies?" Spoken with a little disdain. Becky didn't really talk a lot about kids or have any of her own, but she had been good with Lindsey.

"How about a compromise? Light-hearted adult movies?"

"Rom coms? I'm always in the mood."

"We'll discuss entertainment once you arrive." Amanda pulled back her phone and saw it was going on six fifteen. "Come by at seven?"

"Works. See you soon."

Amanda made her next call, waving goodbye to an officer passing her desk. Given the bounce in his step and his call out of "have a good weekend," she'd say he wasn't due back until Monday.

"Hello?" Erica answered her phone in the middle of the second ring. She sounded like she was in a pleasant mood, but then again, it was Friday night, and she probably had the weekend off like that chipper officer.

"It's Detective Steele from Prince William County PD."

"Ah, yes, Detective, is everything all right with Zoe?"

Amanda took a few moments to formulate the answer but went with the broad stroke. "She's doing fine."

"Good. What can I help you with?" There was noise in the background, and Amanda surmised the woman had already secured herself a spot at a local bar.

"I just thought it best to run something past you," Amanda began, deciding to go outside now. It would give her some fresh air. "It's regarding Zoe's care this weekend."

"Oh, do you need me to place her somewhere else?"

"I just need to leave her in someone else's care tomorrow during the day."

"Well, I can arrange something."

"Actually, I have someone in mind. It's another police officer. She's from the Dumfries PD." Amanda stepped outside the building and inhaled the evening air—a little cool with a light breeze.

"Oh, okay." There seemed to be disappointment enclosed in the woman's response, and Amanda wondered if it had to do with the fact that Erica might have to run a background on Becky, thereby interfering with her evening plans.

"Do you need to run a background on her, or do you trust my opinion? I can speak to her exemplary record."

"She's a friend of yours?"

Amanda smiled, impressed by the woman's quick deduction. "She is my best friend."

Erica was silent.

Amanda continued, stating her case further. "I realize the upset that Zoe could experience by being shuffled around, and I plan to limit that as much as possible. I was going to have Becky Tulson, that's the officer, stay with her at my house—someplace Zoe's familiar with."

A few seconds ticked past without anything being said by either of them, but there were voices in the background. One sounded like they were addressing Erica and confirming her drink order. Amanda saw a crack.

"I realize you must typically have to run everyone through a background check, have them sign off like I did, but I can vouch for Becky. She'll keep Zoe safe. You have my word on that."

"Uh."

"I'm not sure what you mean by that… But I assure you that if anything does happen, I'll say I never touched base with you. Come on, what do you say?"

It was getting a little louder around Erica, and Amanda imagined it was the social worker's growing crowd of friends gathering for happy hour on a Friday night.

"Fine. But if anything happens—"

"Trust me. Zoe will be safe." She was saying the words and speaking the promises, but she really couldn't let the words sink in. The thought of anything happening to Zoe tortured Amanda.

"Okay, Detective Steele. Call me if anything changes." Erica went on to wish Amanda a good weekend, and Amanda reciprocated. No need to point out she wouldn't get much of one.

But as the thought of the two days ahead worked their way through Amanda's mind, something else occurred to her. The family dinner at her parents' house on Sunday. Her sisters and brother and nieces and nephews would all be there. Her father.

How could she even look at him after knowing what he'd done to her mother? How greatly he must have hurt and humiliated her. And then to have it all resurface in public... in *court*. It would have been mortifying. Sunday would be a tough day.

She could use caring for Zoe as an excuse not to go, but that didn't feel right. She hated it when parents used their children to pardon their behavior. And who knew how much longer her mother had as a free person? This could be the last Sunday dinner with the entire family. Amanda had already missed so much of their lives, having pulled herself away from them after Kevin and Lindsey's deaths. She could ask that Becky sit with Zoe on Sunday as well, but it felt like it was too much of an imposition, and on top of that, she didn't want Zoe to get the feeling she was being passed off. But she couldn't exactly just show up at her parents' door with Zoe. Amanda had to call her mother and give her a heads-up.

She dialed.

Her dad answered the line, and Amanda's breath froze. Eventually, she got her voice to cooperate. "Uh, Dad, I need to speak to Mom."

"Let me get her." He didn't say anything besides that. No defense for his actions—nothing.

Her mother picked up with, "Don't tell me you're not coming on Sunday. You know that—"

"Mom, I'm coming." If Amanda didn't cut in and slow her mother down, she'd just keep going.

"Good. What is it, then? Everything okay? Oh, don't tell me you found out about… Mandy, I don't want to talk about it."

Neither did Amanda—not now or ever. But at some point, it had to be discussed. "I did find out, but that's not why I'm calling. I just wanted to let you know that I'll be bringing someone with me on Sunday."

"Someone? Like some guy you're dating?" Her mother's tone held disgust, and Amanda wasn't sure where the hostility originated from.

"Heavens no." *And am I dating anyone?* That question popped in her mind. She hadn't heard from Logan today and wasn't sure if she would. Considering all that was going unsaid between them, did they have a future?

"Who?" Her voice was marked with curiosity.

"You probably heard about the double homicide in Triangle." There was not a question in Amanda's mind that her mother had. Even with her trial, Amanda imagined her mother keeping up with the news.

"Yes. The Parkers. He worked for some company in Washington?"

"Yes, those are the murders I'm talking about." She wasn't getting into Brett Parker's work.

"It completely makes sense you're on the case. You're their best. Malone knows. I remind him of that every chance I get."

"Mom," Amanda stamped out, like a finger snap, trying to rein in her mother's attention. A few seconds of silence, then Amanda went on. "Their daughter, Zoe, is an eyewitness."

Her mother gasped. "Oh my goodness. She saw her parents get murdered. She's just a little thing, if I remember right."

"She is. Only six, and she's in protective custody. In this case, that's me."

"Working the homicides and babysitting? No one can say you don't multitask, Mandy."

Again, no need to dwell on it. "I'm busy, and I need to get going, but the reason I called is to run something by you."

"By all means, spit it out."

Amanda found amusement in how her mother could get long-winded and take detours in conversation every which way, but if Amanda took a little longer to say something it was, "Spit it out, Mandy."

"I need to bring her with me on Sunday."

Silence.

"Mom, did you hear me?"

"Sure, what's one more? See you both at five. We'll eat at six."

"Okay. I love you, Mom."

"Love you." With that, her mother hung up, leaving Amanda holding her phone.

Her mother might have agreed to let Zoe tag along, but it wasn't hard to figure out that she wasn't too thrilled about the arrangement. Amanda replayed the conversation in her mind. Her mother's tone had changed around the point Amanda said Zoe was six. Amanda could have smacked herself in the forehead.

Her mother had loved Lindsey immensely, and losing her granddaughter had been too much for her to fully absorb. Maybe having Zoe there would remind her too much of Lindsey. Hopefully, her mother would come to see, as Amanda was beginning to, that Zoe's presence was rather healing. And Zoe wasn't Lindsey, but she was a precious little girl.

CHAPTER THIRTY

Pizza loaded with gooey cheese was just what Amanda needed after this week—the worst of which had been jam-packed into the last few days. Amanda, Zoe, and Becky all sat on the couch, Zoe in the middle. The little girl seemed to attach herself to Becky rather quickly. She had curled up on her side, body under a throw blanket, Lucky hugged to her chest, and her head on Becky's lap. Amanda got the feet, and she was tempted to tickle them.

Lindsey used to fall asleep on the couch in front of movies all the time. She alternated between laying her head on Kevin's lap then Amanda's, like she didn't want either one of them to feel left out or like she loved the other one more.

The evening certainly brought up happy memories, and after Becky had left and Zoe was settled into bed, Amanda once again hit the sack early.

When she awoke on Saturday morning, she was pleased to discover that both she and Zoe had slept all the way through the night, uninterrupted by bad dreams or whirling thoughts.

Amanda was starting to realize that recently when she thought of Kevin and Lindsey, she was more happy than sad. Maybe she was finally starting to move forward. Had that been because of Zoe's appearance in her life, as she'd considered last night? Or was it simply because enough time had passed and she was allowing herself to heal?

Becky had shown up at Amanda's house at about a quarter to eight. Zoe had been happy to see her and didn't make a fuss when

Amanda left. She was immensely relieved and grateful for that. It was now nine o'clock, and she was in the car next to Trent on the way to speak with Denise Steinbeck.

Trent pulled into the driveway of a townhouse and said, "This is it."

Amanda led the way to the front door and knocked. No response. She was about to knock again when the door creaked open.

"Ah, yeah, what is it?" The woman, somewhere in her forties, had a bad case of bedhead, and her red-rimmed eyes testified to either a lack of sleep or a hangover—maybe both.

"Denise Steinbeck?" Amanda asked, holding up her badge; Trent was doing the same.

"That's me." The woman's grogginess seemed to vanish and was replaced with wide-eyed curiosity as she took in her visitors.

"We're Detectives Steele and Stenson," Amanda began. "We'd like to talk with you about your husband, Larry."

"What about him?"

Amanda was a little taken aback by her reaction, as it felt a tad harsh. "If we could just have a few moments of your time?" She nudged her head toward the house, implying that she wanted to be invited inside.

"Okay." Denise backed up and said, "You'll have to excuse me. I was sleeping when you knocked. Still waking up." She scratched her head, mussing up her brown hair and causing it to stick up even more than it had been.

"No problem. Do you have somewhere we could sit?" Amanda prompted.

"Thisaway."

She took them to a living room not far from the front door and dropped onto a couch. She stared blankly at Amanda. For someone who'd just had the cops show up at her door about her husband, Denise didn't look too shaken or concerned. Or she was doing a good job of hiding it. They'd checked Missing Persons, and Larry hadn't been reported missing.

Amanda and Trent sat in a couple of chairs that were situated across from the couch.

"We have reason to believe your husband may have had some business to take care of in the Lake Chesdin area," Amanda said, avoiding mention of his suspected death and recovering his phone at the bottom of the lake—for now. "Would you know what that might have been?"

"I wouldn't have a clue." Denise clenched her jaw.

"Are you and your husband experiencing problems, ma'am?" Trent asked.

Amanda glanced over at him. Talk about pulling no punches.

"Huh, you could say that. The bastard up and left me."

Amanda leaned forward, finally understanding the woman's reaction better. "When was this?"

"Last week. Don't ask what day because they've all been blurring together. Twenty years, and this is how he treats me? Despicable."

"Sorry for your troubles," Amanda said, understanding now why the woman might look so disheveled. "You said you've been together twenty years. Have you had your issues before, maybe that led to Larry leaving?" There was no delicate way of asking this.

"We've had our issues, sure, but it's been worse lately."

"In what way?"

"He's been moodier than normal, and he kept to himself far more than usual."

"Do you know what prompted this change in behavior?" Amanda asked.

"Well, he was different not long after he got his new job."

Trent leaned forward. "The one at Sunny Motel?"

Denise glanced at him and nodded. "Uh-huh, that's the one. I'm pretty sure he started having an affair. Access to all those beds, women. It would explain everything. Maybe why he was in Lake

Chesdin too." She flailed a hand toward Amanda. Her expression was pained.

Amanda tiptoed toward her husband's fate and would leave out any reassurances as to his loyalty. For all she knew he was a cheating bastard. "Your husband has surfaced in an open investigation that my partner and I are working."

"Is he a suspect? He did something wrong and you're looking for him?" Denise's brow scrunched up like she had a headache—maybe she did.

"Not exactly." Amanda proceeded gently. "We believe he may have been the victim of a crime." Did she go ahead and say that they believed he'd been murdered and his body dumped in the lake? If she did, Denise's next question would likely be about her husband's body.

"The victim?" Her voice was tight.

"We've recovered some rather disturbing images and have reason to believe in their validity," Amanda said. "We believe that your husband was murdered." There'd be no more dancing around it.

Denise's eyes widened, and she clamped a hand over her mouth. Slowly, she dropped her arm, and her face hardened to stone. "Serves him right. Just reward for him… for him…" She started crying—the ugly sort with tears flying everywhere and snot bubbles and gulps for breath.

Amanda glanced at Trent. Denise was one conflicted individual, slightly off her rocker. "We're sorry for your loss, Mrs. Steinbeck."

"So you're… uh…" She sniffled. "Sure he's, ah, gone?"

"Quite, or I wouldn't have said it," Amanda said gently. "It's sort of a difficult situation because we haven't recovered his body."

Denise's eyes snapped to Amanda's. "You haven't…?"

Amanda shook her head. "We have photographs that show your husband on a boat with two men. He was shot and thrown overboard."

"This happened on Lake Chesdin?"

"It did. Divers went out yesterday in the vicinity of where the incident had occurred but weren't able to recover him. They did find his cell phone, which led us to you."

Denise sniffled, then snatched a tissue from a box on a table next to her. Must have been the last one or close to it, as the lightweight box skittered across the top and fell to the floor. "Damn it to hell," Denise muttered and got up. She went to another room, and from the sounds of it, she was rummaging in a cupboard. She returned with a fresh box. She ripped the top off and plucked out another tissue. She didn't bother picking up the empty box and doing anything with it.

After Denise sat back down, the two tissues clenched in her hand, Amanda took out printed pictures of the two suspects and showed them to her. "Do you recognize either of these men?"

Denise grabbed reading glasses from the table next to her and studied each image in turn. "No. I've never seen them before. Did they have something to do with Larry's…" Her chin quivered, and her eyes pooled with tears. It seemed obvious she couldn't bring herself to say *death*.

"We believe so. Yes. So you have no idea why your husband might have been in the Lake Chesdin area?" Larry Steinbeck could have been taken to the lake for the purpose of killing him and disposing of his body, or he could have planned to meet with the two men in the area for some purpose.

"I don't, but like I said, he wasn't exactly talking to me." Pain and betrayal were evident in her strained voice. "Do you know when he was… um… killed?" Denise blew her nose several times and bunched the used tissues in her hand.

"We believe it was Thursday of last week in the early morning, before sunrise," Amanda told her. "When did you see him last?" The woman had said the days blurred together, but Amanda felt Denise knew when to the hour.

"Oh my God. Thursday?" Denise laid a hand over her heart. "He didn't come home from work that Thursday morning. He does the night shift… Then he wasn't answering his phone. I just assumed he'd up and left me again."

"Again?" Trent asked.

Denise batted a hand. "As I said, we had our issues."

It was beginning to make sense why Denise wouldn't have reported Larry missing—especially if their *issues* meant they'd separate on a rather regular basis. "You and Larry often take time apart?"

"Larry and I had a unique marriage," she began. "We were always on again, off again. Didn't usually rope in other people or anything, but we'd go our separate ways. Had to. We could fight like cats and dogs, but then making up… well, it was heavenly. I called Sunny Motel on Thursday morning, and they told me he had shown for his shift on Wednesday night but had left early. I just assumed we were 'off' again."

"So you had a fight before he went to work? Something else that prompted you to believe that?" Amanda asked.

Denise nodded.

"You said he was moody lately, but is that all?" Amanda needed to get to the meat of what had caused that behavioral shift, and if it might have in any way resulted in his murder.

"He wouldn't talk to me. I asked him to tell me what was bothering him. It was obvious something was, but he refused. He told me not to concern myself with it."

It was possible that Larry didn't want to burden Denise with something. Possibly a pressure at work. Maybe the sex-trafficking ring was wanting to reinitiate a business arrangement with Sunny Motel's new manager. Had they killed Larry because he wouldn't comply? "Did Larry ever mention having problems at work?" Amanda recalled Denise had said that Larry's changes started when he began at the motel.

"Not outright, but he seemed stressed and ragged when he came home, but working at night was a new thing for him. Before the motel, he worked days at a manufacturing plant. Boring, repetitive work on an assembly line. The place paid good, but as they say, all good things come to an end. He told me he was excited about the motel job just before he started. He was happy to be the manager instead of an underling."

"And how did Larry come to have the job at the motel?" She was curious because the line of work he'd been in before was another world from the hospitality one.

"He applied, got called in for an interview, and was given the job on the spot."

She found that interesting—again, given Larry's work experience being a far cry from the new job. There must have been candidates better suited for the management position, but maybe with what had taken place with the previous owners, the new ones had a hard time attracting job applicants. "Did Larry have any experience working at a motel?"

"Oh, back when he was in high school, he worked part-time at one."

Hardly enough to qualify him as a motel manager. "What kind of man was your husband? Was he easygoing or stubborn?"

"Larry? Well, he could bend like a reed in the wind. Whichever way it blew, he went. It was often the source of our arguments. He let people take advantage of him."

"So he was easily manipulated," Trent said.

"He could be, yes, but he also had a fierce stubborn streak."

Amanda had a feeling it was the latter that had led to his death, and the former easygoingness that got him the job—assuming the new motel owner sensed this about Larry and was up to the same tricks as the old one. It was possible the ring approached Larry for his cooperation but he'd refused, gripping onto his stubborn streak and taking a stand against them. That certainly wouldn't have gone over too well, and it could have been what got him murdered.

"Do you know of anyone who might have had something against Larry?" Amanda asked, resorting to one of the most basic questions in an investigation and doing so to re-instill some objectivity.

"Enough to murder him? I can't imagine him stirring up that much of a reaction in someone."

"You said he could be stubborn…" Amanda pointed out.

"Ah, sure, but enough to get him killed? I don't know."

"Did your husband have any close friends? Maybe they know of someone?" Larry could have confided in a friend about what was going on in his life.

"Well, he is—*was*—good friends with a man named Gerald Cunningham."

"Where could we find him?"

"He's a priest here in town. The two of them go way back." Denise gave them the name of the church and where to find it, but Amanda had passed it a million times in her life. "He lives there in the rectory," she added.

"Thank you, Mrs. Steinbeck," Amanda said. "And I'm very sorry for your loss. Is there anyone we could call for you?"

"No, but you can find his body. It's just all so hard to accept that he's actually gone… So hard. And without a…"

Amanda nodded. "I understand. We'll do what we can."

She and Trent saw themselves out.

Once they were in the car, Amanda said, "Let's just hope that even if Larry wasn't talking to his wife, he opened up to Gerald."

"There next, I take it?"

"Yep." Her phone rang, and it was Malone. "Aren't you supposed to be painting?" she said as a greeting. This garnered a side-glance from Trent.

"I'm on a break."

Amanda could hear Ida's voice in the background but not what she was saying.

Malone continued. "I got a call about the Dodge Charger. The APB worked. It was found." He proceeded to tell her where—a rural area of Prince William County.

"I assume it's being processed and brought in?" she said.

"It is. Initial findings show that it was wiped down. No prints recovered yet."

"Not a surprise there if we're looking at professionals."

"No, suppose not. Well, I wanted to let you know, but I better get back to it or the woman will have my—"

"Scott!" Ida burst out.

"Coming, dear." Malone ended the call.

"The Dodge Charger was found," she told Trent. "No prints as of yet, so no lead there."

"As you said, *yet*. Something might come up."

She glanced over at her partner, wishing she could be as optimistic. What if they never found the shooters and Zoe lived the rest of her life in danger? Amanda would do all she could to prevent that, but sometimes the leads dried up. She just hoped they wouldn't with this case.

CHAPTER THIRTY-ONE

Amanda and Trent headed toward the rectory's door. She knocked, and they waited. No response from inside the residence, but the front door of the church swung open, and a man in his twenties came around the side.

"Can I help you?"

Amanda and Trent held up their badges.

"Detectives with the Prince William County PD. We're looking for Gerald Cunningham," Amanda said.

"You're not going to find him." The man lowered his voice in increments as he spoke while closing the distance between them.

Amanda's skin prickled, not sure if she wanted to know the reason. Her mind went wild, wondering if Larry Steinbeck told the priest something that had gotten him killed. "Why's that?"

"He's gone away for the weekend to visit his sister in Pittsburgh, but he'll be back on Monday."

Amanda let out the breath she'd been holding. Pittsburgh, Pennsylvania, was over four hours away by car. There was no way to justify the trip when it might not even yield anything, and talking over the phone limited the ability to read facial expressions and body language. "Who are you?"

"Seth Massey. I work with Father Cunningham."

"Do you know what time he'll be here on Monday? We have something we'd like to talk to him about. It's probably best done in person."

"I'd think he'd be back in the afternoon."

She motioned toward the man. "Could you maybe just call him and ask? Do you have a way to reach him there, or does he have a cell phone?"

"He does." Seth stayed motionless.

"I'm sure he wouldn't mind if you called him," she prompted, making a large assumption. But if Gerald picked up that meant he was still alive.

"Fine." Seth got out his phone, pressed a number from his contact list. "It's ringing... Father Cunningham, it's Seth. Sorry to bother you on your time off, but there are detectives here who want to speak with you... I don't know what about." Seth looked at her with the question enclosed in his eyes.

"About his friend Larry Steinbeck," she told him.

Seth relayed this to the priest. "Uh-huh... Okay... You sure?" Seth locked gazes with Amanda. "He says he'll leave early Monday and do his best to be back at nine in the morning."

"Thank him for us and let him know we'll be back then." She listened as Seth passed that information along to Gerald and waited until he'd ended the call and pocketed his phone. "Thank you for that," she said.

"Yep." The guy turned and went back into the church.

"At least we know Cunningham's alive," Amanda said to Trent.

"You were wondering too, huh?"

She just nodded. She was curious, though, if the priest would be returning early if they hadn't wanted to talk about Larry.

They got into the car, and there was one more stop she could think of making before they called it a day. "Let's drop by Sunny Motel." Surprisingly, for all the times she'd said its name or thought of it, she hadn't picked up on the irony until now. The place had facilitated sex crimes, could very well be doing so again. To be involved with such a dark part of human society, and then to have such a cheery name… A true mockery. "I want to talk to the clerk on duty and see if we get any enlightenment about Larry, also maybe why he left early from his shift Wednesday night."

"Well, for him to be on Lake Chesdin Thursday morning, he would have left Dumfries before that."

"Sure. But the night before? Still, someone at the motel could have seen him leave and know if he was alone. They might even be able to ID the men from the boat."

As Trent drove, she couldn't help but think if it hadn't been for the Parkers' murders, the photographs, and the discovery of his phone, Larry could have just disappeared—gone forever without a trace. It was a good thing Larry had someone like Brett Parker watching out for him—intentionally or not.

The guy at the front desk of Sunny Motel looked bored out of his mind. He told them his name was Bobby Bridges. The introductions were made, and Amanda got to the point of their visit.

"We're looking for Larry Steinbeck, and we understand he's the manager here," Amanda said. She was going to approach it without bringing up his murder.

"He *was*. Rumor is he was fired, and they're looking for his replacement. I might be up for the job." Bobby smiled slyly, exposing crooked teeth, but it was the lecherous reflection in his eyes that gave Amanda shivers.

Fired, murdered: Both past tense and rather final. "When did you last see him?"

"Wednesday, last week."

"That was when he was here for his shift?" she asked, to steer the direction of the conversation.

"Well, sorta."

"What do you mean?" Trent asked.

"He showed up then left."

So Bobby knew about that. "You were working with him that night?" she asked.

"Uh-huh."

The hairs rose on the back of Amanda's neck. "Did you see him leave with anyone?"

"Nah, not that I saw. He just got into a cab and left, never came back. Not Wednesday night, not since. I'd say he's not coming back."

The goons from the boat had probably followed him and taken him then. "Into a cab? He didn't have a car of his own?" They hadn't even looked at that aspect of Larry's background.

"Not that I'm aware of. Never seen him with one."

"All right. What time was it that he left on Wednesday?" Hopefully he'd noticed that.

"Say eleven?"

"Do you know why he left?" Trent asked.

"Nope."

"Very strange. Did he say at all? Even something as simple as him going for a coffee?" Amanda tossed out nonchalantly.

"Nothing. And we have coffee here." He flailed a hand toward a coffee maker.

Amanda brought up the pictures of their suspects—the bald man and the blond—and held the screen for Bobby to view. "Do you recognize either of them?"

Bobby studied the images and didn't look at her or Trent when he responded, "No."

"You're sure?" She was finding it hard to know if he was telling the truth, and she didn't care for his sudden aversion to eye contact.

"I'm sure." He met her gaze now.

She nodded, reluctantly, and put her phone away. She'd try another tack. "What do you think of working here?"

"Me?" Bobby pressed his palm to his chest. "I like it just fine."

"They pay well?" she asked.

"I guess."

"You ever see anything going on here that bothers you?" She tried to voice the question in such a way that it wouldn't be confrontational or reveal her suspicions, but she was struggling.

"You mean do hookers get dropped off?"

She nodded. Bobby had seen right through her.

He went on. "I heard about what was taking place here before, but I haven't seen anything hinky like that."

"And how long have you worked here?" Trent inquired.

"Since the change in ownership… So since June. That's when they had the place up and running again."

Amanda pulled her card and extended it to Bobby. "You think of anything or happen to see something you think I should know about, call me. Number's on there." She flicked a finger toward her card that was now in his hand.

"Okay, but I wouldn't be waiting by the phone." Bobby tucked the card into his shirt pocket, and Amanda and Trent left.

They got into the car and let it idle in the lot.

"The goons from the boat got to Larry on Wednesday night," she concluded.

"Sounds quite possible, but we still don't know if it has anything to do with sex trafficking—not really." He added the latter bit with seeming hesitancy.

"I guess you're right, but I think it does. I think they tried to strong-arm Larry, but he refused. The ring wouldn't like to be told no and probably retaliated."

"I'm not saying it's not the case. We just need the proof."

"Oh, we keep going at it, and I think we'll get the proof." She glanced at the clock on the dash; it was going on one in the afternoon. "Let's resume the investigation on Monday."

"Really?"

"Yeah. We don't do the case any good if we're spinning, and with someone like the congressman in our sights, we want to make sure that we go about everything methodically." Honestly, her mind was drifting heavily to Zoe and Becky. Last night had been so fun, she realized her soul could use some more of that, and they were in a holding pattern waiting for the priest to return to town anyway. There also weren't any leads that required their immediate attention.

"All right. Well, I guess I'll have lots of time to get gussied up for my date tonight."

"Your date?" She faced him. Normally, she didn't dip into his personal life, but the question had just spilled out.

"Yeah. That CSI lady."

"Oh, Cassie Pope." Amanda smiled at him. "Well, good for you." She remembered the instant sparks between the two of them.

"Thanks. I've been going through a dry spell lately."

"I didn't need to know that."

Trent laughed as he put the car into gear and took them in the direction of Central, where they'd get their personal cars and go their separate ways.

CHAPTER THIRTY-TWO

The rest of Saturday was leisurely, and Sunday was proving itself to be rather low-key too. Amanda was loving it, and Zoe also seemed to be enjoying herself. Amanda had some downtime like this during her suspension—relaxation really was underrated.

They'd called Libby again at the hospital and discovered she was being released that evening. The rest of the day was split between watching television, playing board games, and coloring. Zoe's drawings were getting a little brighter in tone.

Amanda was happy for how time had slowed down, but now that she was on her parents' doorstep with Zoe, it felt lightning quick. She wasn't sure she was ready to face her father. She turned to Zoe. "All right, you ready to meet my crazy family?"

Zoe made a funny face and pushed out her lips. "Okay," she said and smiled.

"You'll fit in just fine." Amanda laughed and went to pinch the tip of Zoe's nose, but she juked out of the way.

Amanda knocked, though her family, her parents especially, were good with the "walk right in and make yourself at home" approach for their children. Amanda preferred to announce herself. She wasn't assuming the risk of walking in on something that she wouldn't be able to un-see.

Her mother opened the door, and the look on her face had Amanda rethinking whether it was a good idea to bring Zoe. There was a hint of a frown on her lips and a sadness lingering in her eyes. Amanda wanted to pull her in for a huge hug but had a feeling her mother might crumble apart.

Amanda bent down next to Zoe. "Zoe, I'd like to introduce you to my mother. Her name is Julie. Mom, this is Zoe."

"Well, hello there, little lady. You can call me Jules. Come on in." Her mother lifted her gaze from Zoe to Amanda.

Amanda saw a spark of joy. Maybe the presence of a child was what her mother and the rest of the family needed tonight. It would steer the conversation from less pleasant topics like her mother's trial and her father's adultery.

Amanda and Zoe followed her mother to the back of the house, and as they were passing through the dining room, Amanda made out the sounds of her brother and sisters laughing. Occasionally, her father's voice could be heard over the din. It felt good to know they were having some fun, all things considered.

"Well, look at who finally decided to show up." Kristen got up from where she'd been sitting and hugged Amanda but quickly turned her attention to Zoe. Kristen got down next to her and said, "Who do we have here?"

Really a rhetorical question as Amanda trusted that her mother would have informed the rest of the family of Zoe and her situation. Amanda looked down at Zoe when she didn't respond.

Zoe was hugging Lucky close to her chest and had shrunk back, like Kristen made her nervous and intimidated. Her blue eyes were dancing all over the room and taking in all the strangers' faces. Amanda could only imagine what was going through her mind. And she felt sorry for her. After all, her entire life had changed in one swoop, and now here she was with so many new people—all of whom were staring at her.

"This is Zoe Parker," Amanda said to the group. One by one, everyone around the room said, "Hi," to the new person in their midst.

Ava came over and asked Zoe if she would like to go into another room and play. Zoe's response was to reach for Amanda's hand and tug down.

"I think we'll just stay out here for now," Amanda answered on Zoe's behalf and scanned the room for a place to sit. Sydney, Amanda's youngest sibling, made room on the couch for them. Amanda was very well aware of how the conversation had stopped when she and Zoe came into the room. "Thanks, Syd."

As they squeezed onto the couch, Amanda noticed her brother, Kyle, in particular, had his gaze on her. When their eyes met, she didn't really like what she saw reflected in them. He ended up shaking his head, breaking eye contact, and leaving the room in the direction of the kitchen. Amanda knew that Kyle hadn't approved of her turning their mother in, but Amanda wasn't sure what he really expected her to do—look the other way? She also knew he blamed her for what their mother had done.

Amanda caught Ava's eye and remembered that she went to the school where Libby Dewinter worked. The other night hadn't been the time to ask. "Ava, Zoe here is friends with Ms. Dewinter, a teacher from Dumfries Elementary, where you went. Did you have her as your teacher?"

"Oh yeah, she's great. How do you know her, Zoe?"

Zoe tucked closer into Amanda's side and looped her arm through Amanda's. Lucky was in a stranglehold, and it didn't seem like the girl was going to respond.

Amanda realized her error in judgment. She'd been concerned about her family saying something to upset Zoe, and here she was bringing up Libby.

There was banging of pots in the kitchen—a welcome distraction—and the squeaky sound of the drawer in the oven being opened and closed. Dinner must be getting close to being finished. The smell of cooking roast beef was unmistakable as was the smell of garlic that permeated the air. Amanda's mother was certainly the chef in the household, but her dad always took on the task of piercing the meat and inserting chunks of fresh garlic.

Her mother entered the room and didn't say anything. She just looked at her entire family, and it hurt Amanda's heart just guessing what she might be considering right now. If she was embarrassed about her husband's infidelity coming out, it wasn't apparent. Rather, the way her mother's gaze took everyone in, it was like she was committing every nuance of this moment to memory—and for good reason. Tonight could be the last occasion they were all together as a family for a long time. It all depended on how the trial went and what the jury decided. And if she was convicted, how long her mother went away for would be contingent on whether the judge wanted to make an example out of the wife of the former police chief.

Amanda's sister Emily called out from the kitchen, "Dinner will be ready in five minutes. Everyone might as well get to the table."

Amanda's father, her siblings, and nieces and nephews didn't waste any time responding to the invitation. Amanda went to get up, but Zoe held onto her arm, keeping her on the couch. She looked down at her. "What is it, sweetheart?"

Zoe hugged her dog even closer to herself. Her chin quivered, and her eyes pooled with tears. "I miss my mommy and daddy."

She was searching Amanda's eyes, waiting on a response, but there was truthfully nothing that Amanda could say to heal her heart. She went with acknowledgment. "Honey, I imagine that you do." Seeing this little girl breaking down in front of her was torture. No one so young should know this much pain. Let alone have witnessed the murder of her own father.

Tears started falling down Zoe's cheeks, and Amanda scooped her up and swept her hair back. She held her like that and rocked her for a few minutes. Amanda's mother poked her head in the room but backed out slowly. This wasn't the way Amanda had seen tonight going. She'd wanted to be there for her mother and the rest of her family in a stand of support and unity, but considering this little girl's fragile emotional state, it would probably be best if they left. It likely would have been better if they'd never come. "We can go home." *Home?* Amanda swallowed roughly and corrected, "Back to my house."

The little girl's sobs started to subside, but Amanda wasn't breathing any easier. Zoe got off Amanda's lap and stood in front of her. Her eyes were now red, and her cheeks flushed. Amanda tucked a strand of the girl's hair behind an ear. "Do you want to leave?"

A few seconds passed by as if the child were considering. Eventually, she twisted her upper body in a display of "no."

"You sure?"

"Yeah." Her voice was so small, Amanda almost wondered if she imagined her talking.

Amanda gave it a few minutes, got up, and held out her hand toward Zoe. "Well, you're in for a treat. Mom's cooking is the best."

"My mom's was great too." Sadness was burrowed in her voice, but so was pride.

They made their way to the dining table and took their respective seats. Dinner was served up in its usual fashion, but unlike the typical natural flow of conversation, tonight's was more strained. It was like with every passing moment the inevitability of their mother's fate weighed more heavily in the room, becoming tangible.

Amanda was seated across from her brother and tried to make eye contact with him periodically, but he was having nothing to do with it. Honestly, it felt like he was avoiding her altogether, like he wished that she wasn't even there. It was obvious that he didn't approve of her bringing Zoe, though Amanda knew there was so much more to it than that. Getting him to open up about all his feelings would be a lot harder, though. Her brother was a quiet and reserved man, but as the saying goes, he wore his heart on his sleeve. Amanda knew at some point she'd have to speak with him, but it would be her who would have to initiate the conversation. Her brother was also proud and probably one of the most emotionally reserved people in the family, next to her father. He took the prize in that category, and maybe that's where Kyle got the trait.

Amanda glanced at her father now, and their eyes met. He was hurting; that was clear. She gave him a tight smile, feeling for him but not quite forgiving him yet… or understanding.

When dinner was over, and dessert was served and eaten, her father said he had something he wanted to say to everyone.

The room couldn't have fallen any quieter.

Her father cleared his throat. "You all know by now about my mistake twenty-six years ago."

"You don't need to do this, Nathan," Amanda's mother said, and Amanda agreed. What a night for Zoe to be here.

"I want to clear the air. It's my mistake, and I want to own that fact." Her father and mother held brief eye contact, and she nodded. He continued. "I'm not going to make any excuses for what I did or the hurt I caused your mother. I just hope all of you can forgive me over time."

"I forgive you, Grandpa," Ava said.

"Thanks, sweetheart."

"And I have forgiven him," Amanda's mother said, "and I ask that all of you do too. What your father did hurt all of us, but I am his wife and the one he made his vows to. So, this is the last we speak of it." She gave her husband a stern look.

"Actually, Jules, I want to tell them the rest of it."

Amanda's mother dabbed at the corner of her mouth with a napkin. "If you feel you must."

"Did you sleep with anyone else besides… well, you-know-who?" Kristen asked.

Their father shook his head. "She was the only one, and the affair only lasted a couple of months. Which I realize is long enough when it shouldn't even have happened. But now that all this mess is in the open, you should also know that you have a half-brother."

"Say that again?"

"What?"

"Who?"

The questions came in rapid fire from Amanda's siblings, but she was quiet, putting it all together. She'd met Emma Blair's son in April. He was a fireman, looked like he could be in his twenties, and he'd treated Amanda with disdain just like Emma. So blindsided by the fact her father cheated on her mother, she hadn't even considered— "It's Spencer," Amanda said, earning her father's gaze.

"That's right. You know him?" he asked.

"I've met him. Yes."

"Don't hate him, and don't blame Emma Blair either. I'm just as culpable in what happened," her father said, directing these words specifically to Amanda.

"We can just go on like we have," her mother interjected. "Nothing's changed. It's just that now you know about it."

"That right. We know about it." Sydney laid a hand over her heart. "A half-brother."

"I don't know how he'd feel about it—or how Emma might feel—but I'm sure you can meet him if you'd like."

"So he knows about us?" Sydney gulped back a small sob.

"He does," their father admitted. "Just whatever you do, be there for your mother right now as much as you can. She needs your support."

"You knew about Spencer, Mom?" Amanda asked, her insides aching.

"I did. I found out about all of it years ago when your father was in Alcoholics Anonymous."

"Step nine. Make amends." Her father spouted that like he'd been through the program last week, but with the exception of a recent slip this year, he'd been sober for over twenty years.

"Mom, why didn't you tell us?" Sydney asked.

"All of you were children, and Syd, you were just a baby. It wasn't any of your business to know. It was a matter to be worked out between husband and wife."

"I need to process all this." Kristen got up from the table and went into the kitchen.

Sydney ended up saying she needed to leave. The others were sitting in stunned silence. Zoe was looking at Amanda, not seeming to understand anything of what happened. Probably a good thing.

"I know everyone will think I'm leaving because of what just happened, but I have Zoe to consider, and she needs to get to bed at a reasonable hour." Amanda stood and glanced at her father, and while a part of her wanted to offer ready forgiveness, she couldn't get herself to offer it. She needed time to fully process everything she'd found out this week about her family, Emma Blair, and now Spencer.

Everyone mumbled their goodbyes to her and Zoe, except for her mother, who followed them to the door.

"Will you be at court tomorrow morning?" she asked.

Amanda took a moment to consider her schedule for tomorrow. Father Cunningham, Zoe returning to school, and she was still intent on getting concrete evidence to use against Congressman Davis. It would be a bonus if some forensic evidence was recovered from the Dodge Charger. And she should follow up with the crime lab to see if the photos of their suspects netted any hits in the facial recognition databases. "Mom—"

She held up her hand. "No need to say another word. I can see it on your face that you're busy. I understand you have a job to do, and I also trust that you'll be there when you can." Her gaze dipped to Zoe, then back to meet Amanda's eyes. "Do right by her."

"I will."

"And forgive your father." Her mother showed the first crack of sadness on the subject. Her shoulders sagged, and her eyes filled with tears. She pulled Amanda in for a hug and whispered in her ear, "I love you, Mandy Monkey."

"I love you too, Mom."

Amanda and Zoe left and headed home. And there it was again. *Home.* As that word repeated in her head, Amanda's heart bumped off rhythm. Zoe had just entered her life a few days ago, and despite trying to remain detached, the girl was starting to mean something to her. Amanda was also remembering how much she liked being a mother, and maybe that was the toughest pill to swallow. It wasn't just that this little girl reminded her of Lindsey at times, it was the fact that Amanda would never be able to have a child again. But then a child would also require that Amanda find a man that she trusted and loved—to go about it conventionally, anyhow. Right now, that seemed like an even taller order. She liked Logan but wouldn't necessarily say she loved him. And these days with the quietness that stretched between them at times, and the words not being said, it felt like termites were eating away at the foundation of their relationship. If they didn't address the issues soon, things would come crumbling apart.

And she had no idea how she was supposed to handle the news that Spencer Blair was her half-brother. That reveal had really blindsided her.

CHAPTER THIRTY-THREE

It was exactly nine o'clock Monday morning when Trent pulled into the parking lot of the church and neighboring rectory. He parked close to the residence but didn't turn off the car. Rather, he looked over at Amanda. She saw him out of her peripheral, but she was focused more on the clock on the dashboard. She wasn't much in the mood for chitchat this morning after her father's bombshell last night. And Zoe was back at school. Amanda was worried about her, even though she knew that Officer Wyatt would be assigned to watch her.

"Amanda, you good to do this today?" Trent spoke to her gently, wresting her from her thoughts. She hadn't told him what was going on in her personal life, but he was exceptionally good at reading her moods.

"Yeah." She looked over at him and nodded, pressed her lips.

"If you want to talk to me about anything, I'm here."

Despite her rule about keeping professional and private lives separate, she found herself wanting to share with him, but now wasn't the time. "Maybe later," she said and got out of the car.

By the time the two of them reached the rectory door, it was opened, and a good-looking man with dark hair was standing there. He was younger than Amanda had imagined the priest would be, somewhere in his fifties.

"Are you the detectives who were wanting to talk with me?" he asked.

Amanda and Trent were holding up their badges, so the answer to the man's question seemed rather obvious, but Amanda obligingly said, "Detectives Steele and Stenson. I take it that you're Father Gerald Cunningham?"

"The one and only."

"Could we come inside to talk?"

"I expected you'd want to." Gerald stepped back so they could enter his home.

Amanda noted immediately how tiny the space was, but it was clean and functional. From the front door, she could see all the living spaces and the doorways to a bathroom and a bedroom.

Gerald gestured to the sitting room and told them to make themselves comfortable. He sat on the couch, and Trent and Amanda each took a chair.

"You want to talk about Larry. Is he all right?" Gerald asked, and Amanda found it interesting that he'd gone right there.

She hated the thought of being the bearer of bad news. After all, if this man was a close friend of Larry's, the news of his death would deal a hard blow. But she had a job to do, and this man may hold the key to the investigation. "Unfortunately, we have some bad news about Larry Steinbeck. He's been murdered."

Gerald leaned forward, his face a mask of anguish. "Murdered?"

"We came into the possession of some photographs, rather disturbing ones, that may have captured your friend's murder," she said, treading gently.

Gerald stared at them, saying nothing.

Amanda went on. "Would you happen to know what sort of business Larry might have had in the Lake Chesdin area the week before last?"

"Ah, no… I have no idea what he would have been doing there. Is that where you believe he was murdered?"

"It is. We recovered his cell phone from the bottom of the lake."

"So he was there." Gerald took a deep sigh, but there was something in his eyes and body language that indicated he wasn't really surprised by his friend's fate.

"Do you know who could have wanted him dead, and why?" Trent interjected.

Gerald looked from Trent to Amanda. The anguish that had been there before had only deepened. His eyes seemed to sag now with sorrow, and his chest heaved as he breathed. "Just please find whoever did this and hold them responsible. That's all I can ask." He took another deep sigh, and Amanda couldn't resist pushing him. He had just avoided Trent's question altogether.

"You know something that you're not telling us," Amanda said softly. As she looked at the priest, she couldn't help but see the man behind the collar, the person who had been Larry's friend, and he was already grieving. But she couldn't go easy on him because of emotions. This was a murder investigation, and if he had information that could help them catch the shooters, she had to do whatever she could to make that happen, to dredge that out of him—no matter how painful.

"You're right. I do, but I'm just not sure if I should tell you."

"If it's something that will help us find Larry's killer, as his friend, you should."

Gerald's body became rigid, and it was obvious he was having some sort of internal debate. But Amanda also had to wonder if he was afraid of what he knew, fearful for his own safety.

"If you're afraid of someone, we can protect you," she offered. "So if you have this person's name, please tell us. It's plain to see you have someone in mind."

Gerald looked from Amanda to Trent, seeming to weigh his options. Eventually, he said, "I have a pretty good idea who would have wanted him dead."

"Would it help you to know that our investigation has led us to a very powerful man? It might be the same person you're thinking of." She met the priest's eyes, and they widened just slightly. This told Amanda that whomever Gerald was going to name had power and reach. "We can protect you," she repeated.

Gerald rubbed his jaw and perched his elbow on the arm of the couch. He then let his forehead fall into his palm. "It had something to do with his new job."

Amanda felt tingles go through her. It was like all their suspicions were colliding together and forming the truth. "The one at Sunny Motel?"

"Yes, that's the one. I assume you know the history of the place?"

Amanda nodded and said, "We do."

"Then you should know that those people came back, the ones who sell those girls for money. They came to Larry and tried to buy him off. Even tried to hand him a thousand in cash, but Larry would have nothing to do with it." Gerald met Amanda's gaze. "Larry was a good and decent man. He was a loving husband and an amazing friend."

Interesting. "His wife had a different opinion of Larry, and she told us they were on again, off again."

"Oh, they had their share of problems. And I know marriage takes two people to make it work, but it only veered off the rails when Denise went off her meds. She's bipolar. Pretty severe."

Amanda nodded. His explanation made more sense of Denise's reactions during their visit.

"These people who approached him at the motel… what happened after Larry refused to be bought?" Trent asked.

"It wasn't good. At least that's what Larry told me. He said he got a real bad feeling and wanted to quit his job, but he wasn't in a position to afford such a thing." Gerald stopped talking, but it made Amanda feel like he had far more to say.

"Did they approach Larry only once?" she asked.

"Nope. They were like a bad penny that kept turning up. Now this is where I'm a little apprehensive of saying a name, but you promised that you could protect me."

"We most certainly can," she affirmed.

"Congressman Eugene Davis cornered Larry when he was getting ready to leave work one night. He told him that he would make it worth his while if he'd just cooperate and look the other way. If it was a matter of money, he'd give him whatever he asked for."

Amanda glanced briefly at Trent. It was so rare that information like this just came to them, and as good as it was, she still wasn't sure if it was damning enough. If only they could catch the congressman in the act.

Gerald started fidgeting on the couch as if he couldn't get comfortable suddenly. "I will take you up on that protection. I'm also in possession of something you may want to have."

"We'll arrange the protection before we leave here." She was trying not to get worked up about what this thing might be. "What is it?"

Gerald got up from the couch and went into the bedroom. He returned in less than a minute, and between two fingers he held a USB stick. He handed it over to Amanda, and then he sat down again.

"What is this?" she asked.

"What you probably don't know about Larry is that when he felt strongly about something or he wanted to right wrongs, he took it upon himself. He was fearless that way... And look where it got him." Gerald's voice turned gravelly.

Amanda held up the data stick. "You're an incredible friend for stepping up and helping him." She wished she could come out and admit their investigation had led them to the congressman, but affirming that could instill more fear in the priest. "What will we find on this?"

"I never put it into a computer. Larry told me it was just for safekeeping and that if anything happened to him, I was to come forward with it. But only if cops came to me, and I trusted them."

"Do you know why he wouldn't have left this with his wife?" Amanda asked, figuring it probably had to do with her mental instability, but maybe there was more to it than just that.

"I told you about her health, but he just wanted to keep her out of this—not that I know what *this* is—but I got the impression it was serious. He probably wanted this as far removed from her as possible, just in case. Separation and deniability never hurt."

"I appreciate that you're entrusting this to us," she told him.

"I'm quite sure you'll find what you need to go after the congressman, but as I said I never looked at what was on there. I just know what Larry told me—that what's on there was his insurance policy. Now…" Gerald dropped his head and shook it. "He must've known he was in danger."

The priest's forthright words amped her curiosity about the data drive even more. "Thank you so much for your time and your help. And we're deeply sorry for your loss. I'll call my sergeant and get protection set up for you."

Trent and Amanda saw themselves out, and Amanda made the call she'd promised to as soon as they reached the car. She told Malone about their visit with Cunningham, and by the end of her briefing, he was cussing under his breath.

"Isn't this a good thing? We could have him, a real solid means to go after Davis and shut down the sex-trafficking ring once and for all." She knew she was being extremely optimistic.

"Well, don't go getting ahead of yourself. Let's have a peek at what's on that USB drive and go from there."

"Could you just get an officer to watch over Father Cunningham for now? You can revisit whether he needs protective housing arrangements later. Once someone arrives at the church, Trent and I will get back to Central ASAP."

"Consider it done." Malone ended the call.

Trent had the car running, just to fend off the bit of a chill that was in the air. But it also felt like there was a little bit of an energetic chill, a knowing that they were getting close to exposing something huge. Amanda knew Malone was right, and until they knew for sure what was on that USB drive, she should reserve optimism. That normally wasn't a problem for her, but she had this strong feeling they were getting very close to being able to arrest the congressman. And if they succeeded in bringing down the sex-trafficking ring, words wouldn't be able to describe how she'd feel. Just thinking of all those young girls being exploited was absolutely sickening.

CHAPTER THIRTY-FOUR

It hadn't taken too long for an officer to show up at the rectory, and for Amanda and Trent to get set up in a conference room down at Central. Malone had joined them there.

"Load it up, Trent, and let's see what we've got," Malone said.

Trent plugged the USB drive into the side of a laptop and opened the file directory. "It looks like there are a variety of things on here. JPEGs, so pictures, but there are also MP3s. Audio."

Amanda's heart sped up with the possible implications. Did that mean Larry had gotten hard proof of the congressman doing something illegal? "Click on something," she blurted out, and it had both men looking at her.

He opened the first picture and revealed a nighttime shot of young girls outside of a motel room.

"That's at Sunny Motel," she said. "I recognize the exterior. So… what? They were dropping girls off there despite Larry's refusal to cooperate?"

Trent backed out of the photo and looked at the list of files. He dragged his finger down the screen and said, "It looks like the oldest file on here is an MP3."

"Open it up," Malone directed.

Within a few seconds, they were listening to two men talking. Trent said, "Is that the—"

"The congressman? I believe so." Amanda glanced at Malone.

He gestured toward the laptop and gave her a look that told her to zip it for now.

She did.

They heard the other man identify himself as Larry Steinbeck. He told the congressman that he'd accept money from him to look the other way when girls were dropped off at the motel. The congressman sounded pleased. He made some comments about welcoming Larry to the family, and that had Amanda's stomach lurching. The congressman really had such a warped view that he considered his sex-trafficking ring a family? Beyond nauseating.

They listened through to the end; the recording was about seven minutes in length. But it was solid evidence to use against Congressman Davis and to charge him with human trafficking.

"Where do you think this was recorded?" Trent asked.

"Why would that matter, Trent?" Amanda volleyed back.

"It's just… did the congressman know he was being recorded? Is this something a judge can throw out as inadmissible?"

Amanda glanced at Malone and said, "It doesn't really matter if he wasn't aware. As far as I know, one-party consent is all that's needed in Virginia and DC."

"That's right," Malone said.

"So we just prove this is the congressman's voice and we have him?" Trent's voice held a bit of a gloat to it, and he sounded just as eager to slap cuffs on the politician as Amanda was.

"We have him." It was Malone who affirmed this, but he didn't sound overly enthusiastic about it.

"Shouldn't you be happy?" Amanda challenged him.

He met her gaze. "Oh, I am. It's just that there's a lot of red tape to cut through when you go after someone like Davis."

"Something you're more than capable of." Amanda wasn't sure entirely what was weighing on Malone's mind. She hated to think that maybe he was concerned about his own career and that somehow going after Davis would have bad repercussions in that regard. She always thought of Malone as someone who put the law and people's welfare first.

"Don't you worry. I'll take care of this. I'll get the paperwork in order and rope in the Metro PD in DC where he lives. But not until every t is crossed and every i is dotted. Do you understand me?" He took a moment to properly glare at each of them.

"We understand," Amanda said. "We want this guy to go to prison for life, and we're both smart enough to realize that means we get our shit together first."

"That's great to hear."

Amanda's phone rang, and she checked the caller ID. "It's CSI Blair," she announced, only finding it odd she had done so after the fact. She answered and said, "I'm going to put you on speaker. I'm here with Trent and Sergeant Malone."

"I have some good news for you, Detective." Blair carried on as if she'd never even heard Amanda mention Trent or Malone. "I'm not really sure exactly where to start, but so far there's been no forensic evidence in the car to lead us to any specific person."

"Suspicious right there," Amanda said. "It was obviously wiped down before the car was ditched."

"I'm not going to deny that, but where they messed up was with the bullet casings left behind at the Dewinter property."

Amanda inched forward on her chair. "Are you telling me we got a hit?" She remembered Malone saying they had prints.

"We did. A guy by the name of Corey Sutton."

"Address?" Amanda asked.

Blair proceeded to rattle that off, and Trent recorded it in his notepad. At least it was local—specifically, in Dumfries.

"Those pictures that Trent sent over, of the men on the boat, gave us a hit on Sutton but not on the other two."

"At least we have Sutton," Amanda said. "Is there anything else or—"

"I thought you'd be happy with this much." Blair's tone was all too familiar to Amanda. Normally the woman made her feel like she was an intrusion and interruption to her day, a major pain in the butt. Now Amanda understood why and actually found herself feeling empathy for the woman. Her father had left her pregnant and gone back to his wife. He probably never spent any time with Spencer either. Hopefully, her father had at least sent financial support their way.

"I didn't mean to sound ungrateful," Amanda said. "I was just wondering if you had something more. That's all." She did her best to keep all confrontational nuances from her voice. Then she added, "Thank you for this."

"Uh-huh." Blair ended the call.

"When it rains, it pours." Malone got up, turned at the door, and said to them, "You get on Corey Sutton, and I'll get things started regarding the congressman."

Just then the door opened, and Police Chief Hill ducked into the room. She stepped back as if Malone had startled her because he was standing right there, and she laid a hand over her heart. Her gaze swept the room, landing on Amanda for a few seconds too long. Then the woman shifted her attention back to Malone. "I was just looking for you. Do you have a minute to talk?"

"Sure do. Let's go to my office."

Hill backed up to let Malone lead the way down the hall, but she remained in the doorway, giving Amanda one more look. Her eyes and demeanor were cold, and it had Amanda curious why the chief was seeking out Malone at that moment.

Maybe Amanda was being paranoid. After all, the congressman was Hill's brother-in-law, and they'd just heard damning evidence against him, but there was no way Hill would have known what they'd been up to or what they just heard.

Amanda pulled the USB drive from the laptop and decided to set a trap. "Good leads right here," she said to Trent. "I'm going to put it in my desk drawer before we head out."

That's when Hill slithered down the hall, and Amanda met Trent's gaze.

"You just set her up," he said.

"Yep. Time to find out how dirty she is."

"You can't risk her taking it and losing the original."

"Don't you worry. We'll be putting a blank drive in my desk, but we will make another copy. We'll log it into evidence, while I'll keep the original on me just in case the other one goes missing from lockup." Amanda wouldn't put anything past Hill at this point, but there was no sense arming her with the actual intel if she did take the one from the drawer.

"Oh, sneaky." He smiled at her. "I like the way you think."

"Why thank you very much. And right now I'm also thinking we need to go bring in Sutton. Maybe we can get him to talk, and he'll lead us to who killed the Parkers and Steinbeck. He might even give us more to use against the congressman."

"Always a good time for an arrest." Trent smiled at her.

"Absolutely."

CHAPTER THIRTY-FIVE

Before leaving Central, Amanda pulled the background for Corey Sutton. He'd served a few years for breaking and entering in his early twenties, but she wondered how long he'd been getting away with murder. He was now thirty-nine.

She had called on a sergeant in the uniformed officers division of the PWCPD and had a patrol car watching over Sutton's apartment building. They were still waiting on the search and arrest warrants to come through for Sutton, but she didn't expect that would take too long.

The clock on the dash told her it was just past noon, and her stomach grumbled that it was time to eat. "You might as well take us through a drive-thru, Trent."

"Okay…?" He'd dragged the word out and made it sound like a question. He looked over at her from the driver's seat. "I'm just not used to you stopping and actually, you know, taking care of yourself."

She met his gaze, and she wished she could dispute what he'd just said, but it was right on the mark. Normally she would just push through, past exhaustion, past starvation, past a desperate need for coffee. But she wasn't going to own up to that—not outright. Instead, she said, "It's never a good idea to make an arrest on an empty stomach."

Trent grinned and faced out the front window. "If you say so."

She wouldn't have thought she'd ever like a partner who could call her out, but she found some comfort in the fact that Trent knew her so well. It made her feel like he had her back, no matter what storm came at them, and that soothed her and gave her something solid and reliable in her life. "Yes, I say so." She smiled at him.

They got some burgers and fries and munched them down in the car.

"Is now a good time to tell me what you wanted to earlier?" he asked after swallowing a mouthful of fries.

She looked over at him, considered. "Not really, but I will." She let out a deep breath. "I'm just going to say it fast. My father had an affair with CSI Blair, and her son, Spencer, the fireman… well, he's my half-brother." Trent had met him back in April at the same time Amanda had.

Trent was staring at her, his mouth agape.

"Say something," she prodded.

"I don't know what to say."

"Right? Neither do I. Complete shock, but it all came out because Blair's testimony was removed from my mother's trial due to a potential conflict of interest. But there's been a lot of water under that bridge. You didn't hear about this when you were in court?"

"No, I swear. Wow. Spencer's, what, twenty-something?"

"Twenty-five, thereabouts. My father had the affair twenty-six years ago, and it lasted a couple of months."

"Whoa."

"Yeah. Now, off me and onto you. How did your date go?" She surprised herself by asking and stuffed a fry into her mouth. But the inquiry would shift the focus from her.

"It was good. Think we'll see each other again."

"Nice." It was sort of strange having this type of back and forth with Trent—a little awkward but comfortable at the same time. Her phone pinged—the warrants were in. She held up her phone. "Here we go."

They wrapped up what they hadn't finished, and Trent put the car into gear and took them in the direction of Sutton's home.

It didn't take them long to reach the apartment building where he lived. It was one of the nicest ones in Dumfries. Not that Amanda was surprised. Being a criminal typically paid quite well—if you were doing it right. But in exchange, one had to sell their soul. Thankfully, that sacrifice was too great for most people.

Officers from SWAT were already on location and had cleared some tenants from Sutton's apartment building. They were approaching things as if Sutton were armed and dangerous. Just thinking that reminded Amanda of her injured arm and her close call—if one wanted to consider the graze of a bullet that. She didn't, but some would.

Amanda banged on Sutton's door; his apartment was on the fifth floor. "Prince William County PD! Open up!" She waited a few seconds in silence, then repeated the process.

There was no response from inside, and everything seemed quiet. She stepped back and gestured to one of the SWAT officers shadowing her and Trent. "Get us inside," she said.

It didn't seem to take him any amount of time to bust the door from the frame, and they were in. The place stank of stale food, and there were dirty dishes on the counter and empty takeout containers. From the front door, she could see the living room, and there were empty beer bottles that lined the coffee tables.

"Corey Sutton, Prince William County PD!" she announced again but was met with ringing silence. She turned to the SWAT officers and Trent. "We'll take a look around, but I think it's safe to say Sutton isn't here."

The apartment was furnished with rather expensive-looking furniture, but the footprint was small. Though for someone living alone, it would have been appealing for its lack of upkeep—not that it seemed that was one of Sutton's concerns.

They went down the hallway with two SWAT officers, and she ducked her head into the bathroom. She found bloodied gauze in the open trash can next to the toilet, and she got the feeling that she'd probably struck him in the exchange of fire at Dewinter's house. The thought made her feel good. Maybe a childish tit for tat, but it was the least of what he deserved.

She called Trent into the bathroom and shared her find with him.

"Do you think he's still alive?" Trent asked.

"I have no reason to think otherwise, but whoever treated his injury didn't do it in a hospital or clinic, it seems. We never got a hit from either one."

"Well, it shouldn't surprise us to think that there'd be a doctor who Sutton could have seen off the books."

"Nope, no surprise at all. Especially now knowing who we're dealing with. He's got money and power on his side. Guy makes me sick."

"Me too. But we're going to get him. We will. You can count on that. We've got the proof. We're just waiting until all of the paperwork is lined up."

"It can't come fast enough."

Just then, the SWAT officers returned from where they had continued down the hall. The one who had breached the apartment door said, "It's all clear. No sign of Sutton."

This was really the worst-case scenario. Well... second, she supposed, to a showdown in a hail of bullets. Still, it left them without a talking lead, someone to pressure.

"We'll take a good look around and then clear out," the one SWAT officer said. "We'll keep officers posted on the building, and if Sutton shows up, we'll grab him."

She just nodded. She couldn't bring herself to say anything. The disappointment about Sutton not being there was almost overwhelming. A small part of her wondered where he was. Did he know they were searching for him? And if so, how? Did his absence have something to do with Hill? Had she somehow found out they were coming here and warned him?

Her phone rang, and the caller ID showed it was Dumfries Elementary School. "Detective Steele," she answered. As she listened to the person on the other end, her legs buckled beneath her. "Trent, get us to Zoe's school. Right away."

Trent didn't say anything in response, but he was quick about getting into the car, turning it on, and hitting the road. He had to be driving well past the speed limit, but to Amanda, it didn't feel fast enough. She could never forgive herself if something happened to Zoe, and with that thought, she realized how often life forced her to realize her vulnerabilities over and over again.

CHAPTER THIRTY-SIX

Amanda's caller had been the principal, informing her that Zoe hadn't returned from lunch, and they hadn't been able to find her. Lunch had been two hours ago!

She kept trying Officer Wyatt, but his phone repeatedly went to voicemail. "It's Amanda. Call me back immediately." She looked over at Trent. "He's not picking up. It makes no sense. Where is he?" she asked, not really sure she wanted the answer. The person or persons they were after had killed before. They had shot Libby to get to Zoe. They probably wouldn't think anything of killing a cop to take their target. As much as she worried about the officer's welfare, it was Zoe at the top of her list. She was a little girl, defenseless in the face of an armed man. Amanda really couldn't entertain other thoughts that crept into her consciousness. It was what these men did with little girls. What if, as she'd thought before, it wasn't just a matter of silencing Zoe, but something even more sinister—a lifetime sentence in hell? What if they planned to exploit her?

She gasped so loudly that Trent tapped the brake and looked over at her.

"As Malone is always telling me," he said, "and you're always backing him up, let's not get carried away. Officer Wyatt could have a good reason for not answering his phone. We could find Zoe and him just fine."

She glanced over at her partner and realized her eyes were full of tears. "I sure hope you're right." She sniffled and let the tears fall, but she wiped them away. More furious than sad at this moment.

Trent took the last turn, and they went down the street the school was on. As Trent got them closer to the school, Amanda was looking for a police car, but she wasn't seeing one.

"Where is he?" The question came out as a strangled cry.

Trent pulled into a parking space, and she was out of the car before it came to a full stop. She ran toward the building, then inside and toward the principal's office, bypassing the secretary. The principal looked up from his desk and appeared shocked at her intrusion.

The secretary was coming after Amanda, saying, "Excuse me, ma'am, but you can't be in here."

Amanda flashed her badge, keeping her eye on the principal. "I'm Detective Steele. We spoke on the phone. Have you found Zoe Parker?"

His face went downcast, and he shook his head. "No. We've looked everywhere."

"You haven't looked everywhere if you haven't found her." She was near the point of screaming, and Trent tugged on her arm.

"Can you page her to your office?" Trent asked calmly. "She's been through a lot; she could be hiding somewhere." He looked at her, and she nodded.

The principal gestured to the secretary, and she retreated to her desk. Next came her voice over the speaker system: "Zoe Parker, please report to the principal's office."

"Do you"—the principal pulled on his shirt collar—"think something's happened to her? I thought Zoe had an officer with her."

The principal was probably sincerely concerned, but Amanda hated that even for a split second she considered it might have more to do with him not wanting any blame to fall on him for Zoe's disappearance. "If someone took Zoe," Amanda began, "then it is the shared responsibility of every adult in this school, as well as officers with the PWCPD. But I'm less concerned about blame, and more concerned about the welfare of a young girl. Are we on the same page?" She heard every word come out at a higher pitch than the one before, but it was taking all her willpower not to just scream at the man and unleash her frustration on him. She'd gone against her better judgment to allow Zoe to go back to school—even with an officer watching over her. They should have arranged for her to be home-schooled for a while.

Amanda went out to the secretary's desk and said, "Page her again."

The woman did as Amanda asked, and with every word of the request coming over the speakers, it was like another blow to Amanda. She had this sinking feeling there would be no response.

She tried calling Officer Wyatt again. This time, he answered. "Where are you?" she rushed out.

"I, ah…" Wyatt sounded taken aback by her question. Or maybe her aggression. She wasn't sure.

"Just tell me where you are. Do you have Zoe with you?"

"Ah, no."

Amanda was going to be sick. "What do you mean you don't have her? I thought you were charged with watching over her."

"I was relieved from that duty."

Now it was her without the words. "By whom, and did somebody replace you?"

"I don't know about the latter, but my sergeant told me I was good to go."

Amanda was trying to process what she'd just been told. Was Wyatt's sergeant working for the wrong side, or was something else going on here? She had to find out where that sergeant received the directive to relieve Wyatt from his post. She hung up on Wyatt and turned to the principal. "We need to search every inch of the school. Again."

The principal was pale and seemed slow to movement.

"Now!"

He rushed into action and first stopped at his secretary's desk. He told her, "Page for everyone to look for Zoe Parker."

The secretary's hand was shaking as she lifted her receiver to do as he'd asked her.

Hearing the desperate plea only made this dire situation that much clearer.

Zoe had been taken.

Amanda clenched her chest and started breathing in gasps of air. Trent was looking at her with concern. Or was it pity? She hated to think the latter, but now in the face of losing Zoe forever, it was clear she was dearly attached to the girl. It was something beyond a cop caring for an eyewitness. She wanted to protect her, care for her, love her, and, truth be told, watch her grow up.

"We've got to help out, Trent." She took one more heaving breath and left the principal's office.

As she moved, she called Malone and gave him the update. "Zoe's missing."

"What do you mean?" he rushed out.

"She was taken. Someone came into the school and took her."

"With Officer Wyatt there?"

"He was called away." She entered the library and went up and down each row.

"Shit."

"Wyatt said his sergeant told him he was good to leave his post for the day."

"And he just left?"

Amanda appreciated where Malone was coming from, but being mired in shock wasn't going to get them anywhere. "Normally officers are in the habit of obeying their superiors. But what I want to know is why he got that order."

"I'll talk to the sergeant the minute I get off the phone with you."

"And get out an Amber Alert. Sutton wasn't at his place. He could have taken her."

"Done and done."

"Where are we with the congressman?" she asked.

"Things are rolling forward, but I was delayed by Chief Hill."

Of course you were… Amanda would ask how exactly, but she didn't care right now. She just needed to get to Zoe.

Malone ended the call first, and she finished up in the library. No sign of Zoe.

Trent put a hand on her shoulder. "We'll find her."

She understood what he was trying to do, but the repeated, baseless encouragement was starting to grate. It was like pouring salt on an open wound. There was no way of knowing whether they would be able to save Zoe. But they weren't without options. Malone was making progress on getting the congressman brought in. If necessary, and if the Metro PD would allow her, she could grill him for hours to get Zoe's location. But was there an easier way?

She racked her mind for something, for a lead, assuming the people who took Zoe were going to leave her alive and hadn't already killed her. And here she found herself putting faith in the monsters who pimped out little girls, who viewed them as merchandise. They would, after all, see Zoe as that. But she wouldn't just bring them profit—as sick as that thought was—but as their victim, they'd also have her silence. "Where would they take her?" It was a question she asked the void, not expecting that her partner might have an answer.

"I just thought of something," Trent said. "And it might be a reach…"

"Whatever it is, spit it out."

"Well, we have Sutton's car. It's a newer model. It would have a GPS system, and it—"

"Oh my God, Trent, you're brilliant! We can find out where the car had gone in the past, and it very well might lead us to Zoe's location. It will probably be an address that shows up repeatedly."

"Yep. We can also try tracking Sutton's phone."

At least one of us is thinking clearly. "Again, brilliant." She pulled out her phone and called CSI Blair directly. As soon as the investigator got her greeting out of the way, Amanda floored ahead. "The Dodge Charger. I need you to send us over the GPS history as soon as possible."

There was silence on the other end.

"CSI Blair," Amanda said firmly, "the little girl in this case, Zoe Parker, has gone missing, and what's in that GPS system very well might save her life." Now wasn't the time to pull any punches.

"I'll get it over to you right away."

"We'll also need a phone traced. That is, if you can find one associated with Corey Sutton."

"Consider it done—if there is one."

"Thanks." Amanda turned to Trent. "Now we wait, and we hope."

CHAPTER THIRTY-SEVEN

The Amber Alert had been issued for Zoe, though Amanda wasn't breathing any easier. The school had some surveillance cameras, but it was taking time to get the footage. Amanda was hinging a lot of her hope on the GPS history from the Dodge and the phone trace. Malone still hadn't gotten everything he needed for the Metro PD to haul in Congressman Davis, and the delay was driving Amanda mad. But not as mad as knowing Zoe was out there, somewhere, with evil people.

Officers were called in to conduct a thorough check of the school property, freeing up Trent and Amanda to return to the station. The first thing she did was check her desk drawer.

"Trent." Nausea seized her gut. "The USB drive is gone."

"She took it."

They locked eyes, and Amanda's phone pinged with a text from Blair. She shared the gist with Trent. "If Sutton has a phone, it's a burner, and Blair has emailed us the car's GPS history."

He went to his desk and clicked away. She was standing over his shoulder, and they reviewed the report together. There were a few addresses that popped up several times.

Amanda's phone rang, and it was her brother, Kyle.

"You couldn't even bother to come to court today?" He was obviously angry and hurt.

She took a few deep, steadying breaths. "I don't have time for this right now."

"You're working the case for the murder of that little girl's parents? Yeah, I know. Mom told us all about it before you arrived yesterday. But that's no excuse. You—"

"No, you hold up." With every word out of his mouth, her redhead temper was ratcheting. "You don't have any right to talk to me this way."

There was silence on the other end.

"I know you're mad at me, that you hold me responsible for what Mom did." She pushed this out even though this was probably the worst time for this conversation, but life wasn't scripted.

"Damn right I do."

And there it was… Out in the open. She thought that once he admitted as much she'd feel better, but that wasn't the case at all. "I… ah… don't know what to say, Kyle." She walked over to her desk, dropped down in her chair.

"There's nothing you can say that will fix this. Our mom killed a man, Amanda, because you thought you were—what?—doing us all a favor by pulling away after the accident? Did you even stop for one second to consider how much you hurt everyone by turning your back on them like that?"

She noted how her brother's speech separated him from the rest, as if he hadn't also been affected. "I can't go back and change the past." Her voice was small and pleading.

"I know," he huffed out.

"How did things go today?" she dared to ask.

"Still moving forward. Hard to say right now where the jury will lean."

His statement was a mine laid and rigged to explode with little provocation. "That little girl, Kyle…" She paused there when she heard him groan, but he didn't end up saying anything. "She's missing. More accurately, she's been taken." She was breathing in gasps for air now, and none of them were proving satisfying.

Eventually, Kyle confessed on a sigh, "I saw the Amber Alert."

"But you still chose to call now." She clenched her jaw.

"Yeah, I'm an ass."

"You're certainly acting that way."

"Who do you think did this?"

"We have a suspect, but no one saw him around the school, so…" She sniffled.

There was a span of silence in which Amanda imagined his next accusation. Something along the lines of, *Weren't you in charge of her protection, Amanda?*

Instead, he said, "Well, you've got to find her." He spoke like he was rallying the troops.

"We're doing all we can."

"I trust you are."

At the expression of her brother's faith in her, it felt like something was slowly on the mend between them, but it was still a long way from being healed. "Thank you," she said. "And I'll get to court for the trial as soon as I can. Please trust me on that too."

A few seconds ticked off.

"Okay," he said. "Good luck finding her."

"Thanks." She hung up, probably beating him to doing so, but her emotions were wrenching in her chest. Zoe being taken and then the conversation with her brother. She supposed the latter had been a good thing because it was a start to clearing up the conflict that boiled between them. And she really wanted her relationship with her brother to be repaired. They used to be so incredibly close.

"Ah, Amanda." Trent peeked his head over the partition.

"Yeah?"

"I think I have someplace worth checking out."

She popped out of her chair and was in his cubicle in seconds.

"It's an old warehouse in Woodbridge, and it doesn't appear to be in business now. I checked the property records, and it's tied to a numbered company."

"Bet it's Davis. Let's go!" She spun and bumped right into Malone.

"Oh, no, you don't. We do this by the book." He stared her down, and she was propelled to the past, to April specifically, when she'd gone ahead of SWAT and without legal clearance.

"Fine." She knotted her arms. "Trent's got a place that seems a likely spot for where they might have Zoe."

He frowned. He didn't need to say what he was thinking because it was stamped all over his expression.

"She's still alive," Amanda pushed out, more for herself than anyone else. She just hoped the little girl didn't wish she were dead. Amanda had to shake the darkness aside; it did her no good right now and certainly didn't get her any closer to saving Zoe.

"I'm sure she is," Malone responded.

"But what do we know?" she hissed, feeling foolish for entertaining a positive outcome—no matter how brief it had been.

"No, you were right, Amanda. Would you rather we give up all hope?" Malone shot back at her.

"No."

"Well then." Malone started barking out orders and directions were followed. SWAT was heading up the operation, but Amanda pleaded that she and Trent also be active on the ground when the breach happened. There was no way she was going to stand on the sidelines and get updates through an earbud. Zoe had been in her charge, and it would be her who made sure the girl was retrieved safely—no one else.

CHAPTER THIRTY-EIGHT

It was torturous waiting for every second to pass as SWAT organized the approach. It wasn't until nine o'clock that, with the warehouse fully surrounded, they started to move in.

Amanda tugged on the heavy Kevlar vest she wore, feeling the extra thirty pounds today more than some others. Maybe due to the reason she needed to wear one, or because she was already loaded down with emotional weight. It wasn't like she'd never worn a bulletproof vest before. She was also armed with a new accessory—night-vision goggles. This was because SWAT had arranged for power to be cut to the building. They'd be going in dark.

SWAT went into the warehouse, and Amanda listened as the officers called over the comms with status updates. She and Trent moved with them at a set distance behind. Amanda flicked a button on the goggles to activate them, and everything became shades of green.

Everyone held their guns, ready to fire, fully expecting the need to pull the trigger before this night was over. The place was shrouded in darkness and towering shadows.

The warehouse was ten thousand square feet. Not small by any means, but there were vehicles outside with registrations tying back to the same numbered company as the warehouse.

While Amanda, Trent, and fifteen officers from SWAT breached the warehouse, the property was surrounded by cruisers and officers, all poised and ready to fire as well. A two-block perimeter had been set up to avoid any possibility of civilian casualties.

On site also was Chief Hill, and she was standing with Malone by his SUV. Amanda didn't like that she was there, but she didn't exactly have a say in the matter.

There were several large shipping containers in the main bay, and each were checked in turn.

The repeat of "all clear" came back with a sickening feeling.

Amanda was behind a SWAT officer who opened one of the containers.

"Oh." He stepped back, coughing, and held his arm in front of his nose.

The ripe smell of human decomp was overpowering and had Amanda's eyes watering. Yet, she moved closer to get a good look. Despite trying to place herself out of her body for this, her gag reflex was in full effect. She swallowed the bile that rose in her throat as she closed in. She'd never met this man in life, but she'd seen his face in photographs. "It's Larry Steinbeck..." She turned her back on the corpse and fought like hell to avoid puking and contaminating the area.

"They must have gone back to the lake and retrieved his body after knowing they'd been spotted," Trent said, stating the obvious.

"I'd say so." Amanda noticed that she and Trent were alone now. SWAT had moved on to another container.

"And another body," came over the comms.

She went in that officer's direction. Inside that container was Corey Sutton. There was a large, jagged slash to his neck—an obvious cause of death. Given the arterial spray and the amount of blood, he'd probably been murdered right here. She exited, rounded the container, and stopped.

At her feet was a stuffed dog with floppy ears. *Sir Lucky.*

"Zoe Parker was here," she said through the comms and picked up the doll.

Everyone started moving faster, herself included, and she pushed aside her fear. Zoe loved that stuffed animal and wouldn't be without it unless she had no choice. And it was the toy she'd had with her when she'd witnessed her father's murder. It was more than a stuffed dog; in the child's mind, it was her best friend, confidante, maybe even a piece of herself.

Amanda stuffed the dog into a pocket of her vest, and she and Trent carried on.

Suddenly came the thunderous cracking of metal pinging off the containers. They were being fired upon. She ducked behind a container, seeking cover. Trent was beside her. She peeked out and searched the second-story catwalk. There were numerous assailants, their forms easy to pick up with the goggles.

SWAT was firing back, both sides squeezing off bursts from automatic weapons. Her and Trent's Glocks wouldn't be much use in this kind of gun battle. She'd let SWAT handle it, and while the bad guys were distracted with defending their turf, she and Trent would see if they could locate Zoe.

"Come on," she said to Trent and motioned for him to follow her.

They went along the far edge, out of the line of fire, or at least it was at the moment. She kept scanning the area immediately above their heads, but it was empty on the catwalk. The action seemed to be concentrated on the other side of the bay. But then she spotted a man through a window on the second floor. He'd just passed the glass and left. There must have been an office space there. "Zoe could be up there." She pointed it out for Trent and headed to a nearby staircase.

They both went up. A man was definitely inside that room, as he kept sweeping past the glass. She and Trent had one play here. They had to swoop in quick.

To the right of them, the gunfire continued in a deafening staccato.

She reached the top of the stairwell and twisted the handle. "Locked," she mouthed to Trent. She considered their options. She couldn't exactly shoot and have her bullet go into the room blind. What if Zoe was in there?

She knocked.

"What are you—" Trent pulled her back.

She hitched her shoulders, and the figure passed the window and opened the door. He was armed and lifting his gun on them when she squeezed her trigger. Her bullet found purchase in her target without him getting a shot off.

They waited a few moments and then moved in. No more assailants in the room. No Zoe either.

"She's got to be somewhere else in the building. She's here. I just feel it," she said to Trent.

She looked around, thankful that they'd gone unnoticed by the assailants, who remained occupied with spraying bullets at SWAT. But the tactical team were holding their own. She and Trent moved along the landing. Next to the office, there was another door with a window. A stairwell behind it. She turned the handle, and it cooperated. They took the stairs down and continued with caution. They kept their steps light and their senses alert.

They reached the end of the stairwell, and a plaque on the wall next to another door said *B*. She'd guess that stood for Basement. She went through, and there was a maze of hallways. She wasn't prone to swearing a lot, but she could let off a string of expletives right now. How were they ever supposed to find Zoe in this building—assuming she even was there?

But she didn't say as much to Trent. She just kept forging forward. Every room they checked was unlocked and empty. Then she hit one that was locked. There was a small window, and she peeked through, highly aware of the fact that if there was a bad guy in there, she was as good as dead. But she couldn't risk missing Zoe.

Nothing.

They moved to the next door, and the next, with Amanda playing gopher and imagining her head blowing off. Each time she got away unharmed, her adrenaline was building up in her system. She was starting to almost feel untouchable. She peered into the last room in this hall.

Finally! Zoe was huddled in the far corner, knees to chest, but wasn't moving.

Please tell me she's alive!

"Zoe," she called out. "I'm here." She tried the door, but it was locked.

Zoe popped her head up.

"She's alive," Amanda said to Trent, then, "I found her!" through the comms for everyone to hear. She went on to say, "Basement, northeast corner, last door on the right."

"Copy," said a female voice.

"The door's locked, Trent. How do we…?" Amanda looked around, but only one solution presented itself, as much as she hated it. She directed Zoe to move to a corner out of the way and waited until she had.

"You're going to shoot the lock?" Trent gulped.

"Don't see what other choice we have."

A bullet zinged past their heads, and the two of them ducked. They'd been paying so much attention to Zoe, they'd missed the large bulk of a man heading down the hallway right for them. It was the bald man from the boat!

Another bullet, and Amanda and Trent remained tucked down. Trent fired off some shots, and so did Amanda.

Next thing she knew, she felt herself being pushed backward. She'd been hit, center mass right in the vest. That didn't mean it didn't hurt like a— She roared and squeezed off a few consecutive rounds, and she found herself stepping toward her assailant, closing the distance between them. Then, finally, one of the bullets found flesh. The large man fell in a heap.

"Thank God! I thought we were going to die." Trent was heaving for breath.

"Not if I can help it." She'd been trying to figure out how to get to Zoe, and now this man might have delivered a key right to them. She approached the prone body with caution. She'd learned a long time ago never to assume a perp was dead. But this one was. A bullet had nailed him right in the throat. His gun had fallen from his hand, but out of habit, she still kicked it aside.

She hunched down beside him, and Trent came in close.

"It's the shooter from the boat, and the man who killed the Parkers," he said.

"Yep. Just noticing?" Though they had been rather busy with trying to stay alive. She proceeded to go through the man's pockets. "If you pray," she said to Trent as she stood, "start now." She found a loaded keyring.

"Started the minute Zoe went missing."

She patted his shoulder on the way past him to the room. She kept feeding keys into the lock, but none of them were a fit. Not until the last one.

She had a flashlight on now to give Zoe some light, but Amanda still had her goggles on. She holstered her gun and swung the door open. "Zoe!"

"Amanda!"

The little girl burst across the room to her, a tangle of arms and legs, and Amanda lowered down to receive and give. They shared a tight embrace, and Amanda hissed but did so as quietly as possible. She in no way wanted to discourage this. The little girl laid her head on Amanda's shoulder for a few moments then pulled back. She pointed at Amanda, a smile on her face.

"You found Lucky!"

"Oh, yeah, I…" Amanda hesitated there. Hopefully, dingus hadn't shot the dog, but he should have been protected by the

Kevlar in that pocket. She pulled the toy out slowly. "Here you go."

Zoe hugged Amanda again. "Thank you!"

Amanda was absorbed in this happy bubble but cutting through it was the sound of footsteps tapping down the hall. "Trent?"

"Already on it." He pulled his gun and peeked into the hall.

"Zoe, get in the corner again, sweetheart," Amanda told her, and the girl obeyed.

"It's the chief," Trent told her, and Amanda joined him in the hall. He hadn't holstered his gun, and the chief's presence had Amanda pulling hers again and loading a fresh magazine. Something was completely off here. There was zero reason for her presence.

"Chief Hill," Amanda said as she dared to step into the corridor. Trent was at her six.

"I heard you found the girl," Hill said. "What a relief." She put a hand to her chest as if she was filled with relief, but the skin tightened on the back of Amanda's neck.

Hill got down near the dead body and started rummaging in the man's pockets.

"What are you doing down here?" Amanda asked stiffly.

Hill didn't respond.

"What are you looking for?" Amanda persisted.

"I should be asking you why you're still here, Detective. You found the girl. Take her and leave. Let us clean up here." Hill didn't stop her scavenger hunt.

"Chief," Amanda blurted out, and the next thing she knew, Hill had pulled the man's gun on her and Trent.

Amanda cursed herself. She should have collected it, just in case an opponent came down the hall and had use for the dead man's weapon, but she'd been so concentrated on Zoe.

"Whoa!" Trent said. "You don't want to do this."

Hill leveled the gun on Trent and said to Amanda, "Tell your partner here, I very much do."

Amanda's heart was racing. She was terrified Hill was going to shoot Trent. "Why, Sherry?" There was no way she'd be addressing this woman by her title; she didn't deserve it.

"The pay is extremely high."

"Little girls, Sherry." The appeal came out as if it would have impact, but was the woman even capable of human feeling? "You're in on the sex-trafficking ring with your brother-in-law."

"Ding, ding, ding."

The woman wasn't even decent enough to show remorse or plead her case, tell Amanda why she'd turned to that life. Surely, it had to be more than money that had lured her into exploiting children. But what Amanda couldn't figure out was why Hill had come down here and risked exposure. She could have just stayed in hiding.

Then it hit. There had to be something incriminating on the dead man. Amanda focused on what Hill had in her hands. It was a cell phone. Something was on there that tied back to her.

Hill smiled. "And don't think about calling for help. I cut off your comms from everyone a while ago. Well, everyone but me."

"You're the one who said 'copy' when I announced we found Zoe," Amanda said, recalling it had been a woman. A chill came over her. Hill was going to make it look like Amanda and Trent were victims of the ring and walk away. She'd probably explain away the communication gear "failure."

"Put your guns on the floor, or I'll shoot you where you stand."

"You won't get away with this," Trent pushed out.

Hill scoffed. "Of course I will. Ballistics will say that Damien Vaughn shot you. That's the stiff by the way, and this is his gun." She dangled it in the air.

"Your prints," Trent countered.

"Not after I wipe it down. Any last words?"

"Actually…" Amanda was taking her time, talking slowly.

"Yes, Detective?" Hill rolled her eyes.

In an instant, and in the subtlest of tells, Amanda motioned for Trent to duck back into the room. He moved swiftly, and Amanda pulled her trigger. "Say hi to the devil in hell!"

She rolled into the room as a burst of bullets thundered from the assault rifle—the result of Hill squeezing the trigger as she fell to the floor. Then there was silence.

CHAPTER THIRTY-NINE

Friday, Four Days Later...

Four SWAT officers were in the hospital due to gunshot wounds sustained during the raid, but all of them were expected to pull through. Overall, everything had worked out better than expected, and there was a plethora of evidence.

They were able to confirm that Damien Vaughn was in communication with Congressman Davis and Sherry Hill. Her number was also in the call history of the burner phone recovered from Corey Sutton's body.

Officer Wyatt's sergeant came forward to say it had been Hill who'd told him to pull security on the girl, and he'd just followed orders. This claim was confirmed with his phone records, but he was still facing an investigation, just to make sure he wasn't caught up in the scam and paid off in any way. A search of Hill's residence turned up more evidence that she was crooked and involved with the ring, and they'd found the USB drive from Amanda's drawer on Hill's person.

Malone had joked, rather inappropriately, but accurately, "Just because you didn't like her didn't mean you had to kill her."

Congressman Davis was keeping a prison cell warm as he awaited trial. The judge had denied bail, correctly viewing him as a flight risk. Ownership of the warehouse traced back to Davis. Also, Patty Glover from Sex Crimes was still working through all his financials, but she had been able to confirm Davis's connection to the numbered corporation associated with the ring. He was wearing a chain-link bracelet when they brought him in, and it had a hidden data stick in the clasp with more incriminating evidence. He'd be going away for the rest of his life—thanks in part to Corey Sutton's pang of conscience.

The search of his apartment had turned up a key that led to a safe-deposit box, which held a USB drive. On it was a letter saying he never wanted to harm Zoe, and even though he'd be the one to take her from the school, he'd do whatever he could to keep her safe. He even said that he'd ditched the Dodge Charger hoping it would lead police to the sex-trafficking ring. He'd also included evidence to be used against the congressman, Chief Hill, and Damien Vaughn. He listed the crimes he was guilty of himself. In addition, he'd noted several locations where girls were being held throughout Prince William County and Washington, DC. There would be lots of girls reunited with their families.

Sutton must have figured his days were short. The medical examiner had put Sutton's time of death within a few hours of Zoe's abduction. It was believed that he was killed not long after delivering Zoe to the warehouse. Libby wouldn't be getting full restitution with Sutton's murder, but he wouldn't be hurting anyone else, and that appeased her. Thankfully, Libby was well on her way to a full recovery.

And while the man who killed Larry Steinbeck and the Parkers would never live a day behind bars, he'd paid the ultimate price for his crimes too. In that, there was at least closure. But all this didn't change the fact that it left a little girl without her parents.

Amanda was at Central—not in an official capacity, though. Not for a few more days anyway. The hit to her chest had resulted in a cracked rib and granted her some sick leave.

She was outside the room where Zoe was with Colleen Frost and Erica Murphy. With the threat against Zoe eliminated, the child would be able to resume her life. Or at least start to assemble the pieces back together. Amanda had expected Libby Dewinter to jump at the chance to adopt Zoe, but Amanda learned that she wasn't in a position to do so. And Amanda respected that. Choosing to raise a child wasn't a small decision or a minor responsibility.

Colleen and Erica looked out the window at Amanda and waved her in, just as her phone rang. Caller ID said it was her mother. She held up a finger to the women and pointed at her phone. "Mom? Everything—"

"It's over, Mandy. I'm free." Her mother was crying.

"You're free?" It felt like her throat was closing.

"They found me not guilty, sweetheart!"

Tears sprung to Amanda's eyes, but she was confused. "But the evidence against you…"

"Not strong enough to convict beyond a shadow of a doubt. A lot of the evidence was coincidental without hard proof. You are happy?"

"Yes, of course I am, Mom. Great news." Amanda *was* happy but also felt a cacophony of conflicting emotions. Her mother had confessed to committing the murder, to her, but not on the record. There was no doubt in Amanda's mind as to her mother's guilt, but the daughter in her was relieved her mother would remain a free woman. Still, she had this underlying sense that the justice system had failed.

"Come over to the house, bring Zoe if you'd like. It's time to celebrate."

"I'll get there as soon as I can." Amanda ended the call, still a fluster of conflicting emotions, but she'd push them aside and deal with them later. Right now, she had something else to do.

She took a deep breath, shook her arms, and went inside the room. Just the thought of saying goodbye to Zoe broke Amanda's heart, but she entered and smiled at the girl. Zoe got up and came over to hug her. She wasn't holding Lucky, but she had a drawing in her hand.

Amanda went to reach for it, but Zoe pulled it back. "Before I show you, I want to say I'm sorry."

"For what, sweetie?"

Zoe's eyes darted to Colleen and Erica, and Zoe leaned in toward Amanda and cupped her hands around Amanda's ear and whispered, "For peeing in Lindsey's bed."

"Ah, I appreciate you saying that. Thank you."

"Now, you can see!" Zoe waved the paper and let Amanda take it from her this time.

There were two stick figures. One, a little girl holding a dog, and the other, a woman holding something yellow in one hand—Amanda and her badge again. The two of them were holding hands. Behind them was a line house. Above their heads was a heart and scrawled writing that read *thnk you.*

"This is… ah…" Amanda pinched her nose, fussed. She couldn't hold herself together. She scooped Zoe up, lifting her off the floor, careful not to hurt the most beautiful drawing she'd seen since Lindsey had adorned her fridge with her creations.

She let her tears fall in the girl's hair.

Logan had been right about her job being too risky. It had ultimately been what ended their relationship a couple days ago. He didn't handle the news of her being shot *again* very well, and she didn't fight for him to reconsider. The truth was, her heart was more open than it had been in years, but there was only so much room. And this little girl, the one in her arms right now… well, she had claimed it. And when Amanda looked at her, somehow all the risks she'd taken seemed worth it. For the first time since Kevin and Lindsey's deaths, she felt somewhat whole again, like a part of her she'd never thought would heal had finally stitched together.

There was no way she could turn and walk away from Zoe. Amanda knew exactly what she had to do.

She set Zoe down and tapped a kiss on her forehead. She looked at Erica Murphy. "Could I talk with you out in the hall?"

A LETTER FROM CAROLYN

Dear reader,

I want to say a huge thank you for choosing to read *The Silent Witness*. If you enjoyed it and would like to hear about new releases in the Amanda Steele series, just sign up at the following link. Your email address will never be shared, and you can unsubscribe at any time.

www.bookouture.com/carolyn-arnold

If you loved *The Silent Witness*, I would be incredibly grateful if you would write a brief, honest review. Also, if you'd like to continue investigating murder, you'll be happy to know there will be more Detective Amanda Steele books. I also offer several other international bestselling series and have over thirty published books for you to savor, everything from crime fiction, to cozy mysteries, to thrillers and action adventures. One of these series features Detective Madison Knight, another kick-ass female detective, who will risk her life, her badge—whatever it takes—to find justice for murder victims.

Also, if you enjoyed being in the Prince William County, Virginia, area, you might want to return in my Brandon Fisher FBI series. Brandon is Becky Tulson's boyfriend—not that he came up in this book, but they meet in *Silent Graves* (book two in the series). This series is perfect for readers who love heart-pounding thrillers and are fascinated with the psychology of serial killers. Each installment is a new case with a fresh bloody trail to follow. Hunt with the FBI's Behavioral Analysis Unit and profile some of the most devious and darkest minds on the planet.

I love hearing from my readers. You can get in touch on my Facebook page, through Twitter, Goodreads, or my website. This is also a good way to stay notified of my new releases. You can also reach out to me via email at Carolyn@CarolynArnold.net.

Wishing you a thrill a word!
Carolyn

Connect with CAROLYN ARNOLD online:

carolynarnold.net

@Carolyn_Arnold

AuthorCarolynArnold

ACKNOWLEDGMENTS

This book was possible with the help of a lot of people. As they say about raising a child, it takes a village to publish a book. First, I'd like to thank George, my husband and best friend. He sees me through the ups and downs that come with writing—every step of the way. To another twenty-five *plus* years of marriage, George!

Thank you to my editor, Emily Gowers at Bookouture, for her unwavering faith in my writing and Detective Amanda Steele. I also am thankful for the team at Bookouture—the numerous editors, those in marketing and social media, audiobook production, design and formatting, and countless others who work behind the scenes to make it all happen.

Gratitude goes to the friends of mine who serve as police in their communities and are always only a message away if I have questions about procedure or forensics.

I hope those in Prince William County and who serve with the PWCPD will accept that I've taken creative license with their hometowns and the layout and organization of Central Station in Woodbridge.

Lightning Source UK Ltd.
Milton Keynes UK
UKHW010615221021
392643UK00006B/209